NO LONGER LOST

SECRETS OF STONE: BOOK NINE

ANGEL PAYNE & VICTORIA BLUE

This book is an original publication of Angel Payne & Victoria Blue.

This is a work of fiction. Names, characters, places, and incidents either are the product of the author's imagination or are used fictitiously, and any resemblance to actual persons, living or dead, business establishments, events, or locales is entirely coincidental. The publisher does not assume any responsibility for third-party websites or their content.

Cover Design by Emmy Ellis
Cover Photographs: 123RF

Paperback ISBN: 978-1-64263-130-2

NO LONGER LOST

SECRETS OF STONE: BOOK NINE

ANGEL PAYNE & VICTORIA BLUE

For my beautiful boy, now my handsome
young man—forever my perfect prize.
The world is a better place because you're in it.
I love you, Kadin, and I'm so proud of you.

—Victoria

For my Thomas.

I'd be lost without you.

—Angel

CHAPTER ONE

Taylor

The geraniums I'd planted two springs ago were leggy and fighting weeds for space in the overgrown flower bed outside Mom's dingy trailer. The door slammed shut behind me, the spring of the rusty hinge squeaking with neglect—a lone voice of protest speaking up for the rest of the property.

Preach on, sister hardware. Preach on.

The afternoon I'd spent planting the flowers around this shoddy place had been a hopeful one. I'd been so sure Mom was on the right path toward sobriety. She'd landed a job at a nearby warehouse a short walk away, and she'd be able to make her shifts without problem. Of course, within a month she'd been fired and was back to spending her time at the corner bar instead.

I straightened and stretched my back, looking over to where I'd hastily parked my Nissan in the gravel parking space beside my mom's double-wide. I let my thoughts travel even further into the past. The day she'd moved into the place, she'd been so proud. Her boyfriend at the time had promised her the moon and was one of the few who had started to deliver. That was before his wife had caught wind of the affair he was having and put a screeching—literally and figuratively—stop to the whole thing. Later, my mom found out the woman had threatened a messy and public divorce, making the trailer an elaborate consolation prize. Okay, more like a parting gift. Oh, screw it—sometimes a spade was just a spade. The thing was a payoff, plain and simple.

One of the few things about Janet Mathews that *was* simple.

But as her life had gone, time and time again, being that man's curse had transformed into her blessing. Because of the "cheater with the screecher," as she'd wryly started calling the bastard, she had a roof over her head. I paid the rent and utilities on the lot at the mobile home park and hoped my mother wouldn't squander every cent of her welfare check on drugs and booze. That way maybe I'd at least get a small contribution toward her bills. But I knew better. Relying on her for that—or anything else—was buying a one-way ticket to disappointment.

After tossing the weeds, I got back into my car and shut the door with a tired *whump*. I blew out another resigned sigh while resting back against the headrest—and gritted my teeth against the approach of angry tears.

Stupid. So stupid. This isn't worth your tears. None of it has ever *been.*

This really wasn't ever going to end. I would never get out from under the burden of caring for my mother.

And just because I needed the day to get worse, my memory blazed to life with the text of Mac Stone's *Dear John* letter. Or in this case, the *Dear Taylor* letter. Not that it mattered. The gist was the same; the results couldn't be altered. I could never be the woman he wanted me to be—or even the one I pretended to be. What I gave the world on the outside was a woman who took life by the horns, wrestled it to the ground, and did things her way.

The reality was horrifically different.

I would forever be the victim of my mother's shitty life choices and bad habits. And no, there was no other choice. That would mean turning my back on the only bit of family I had, and I just wasn't cut from a moral cloth that could allow that to happen.

But why did it have to be that way?

I knew that answer already. I just hated facing it.

And was furious with him for making me.

Why had he made it such an ordeal? Why did being happy with him have to mean not looking after my mom? People took care of their parents *and* had meaningful relationships. All the damn time. Even with sex that made my eyes cross and toes curl. The kind a man like Mac Stone was able to give. And give. And *give...*

But deep down, I knew this was different. That "taking care of" someone didn't mean enabling them to continue abusing themselves and using others. I just didn't want to face the reality of it. The reality was I was enabling my own mom.

And would have to give up a man like Mac.

God, I really liked him. All right, maybe more than "liked." Surrendering him hurt more than I wanted to admit. He made me laugh and feel good about myself. He was smart and witty. And did I mention the part about the man being sex on wheels? The kind of experiences I'd never encountered before in my life.

No. I wasn't ready to let any of it go.

But he wasn't giving me a choice.

"Shit," I muttered, lowering my forehead to the steering wheel. But there was the truth, plain and simple. I had two options. Crappy and crappier. And all I wanted was to be happy. I didn't think that was too much to ask of the universe. It wasn't being selfish or greedy.

Mac's smug words blared into my mind, pissing me off all over again.

If you decide you deserve me.

"Shit!" A spew of venom this time. What the fuck did that mean? Where the hell did he get off? Was the bastard chugging hallucinogens during his three-second breaks at the hospital?

I wanted to start the car, drive straight to Oceanside, and crash through the pretty glass of his pristine beachfront place, and then get out and kick him in the balls—all for that comment alone. He was so effortlessly arrogant. So ridiculously self-righteous. He was so...*so*...

A stupid grin spread across my lips.

He was so perfectly Maclain Stone.

So much of everything I was fucking addicted to. That confidence. That self-awareness. That outright, undeniable sexiness. I'd be lying if I tried to deny it.

Bastard.

Alluring, smooth, carved, cocky bastard—all true. But *bastard* nonetheless.

A bastard I could really lean on right now.

But even having the thought made me hate myself more. How did I get to this place? *Lean on him?* I mean, could I hear myself? I'd never leaned on anyone. Never *needed* anyone. That kind of behavior only led to one kind of situation.

The one I was in at this exact moment. Abandoned. Alone. Vulnerable. *Weak.*

A place I swore I'd never be.

A tightness I swore I'd never feel.

Tears I swore I'd never be battling.

"This is utter bullshit."

I stuffed the key in the ignition, turned it, and prayed—a little ritual that had become a new habit. "Please start, Missy. Please start. Come on, girl." I'd only recently started calling her Missy. If she was known to be a drift missile, then Missy was the perfect alter ego for her. I just wished I'd come up with the name sooner. We seemed to have a new bond these days, and thank God it was still working. The engine turned over. I gave the dash a little pat of gratitude and began to back out.

For today, my work here was done. Mom was tucked into bed, with ibuprofen and water at her bedside for the middle-of-the-night cotton mouth and headache. She'd know what to do. She was damn near a professional at this point—though if they really *paid* people to get strung out, I didn't want her knowing about it. Besides, Janet usually went with the hair of the dog approach, and I refused to be a part of that.

While heading back into the more populated part of San Diego, I turned up the radio in an attempt to leave the shitty evening behind me. But even humming along to the angsty alt-rock station wasn't helping. More words from Mac's letter kept taunting me, a great reminder that I had to set the damn thing on fire when I got home.

Willing to be in a healthy relationship...

I crunched a frown until actually feeling the furrows in my forehead. "All right, Clown," I gritted. "Are *you* willing to be in one? Do *you* even know what that looks like?" I finished with a satisfied snort. When I'd first met the ass, he'd been working so many days straight that he didn't know if it was day or night. Forget other basic *relationship* stuff like, say, remembering names or faces.

Though every time you were beneath him, he swore off every other name but *yours...*

Reflections that were *not* needed. *Not* now. *Not* for this process.

Nope. I definitely didn't need awesome sex replays. What I needed were *answers.*

A healthy relationship. What exactly did that look like? Did such a thing even exist? Even Claire and Killian Stone, likely the most happily married people I knew, had one hell of a roller-coaster ride getting to where they were today. And according to the rest of our mutual friends, it was a lot of work keeping things functioning well, no matter what stage a relationship might be in. It required honesty and bravery, fortitude and forgiveness, patience and persistence.

So what the hell was Mac basing his comment on? His own personal "experience" with "healthy"? And where, exactly, was *that* acquired? His psychotic mother was on her third husband, if I remembered correctly. No *Leave it to Beaver* theme song for *that* upbringing. And as an adult, he'd spent the better part of his life hopping from operating rooms to race cars to strangers' beds.

Maybe he was a neurosurgeon with a minor in family psychology. Now wouldn't *that* explain a lot? At least the musing made me laugh out loud before adding a little pressure to the gas pedal. Mac's love of driving had been rubbing off on me. I guess his promise of letting me drive on the track at Thermal was as empty as all the others he'd made.

The sign for my apartment complex came into view in record time. The nearly empty late-night roads coupled with my complete disregard for the speed limit got me home in no time at all. I pulled into my space as Evanescence blared

"Going Under," one of my favorites of all time. The lyrics were perfectly, painfully meaningful tonight...

★ ★ ★ ★

"Will you grab the potato salad from the refrigerator in the laundry room, honey?" Talia had her hands full with an elaborate fruit salad loaded into a basket carved from the shell of a watermelon, so when I asked if she needed a hand, she took me up on the offer.

"Through here, right?" I pointed toward a doorway to my right. The home she shared with her two husbands, Drake and Fletcher, was enormous and complicated. I couldn't remember which door led where, though I'd been inside it more times than I could count.

"Yep, right there. The light is on your left." She called it over her shoulder while heading in the opposite direction toward the sliding-glass door. Just beyond that was the backyard where she, Drake, and Fletcher had gotten married last September.

"Wow," I mumbled. It had been almost a year since that memorable day. Crazy how much had changed in just eight months.

So much...

I found the switch and flipped it on, illuminating the room. The large stainless refrigerator was in the opposite corner alongside a front-loading washer and dryer. I took out the potato salad and then turned to head back toward the kitchen. At the same time, the other door from the garage swung open, almost knocking the bowl out of my hands. I dodged out of the way just in time...

Only to look up into jade-green eyes as intent and beautiful as I remembered.

Surrounded by that face, as strong and chiseled as I remembered.

Turning my stomach inside out, in every incredible way I remembered.

Would walking into the same space as Mac Stone *ever* fail to do this to me? Did I want it to?

Judging by the looks on his and Fletcher's faces, they'd been gawking at Fletcher's new car. The guy was almost as obsessed with high-speed performance vehicles as Mac, but Talia absolutely would not allow Fletch on a racetrack after the accident that had nearly taken his life. So he filled his need for speed with the brand-new 520-horsepower addition to BMW's lineup, the 8 Series coupe.

Apparently I'd walked in on the middle of Fletcher confiding to Mac that he was "working on her." I was damn sure he meant Talia and not the car but wisely kept my lips compressed. Talia had confided in *me* about the man's specific "persuasive techniques," leading to my quick conclusion that he might just end up getting his way after all.

Fletcher visibly brightened as I appeared in the doorway, a smile surreptitiously crossing his boyishly handsome face. "Hey, Taylor! How's it going?"

I grinned at him knowingly. I'd seen the same genuine, excited look on Mac's face so many times when he talked about his "babies," as he called them. "Doing good, Fletcher, thanks."

Quickly turning a shade of pink I was certain I'd never seen on his face before, Fletch scooted past me, grabbing the bowl from my hands as he went. And that was how the tables officially got turned on me inside ten seconds—ensuring *I* had heat-flushed cheeks to answer Fletcher's shit-eating wink.

"I'll get this to Tolly," he drawled. "You're welcome."

I arched both brows. "Are you kidding me?"

He waggled both of his. "Why don't you two kids stay out here and have a nice chat?"

I grimaced. Then huffed. There were such things as surprise setups, but then there were things such as full-on ambushes. I wrote myself a quick self-reminder. *Next time Talia asks for help with the potato salad, pretend I'm late for a wax appointment.*

"Shit." We muttered it in tandem as Fletch shut the door, sealing us together in the massive laundry room.

"So." I tried for nonchalance, certain I sounded like an idiot instead. "How's it...uhhh...going, Mac?"

"Good, good. You?" His grin infuriated me and turned me on at the same time.

"Okay." I shrugged, convinced I sounded like an idiot. *Idiot.* "You...uh...look good." I inspected the floor while I spoke this time.

"Thanks. And you...do..."

His voice trailed off as we finally looked up together, right into each other's eyes. I sucked a breath in. *Holy shit.* The awful-letter-writing clown was more gorgeous than I remembered. Those piercing green eyes. His umber hair messy yet perfect, like he'd just been for a ride with the top down and loved every second of it.

"Damn it."

"What?" he prompted, taking a slow, purposeful step closer.

"You look better than good."

I clapped my hand over my mouth, yearning to take it back

the minute it slipped out. *Shit, shit, shit, shit!* Giving this man and his ego the upper hand was the last thing I wanted to do.

"Yeah?"

"You're wrecking it by talking though." My grin grew wider in proportion to his.

Until he wasn't grinning anymore. Instead, as he reached out and touched my cheek, he was damn near somber about murmuring, "I've missed you, Taylor." But the caress was over as soon as it started, and I instantly missed his warmth before he pulled away, betraying what looked like his own loss.

"Mac." My voice was quiet, plaintive.

"Oh, sassy girl." Without hesitation, he stepped right back in. He brought up his hand again, cupping my cheek with deeper pressure—but then, pausing there, his breath snagged and held as he watched me carefully, waiting for me. Needing my approval. Craving my *yes*...

I wanted to. Dear *God*, how I wanted to.

And was a split second from caving...

But stepped back instead.

Traitor brain! *Why?* My heart and body wanted to jump on him like a monkey, wrapping my arms and legs around him and never letting go. What the *hell* was this stepping back bullshit?

"I... We..."

"What?" His gaze turned the shade of a haunted forest, the green nearly turned to black. Oh holy crap, did thick and needy lust look fantastic on him. "What is it?"

Hard gulp. Swimming senses. "This—This isn't the place," I blurted with trumped-up conviction. "We're way too fucked up for a quick make-out session in someone's laundry closet, and we both know it, Mac."

The forest gained new shadows. The beautiful planes of his rugged face turned the texture of dark concrete—except for the twitch of a smirk at one corner of his firm lips.

"Firstly, I had no intention of being quick."

He closed the step I'd just taken, actually thinking I could create a buffer between us. We were only inches apart again.

"Secondly, if this is your idea of a closet, I'd better ask for a raise."

He lifted his hand to the back of my neck, cradling my head in his big palm.

"And...third?" I husked, though the effort was a challenge. Damn, how he affected me. Aroused me. Seared every inch of my bloodstream with the knowledge of his nearness...and my inevitable reaction to it.

"Well." He wet his lips, making me do the same. "Third is..." He held me captive the entire time he spoke, and his words prodded incessantly at my wounded heart. "You're right."

I blinked. "I...am? About what?"

"We're pretty fucked up right now," he finally murmured. "But at least we both agree, and at least we're both still using the word *us*."

And *now* I really and truly couldn't speak. So I just stared up at him, not even beginning to process everything he'd just said. *A raise?* Like we'd be buying a home together in the future? And *us*? Not quick about it? "It" what? My heart throbbed. My body tingled. And worst of all, my head spun like it usually did when this infuriating and sexy bastard was near me.

"Mac..."

"Hmmm?"

His mouth was inches from mine. I fixated on the deep dip in the upper part and how the edges curled up a little. I wanted to trace all those enticing hills and angles. Memorize them. But that would have to wait—because right now, all I wanted to do was kiss him.

Deeply.

Thoroughly.

Not stopping until our tongues were eagerly meshing, our lips were passionately pressing, and our breaths were nearly matching. Hot for hot. Fire for fire. Lust for lust. Nothing had changed. No; it was better. More consuming than I remembered. More primal. More desperate.

More...of *everything...*

"Taylor. God*damn*." He rushed it out between feverish pants, but only until I grabbed his hair and hauled him down for a crashing collision. I was a woman possessed, starving for the spice-and-wind taste of him. Thrumming for the steel-and-sin feel of him. Aching for the complete and total dominance of him. "Can...can we go somewhere?" he finally snarled against my lips. "Will you come back to my place?"

I held back a conflicted mewl. *Oh, God.* The heat of his body and the hopeful desire in his eyes were so damn hard to resist...and nearly impossible to turn down.

"No. I mean, yes," I stammered. "*No.* Wait. I mean, not right now. I mean, we just—*I* just—got here." I closed my eyes, sealing myself from his gorgeousness so I could wrestle together the might to move away. It was the only way I'd think clearly. "I promised Talia I'd help her with the party. And I haven't seen the babies yet. And, well. Yeah, no. Not today. But I would like to." *Oh God, would I really like to.* "To see you, I mean. If you still want to. To see me, I mean."

"Oh, Sassy." He chuckled, his arrogance simultaneously enraging me and stoking my lust. Well, more than it was.

Maybe a little more than *more*. Whatever the hell *that* level was. “Are you stoned?”

“Fine.” My retort was the same mix of arousal and aggravation. “Fuck off, Clown.” I disengaged fully, whirling to step away, but he grabbed my hand before I could get too far.

“Eloquent as always.” His wink actually did make me feel lit up—not that I was going to let *him* know that. “Come here. Come *here*.” He gave in, holding his arms out and curling the tips of his fingers in. I took one step closer, making him meet me halfway. The gesture was necessary for me to see. He did it without hesitation, wrapping me all the way into his embrace, and at once I buried my face in his strong chest. And breathed in his crisp, masculine smell. And let myself sink into the knowledge of his safe, sure hold.

Holy shit, I’d missed him. More than I’d been letting myself admit.

We stood there for a few minutes, simply savoring the contact of each other again, before he finally leaned back, letting me see the taut look on his face.

“What?” I prodded.

“You need to take better care of yourself.”

I rolled my eyes. “Oh, for—”

“*Please*. Eat something that’s actually nutritious today.”

“Is that an order, Clown?”

He narrowed his eyes. “Would you listen if it were? You can’t keep doing this to yourself. Eat something other than cereal with a cartoon character on the fucking box. Protein would be a good start.” He folded his arms. “I’m going to get Margaux on my side, and then you’ll be sorry.”

I openly laughed. “Good luck with that, pal. The girl is jealous of *this*.” I waved my hand up and down the length of my vanishing body, attempting to mask a twinge of my own concern. I knew I'd finally see him at one of these Stone get-togethers, just as I knew he'd give me shit about "nutrition." But honestly, eating hadn't been very appealing the past few weeks, and I had lost a few pounds—pounds that probably should've stayed right where they were. It would all come back again in no time; I just needed to put some effort into the game.

Similar to the effort Mac was giving me now, as he continued to glare down his strong nose at me. Apparently the man didn't feel like joking when my well-being was at stake.

"Ease up, chief." I pushed at the muscled wall of his chest. "It's fine. I just haven't been all that hungry. You know very well that I normally have a hearty appetite. Things have been a little stressful lately."

"Your mom?" His words conveyed sincere concern.

"Nah. I haven't heard a word from her in two weeks. Not since the night...well, when..."

I drifted off on purpose, realizing the totally awkward vibe I was projecting but refusing to bring up the letter he'd left on my car. *The* letter. *That* letter. I couldn't think of the damn thing without getting angry all over again, and this time was no different.

"Since the night we broke up?" He finished my thought—which pulled the trip wire on my fury.

"Broke up? Mac, this isn't high school. We weren't going steady. I wasn't wearing your letterman's sweater. Shit. We were fucking. Dating, maybe? Is that what people say in this era? I don't know. But then you kind of threw that out the window, didn't you? With the Dear John letter you so gallantly left on Missy? So brave of you to do that, by the way. Thanks for at least tucking it under the wiper so I'd be absolutely sure to get it. Way to face the music in person."

It all spilled out of me in what sounded like a run-on sentence, the punctuation barely intact. That's how it all felt inside too. Hot and messy and pushy and rude—a monster clawing to be unleashed. Only in that moment did I realize the creature had been prowling for a while, waiting for the right chance to destroy my composure and roar free.

"Missy?"

"What about her?" I barked.

"Did you rename your 240sx 'Missy'?"

"Well, the alter-ego thing, remember? Suits her, don't you think?"

"Of course it does."

His gentle response, along with the recognition that he truly remembered why I'd been calling my car by a different name, settled my tone by a few octaves. All the while, he kept grinning. Because he got the reference.

Because he got *me*.

"Don't try to distract me. I'm pissed at you for leaving that letter there. It was a total ball-less-wonder maneuver."

He broke out into new laughter, half choking between his answering words. "Ball-less...wonder?"

"What? You want to pretend it was courageous to write all that shit in a letter and leave it on my car?" My tone danced on the borderline of bitch, but I didn't care. I'd been ramping up for this moment for weeks. Each day, every day. Ramping. Readying. For exactly this chance. To take enough of a chunk out of the good doctor so he bled too. So he hurt just as deeply as I had on the night he dropped that soul-crushing letter on me.

"It's the only way you'd hear me out, Taylor."

"Hear you out?"

"You heard me. Or did you?"

He was so fucking sane about it. Trying to make the shit sound like...*logic*.

"Sure." I spun around and advanced on him, leading the action with my head. I probably looked like a goose on crack, but I didn't fucking care about that either. "Keep telling yourself that."

"What?" He spread a smile, so gorgeously benign. And then added his stunning stare, full of such tender adoration that I wasn't sure whether to slap him or maul him. "Have *you* ever tried having a serious conversation with you, Taylor?"

I screwed my face up tight. "That's...absurd."

"Well, you know what I mean."

"So it was *my* fault? Am I hearing you correctly?" I whooshed back, both arms up with my palms facing out. "You really should have texted. Easier, faster, and just as high on the douchebag scale."

He paled for a moment as my words seemed to finally sink in. After inhaling and then exhaling deeply, he stated, "I'm sorry, then."

I sputtered. Lovely. Guess it was better than looking like a rehab-ready goose. "You're..."

"Sorry," he filled in, clearly meaning it. "Sorry if I handled things wrong. Sorry if my method wasn't right. I hope you can forgive me for that. But now, I really hope we can work on us"—there was *the word* again—"because I've missed you so much."

I sucked in a long breath of my own. "You...you have?"

"Yeah." He stared harder at me. "I've realized over the past couple of weeks without you that I want you to be a part of my life. All the ways you make me smile and laugh...and yeah, even rage and go a little nuts...I want all of it, Taylor." He braced himself directly in front of me, reaching down to wrap both my hands inside his steady, certain grip. "I want to do what it takes for that to happen."

And finally, he paused again. He just stared down at me with those intense greens, encompassing me in his strong hold and letting me process everything about what he'd said.

His confession was...healing. My fire was cooled, my anger chopped in half. But shit, that meant my resolve was caving. Fast. "I would like that, as well."

See, Doc? I can be an adult too.

He grinned as if I'd just declared we were truly going to Disneyland. "Okay. So maybe we can make some sort of plan?" The hopeful look on his face returned while he dipped his toe in the still-stormy waters of us. But at least now there *was* an *us*.

"Okay," I answered. "What are you doing next weekend? And don't think we're done discussing a certain communiqué."

"I have my first race at Thermal. Finally." His tone changed when an idea struck. "Hey! Why don't you come? The house is finished, and you can stay if you'd like."

"I'll text you. I may already have plans." I was dying to just tell him yes but didn't want to make it too easy for him. Though he smirked like he already knew *that*, as well. *Glorious, gorgeous, pompous ass.*

"Okay." And yep, there went the supremely self-pleased head nod. "I'm glad I saw you here today," he said, tucking a kiss to my cheek. "Now go eat. I, regrettably, have to leave. I'm on call and have to go do rounds."

I paused for a few beats. I didn't want to see him leaving already, now that we were on some sort of mending trajectory.

"Happy Memorial Day, Mac." I looked directly into his carved, forceful face. I couldn't believe life was giving me a second chance with this smart-as-hell, sexy-as-fuck man. But was I brave enough to go for it? To make this happen now?

I prayed the answer was yes.

That somewhere deep inside me, *yes* was really going to happen this time.

"Same to you, Sassy."

He hugged me again, bussing me on the forehead as we pulled apart. I already missed everything about him. The way my arms felt around him, the way he smelled, the way my heart sped up when he was near me... All of it.

I wanted him so much.

And couldn't wait to see him again.

I walked back into the house with a stupid smile on my face, almost colliding with three impatient and expectant women. Claire, Margaux, and Talia, my three closest friends in the world, standing with hands on their hips and grins on their lips, all but tapping their red-white-blue-pedicured toes, waiting for every detail about what had just happened behind that closed door.

But honestly, I wasn't sure I knew myself.

CHAPTER TWO

Mac

Time became the cage that confined me. Something that felt like madness set in as the days dragged on. First there was Tuesday in the clinic and then a dragged-out Wednesday from hell in my office catching up on dictations and paperwork. I welcomed Thursday, as my surgical rotation always sped by. By the time we sutured Mr. Creager's cranial incision, most of the hospital was quiet for the evening.

There was actually a bounce in my step as I walked through the parking structure, readying to go home. Tomorrow I'd head out to Thermal. On the following day, my perfect Taylor would be back in my arms—and then beneath my body, if fortune chose to smile my way.

Fuck, I missed her. Everything about her. Her silly jokes and the even sillier way she always laughed at them. The look on her face when she thought of something kind to do for someone else but then quickly attempted to cover up the softness in her demeanor with some smart remark. All the things she didn't think I knew about her. All the things she didn't even know about herself.

And then there were the more obvious things. All the shit that drove my senses crazy and woke my cock with matching speed—especially when she let me put the pedal to the metal on those urges. Her creamy skin, always smelling like whatever lotion had hit her fancy that week. Her fluffy, fresh-fucked hair that tickled my cheeks when she snuggled against me after I'd screwed her through a few gasping, gorgeous orgasms...

"Shit," I muttered—*after* the long, lovesick teenager sigh that escaped my throat. And what of it? If the shoe fits and all that, right? Well, this footwear fit—in all the best ways. I'd fantasized nonstop about having her in every possible way there was. Holding her. Kissing her. Fucking her. Oh yeah—that part especially. We'd more than make up for the time we'd lost over the past month. I was a man on a goddamned mission, and this week had been an agonizing trip to insanity and back due to my rising level of need for Taylor Mathews. I seriously feared I'd completely consume her when we finally reunited.

An irrational fear. The woman could handle it. She could handle *me*. And she was the one woman I'd ever encountered who deserved my complete conviction about that statement. Not only could she take anything and everything I threw at her, but she also could single-handedly put me in my place at the same time. *When necessary.* Sometimes it was necessary to put *her* in *her* place...

Annnnd that was enough to fire up everything between my legs again.

More than enough.

My cock swelled beneath the thin cotton of my scrubs, and I laughed at the fucker's painful protest as I hit the car's ignition, filling the garage with its palpable rumble. Yeah, just what I needed. That sound *and* a brain full of thoughts about the most exciting, entrancing woman I'd ever met. And not just because of her silky hair, her satin skin, and that body deserving of my full worship. That spitfire and her sassy comebacks... She connected with me deeper than skin, on a real cerebral level. A place most other women left me completely wanting.

Needing.

Jesus, I had it bad.

And was reveling in every incredible second of it.

When Saturday finally arrived, I was pumped for several reasons. I couldn't wait to get on the track for my first race since leaving Chicago. Adrenaline surged in my veins from the anticipation of getting behind the wheel and pushing my car to its limits. I had put in a lot of laps since Taylor and I split up, and the turns of the track were second nature now. My little rocket of a car had become an extension of me. I felt confident. Ah, screw it—I felt fucking cocky. A lot of the local guys had their eye on me as the pretty-boy new kid, but they'd learn what was what soon enough. That they should be judging my skill and speed, not my tenure in town.

And if Taylor wore that crazy wraparound dress again, they'd be jealous fucks about that too.

Not that I really gave a crap about what they thought.

Not when I was about to hand out asses on platters—as a warm-up to the real action of the weekend. In all the best ways...

Fuck, I couldn't wait.

I sent her a quick text last night, telling her I was looking forward to seeing her today and a bid to drive safely on her way out to the desert. I knew she read the message, but in perfect hard-to-get fashion, she'd never sent an actual reply. Not even an emoji.

While gunning the engine as I merged from the 76 to the 15, I cracked a broader grin. The woman had left me with way too much time alone, and my imagination had become a creative and crafty workroom for clever ways to tame her sassy fire. She'd be screaming my name by sundown; I vowed it. My visions of her, under me and on top of me and in other positions with me, meant I'd masturbated more in the past month than most of my teenage years. Well, the monkey was done being spanked. Tonight I'd reclaim what was mine.

My car for the race was in top shape—a stunning Austin Yellow M3. Along with my new crew chief, Ron, I had made a few last-minute adjustments that would hopefully give me an edge on the track. I'd only taken this car on the loop since I'd been living in California, although I brought it with me from Chicago. I just hadn't found the time to make the modifications necessary from a regular street car to a track-worthy beast until I found myself with unclaimed free time without Taylor. The back seat and all the manufacturer's niceties were now stripped from the car. Sweet Recaro seats were up front, waiting for me to strap in and go. A passenger seat was installed as well in case Taylor ever wanted to get back in with me. It was always fun to remember the first time I'd taken her out and opened things up. Fuck, she'd been so adorable that day, especially during her little zigzag wobble right after the ride. But especially after we'd come back from dinner that night and I buried my cock inside her during the night race. With her hands bound and her lush lips pleading for me to fuck her...

Shit.

Maybe it *was* going to be necessary to find a few minutes alone and rub one out.

Somehow, I managed to calm shit down, and then I got my ass to the clubhouse, where I found my name on the board. I'd been slotted into the second heat. At least I wouldn't have to wait too long to use up some of the adrenaline spiking my system. Some, but not all. My girl was going to get what she deserved—namely, every inch of my erection thrusting into her tight, perfect body. *Damn, yes.*

I wore my lucky firesuit because I was feeling a bit nostalgic for my East Coast squad. Plus, I'd never lost while wearing it. Did I worry more about winning the damn race or impressing the girl who'd captured my heart? It seemed like a pretty fair toss-up. When they called through the complex for the second-heat drivers to man their cars, I was so jacked up, I barely felt the pavement under the soft soles of my racing shoes.

The green flag signaled the pack to start. The engine sounds penetrated my helmet, injecting me with the thrill I'd become addicted to as a child. Where a non-motorsport enthusiast would hear loud chaos, I heard a symphony. This thrill wasn't for everyone, and I was thankful it gave me the release I couldn't find anywhere else.

We moved through the first few turns as a pack, and when we reached the initial straightaway, I downshifted to get more power. I pulled away from all but two of the other cars. I knew the next turn ahead would be a great place to edge out another car, so I planned my apex carefully and waited to make a move. Sure enough, the car ahead of me started his turn too late and too fast, causing him to oversteer and head sharply into the turn. I passed behind him, came out on his right, and accelerated at just the point his ass end drifted out behind him, and I shot ahead while he continued to correct for his mistake.

Only one car stood between me and the first-place claim on my heat. And damn it if it wasn't that red Porsche Cayman from the night Taylor and I watched the race—and did other things—on my villa patio. Thoughts of her sexy sounds battled for top billing in my mind while I tried to concentrate on my driving. Shards of jealousy spiked my mind as I pressed down on the accelerator to gain an edge on the bastard my girl had her eye on. I had to remind myself we were doing a bit of role-playing that night, and in reality, this guy had nothing to do with any of it. I still wanted to finish first, so I closed in on his back bumper. Closer...closer...

Until Ronnie's voice blasted through my helmet.

"Back off, Mac! They'll DQ you. Get him in the carousel!"

My crew chief was a nice guy, and damn did he know his way around BMWs, but I wasn't in the mood to be told what to do. I just wanted to prove to all the regulars that I was a force to be reckoned with.

As we turned left into the long roundabout, I cut to the inside instead of holding the center line like I'd been taught when I first started driving. I gave my car a bit more gas, trying to pass the Porsche. He was ready for me though, fully anticipating my move. He dropped lower into the turn and blocked me.

I eased off the gas and waited for another opportunity. I knew that when we came out of the carousel, it was right into a serpentine and then a quick right. I held my ground through the first phase. When I saw the right bank ahead, I decided to make my move. Instead of the hard brake a driver would typically apply, I pumped the pedal a little and came around on the Porsche's right. Once again, he was aware of my position. He widened his turn and clipped across the front bumper of my M3. I held the wheel tightly and kept my ground through the turn, coming out on the far side of the Cayman.

I gunned the gas. I cut the wheel hard to the right to take

the lead and instead heard metal on metal as I clipped across his driver's side front quarter panel.

The white flag with the large black X went up with my car's number below it. All my ambition had gotten me disqualified. I'd be sidelined for the rest of the day.

I pulled into the pits with an angry screech. I was so pissed off, I itched to punch someone—or some*thing*. When Ronnie jogged up to help me out of my gear, he caught one glimpse of the rage in my eyes and wisely didn't speak. Throwing my gloves and helmet into the car, I barked at the pit crew to bring the car over to the garage.

Fuck. Me.

How could I have made such a rookie mistake? Instead of strutting a win, I was taking a walk of shame. "Fuck," I gritted beneath my breath. "*Fuck*."

I left the pits and beelined through the locker room. If I saw that bastard from the Porsche, I'd probably deck him, and then I'd be banned from the club. Poor sportsmanship wasn't tolerated in auto racing, and I knew better than to have such a hot head in this arena. I needed some time to get my shit together and calm down.

I headed out to my villa, though the bar in the clubhouse sounded like a much better idea.

No. Being with Taylor sounded like a much better idea.

Where was my sassy girl when I needed her? I would love to lose myself between her thighs right now, forgetting that shit show at the track had ever happened. I was restless and hot, feeling like an exposed wire. Frying off the rest of my system's adrenaline with some hot, dirty sex sounded like a grand fucking plan.

The villa's front door slammed behind me after I swung

it shut. The pictures on the shared wall jumped when the portal hit the frame. I steadied them and then scrubbed a hand down my face while forcing a calming breath. Taylor had found those pictures for me. She'd been shopping through a knickknack store in Old Town San Diego and had found the set of reprographics of first-generation Formula One cars—or so she'd said. I still had trouble really believing her, because the images and their steel custom frames were perfect for the villa.

Just like that woman was perfect for me.

Where the hell was she?

Another rake of a hand up and down my face. I really had to pull myself together instead of watching the clock like a kid waiting on his prom date. Or hell, maybe she'd already made it and I didn't know it. I hadn't exactly been in a clear state of mind when walking across the property from the track. I hadn't even thought to look for her car in the visitors' lot...

Most of the motorsports complex was visible from the patio, so I slid the glass door open and stepped out onto the terrace. The desert landscape was flat and extended as far as the eye could see, making the complex seem to stretch out forever. Even though I had a clear view of the visitors' lot, I couldn't see every place she might park.

But then...

There.

I swear to God, my lungs squeezed into my throat and my balls swelled beyond a healthy size. Yeah, from just a look. Yeah, from this far away. Too *damn* far away.

She was strutting her sexy stuff over by the small grandstand. She wore some sort of floaty summer dress that picked up when the wind stirred, and she quickly smoothed it down with modesty. I grinned, thinking how red her cheeks would be if she thought someone caught a peek when the fabric lifted. She was my kinky siren in bed and my pretty librarian on the street. The perfect combination.

"Shit," I muttered, slammed with another new mental quandary. How would I explain why I wasn't on the track? Embarrassment flooded me already—to the point that I began to pace.

I could just make something up. Say my car broke down...

But I refused to lie to her. I swore I would always be honest, and I meant every word. Nothing had changed about that oath.

But fuuuuuuck. I'd failed today. Royally. Had been a complete rookie, letting that bastard get the better of me. And of all the people to let under my skin? The dude with the red Cayman? It was almost comical.

Almost.

My phone chirped with a text message. I rushed to grab the device from the kitchen island—and warmed at once, seeing her name and face light up the screen.

Have you raced already? Hope I didn't miss it. Traffic was awful.

Okay, screw the track. All right, so I didn't mean that—but was as close as I'd ever be to doing so. Suddenly, nothing else mattered but making things right with my sweet Sassy again. Life had been aimless and agonizing since I'd begged for her forgiveness at SGC that awful afternoon.

The only good thing that had come of that clusterfuck was a slightly better relationship with my cousin Killian. He'd tried, in all the ways he knew, to advise me on backing away from Taylor. He'd even used all the talk-show therapy words, saying she needed "space" and some "safe place" to "get grounded again." But she hadn't gotten much of that when things had gotten worse with her leech of a mother, and she'd had to deal with the shitstorm as best as she could. God*damn*, how I'd wanted to run to her then, but Kil had turned up his inner Dr. Phil and come back twice as hard at me with all the psychobabble. Through every minute, I could almost hear Claire's voice delivering the words instead. But in the end, it was fair commentary.

So as difficult as it had been, I'd dropped out of her orbit.

Difficult? Fuck that. Reaching down and slicing my own gonads off would've been an easier alternative. But this weekend was going to change all that. Well, it was supposed to have. I still stared at my phone, wondering how the hell to respond to her message when I should have been fixating on the idea of getting lost in all her pale skin. Absorbing every note of her throaty moans. Getting reacquainted with every inch of her tiny frame. Hell, even just holding her hand while she fidgeted.

But I was frozen. Standing here like a pussy. I might as well have had my dick in my hand instead of my phone.

I'd never been afraid to admit my mistakes. But it had been so long since I'd actually made a solid one. I wasn't wired to tolerate the fuckers, especially from myself, so eating crow was as unfamiliar as eating fried crickets. Worse, eating crow in front of *her*.

I was damn sure hives were going to set in next. The thought of looking like anything less than the best in Taylor's eyes... *No*. Just fuck no.

I set the phone back on the counter without typing a

response to her.

Instead, I paced. Not for long but long enough to recognize I should go take a damn shower. I was hot and sweaty from the firesuit. If she did show up at my door, I wanted to present better than a barnyard animal.

I wasted a lot of time under the spray, washing my hair carefully between whiffs of the girlie body wash she'd left behind the last time we were here together. Little reminders of my Taylor were everywhere, and I liked it that way—especially now, as I remembered how I'd made her come against my lips and tongue in this very shower stall.

Where I was hiding out like a fucking loser.

With his goddamned dick in his hand.

This time, pretty literally.

"Damn it!" I spat. I owed her more than this. A *lot* more.

After drying off hastily, I strolled back to the kitchen, white towel low on my hips, and grabbed my phone. Twenty minutes had passed, and a flurry of texts lit up my screen. All received in almost pinpoint accurate intervals of one minute.

Mac. Where are you?

Seriously, WTF?

Someone said you were disqualified.
What does that even mean?

And where are you?

You know what? Forget I asked.

I bolted out onto my terrace again to see if I could still spot her in the stands. My heart lurched as I caught the taillights of her 240sx as she peeled out of the parking lot toward the main road.

"What the fuck?"

Why hadn't she come up to the house? She was pissed, and I couldn't say I blamed her, but she hadn't even given me a chance to explain.

But do you deserve one?

Shit, shit, shit, *shit*.

If I ever recovered from this mess, it would be a miracle. Honestly, I didn't deserve her forgiveness. I let my own pride get in the way of what I desired the most, and now I'd have to pay the price for it.

Paging Dr. Clown. Egotistical douchebag extraordinaire at your service.

CHAPTER THREE

Taylor

Being back at this place was surreal. It seemed like just moments ago that Mac carried me across this exact parking lot at Scripps Green in La Jolla and then drove me home.

And then changed the fiber of my being.

After that night, absolutely nothing had been the same.

I scanned the lot for an available parking space and pumped a quick fist with the minor victory of spotting white taillights ahead, signaling someone else was backing out. I gave them as much room as possible in the narrow lane, flipping on my turn signal in case anyone came along and had designs on the same parking space.

Missy sputtered and chugged as I parked and then turned the ignition off. I quickly checked out the area again to see if anyone had heard her automotive flatulence.

She never did that when he *drove her.*

And no, I wasn't going to dignify the comment by thinking of that *he* for one more second.

But I was already breaking my own rule.

"Get a grip on yourself," I seethed at my hands, still positioned at ten and two o'clock on the wheel. "This is ridiculous. It's Thursday. He's in surgery." At least I was still at *he* and not the alternative. "There is *no* damn way you'll run into him today. Flukes are flukes because they're...well...flukes. And that last time was a *fluke*."

And I'd officially lost my mind. Talking to myself, alone in my car, even throwing in a hand gesture or two.

But it couldn't be helped. I was so pissed at Dr. Maclain Stone that if I saw the man in person, I'd likely stab him.

No.

I'd *definitely* stab him.

Two weeks had gone by since he'd turned me into a humiliated ass—in the middle of the fucking *desert*. Worse, for a woman who'd been raised by the queen of the game players, I hadn't seen through one second of his game. I'd let my hormones become a hurricane that swept me away, lured completely by his sexy smugness and intoxicating allure—all the way up to the moment I realized he'd stood me up. Did I mention the part about being in the middle of the damn desert?

I hadn't talked to him since that Saturday afternoon—if unanswered texts even counted as talking. Now mid-June was upon us, and I just wanted to head out to the beach for some Pacific Ocean therapy. After I donated some blood. My days off were rare, and I cherished them like gold, which made me long for the similarly colored rays atop the breakers along the shore. I wasn't about to waste one more second thinking about a certain clown.

Thinking about *him*.

There. That was much better.

Inside the Bloodmobile, the giant RV the San Diego Blood Bank used as their command center for on-site collections, it was the same drill as every other time. I signed my name on the clipboard hanging on the door and then grabbed another clipboard of required paperwork off the table. I sat down in one of the plastic chairs lined up against the vehicle and searched my purse for a pen.

"Hey, Taylor! Great to see you." John, one of the regular blood bank phlebotomists, popped his head out the RV door to greet me.

I jumped a little, recovering with a laugh. "Hey, John. Sorry. You...uh...startled me. How's it going?" I flashed a friendly smile though struggled to keep it in place. I silently pleaded the fates that he wouldn't mention the last time I was here. Dear God, what a fiasco that had all been. *Supremely uncomfortable, party of one.*

"Not too bad. Nothing too exciting to report." His boyish grin reached his eyes when he spoke. "At least not 'excitement' the way *you* define it."

Crap, crap, crap; here it comes.

"You're, umm, not going to need rescuing again today, are you? That boyfriend of yours..."

"Yeah, well. Can we just—"

"He's a little...much."

I gulped and tried not to break open a hole in the asphalt to dive into. John grinned wider, finishing his comment with a wink.

"Okay, first..." I began the challenge with a good-natured tilt of my head. "How many times have I given blood here, John? You know that whole thing was just a fluke. I never have problems after donating."

John held up his hands. "Fair enough."

I huffed and then nodded. "Glad we're straight."

He winked again, and my stomach did a weird twist. "So... is there a 'second'?"

"Oh yeah, there fucking *is*." I was definitely back on solid footing. Knew exactly what I wanted—*needed*—to get off my chest, despite the fact that it now looked like *I* was freaking poor *John* out. "Secondly, Dr. Stone is most definitely *not* my boyfriend."

I topped it off with a hard glare, all but daring the poor guy to carry the conversation further. As I could have predicted, John held his hands up a little higher.

"Hey, whatever you say. I was just joking around a little bit." He didn't sound like he'd been joking, but I was glad for his tactics switch, at least.

"Sorry, John," I mumbled. "This is all me. It—him—it's all just still a touchy subject, I guess." I resumed digging for a pen and came out with a bright-pink ballpoint. What the hell? I was batting a thousand at maintaining any semblance of dignity at this point. Thank God it was John, with his sweet disposition and ready acceptance.

"Well." He snorted, and the brutal edge of it had me rethinking the "sweet disposition" stuff. On the other hand, it was kind of nice to see someone getting incensed on my behalf. *Damn* nice. Maybe I wasn't losing my mind, after all. "The guy was a fool to let you go. A *fool.* That's all I know."

"Thanks." I eked out a new smile, but John didn't vacillate from his stance. "You're sweet." And why had I just let *that* slip out? The guy wasn't going to let the subject go, which meant the conversation snippets had to come from me. "But really, he never had me in the first place, so there's that." I finally added a nonchalant shrug and then set to work on the papers in my lap. *There. Done.*

"Let me go check if they're ready for you inside. And really, hon, I'm sorry if I offended you."

Another forced smile. "No worries," I said without looking

up. "It's all good here." I didn't look up again until I heard John's retreating steps followed by the RV's closing door, leaving me to let the memories and anger back in.

Damn it. Damn *him.* When would these taunting thoughts stop? I'd nearly been back in control, and then he had to go and stir *everything* up at the Memorial Day party. Had to go and reinsert himself in every cell of my libido...and hope in my heart. Had to go and invade, just as ruthlessly as he had the first time, every corner of my carefully guarded world. The asshole didn't deserve an *inch* of that real estate, either—let alone the miles he was taking up.

But I missed him. Everywhere. All the damn time. My body ached and throbbed for his touch. My lips tingled when I remembered his kisses. My pussy pulsed when I recalled all the bites he peppered across my body, driving me insane with his lusty gifts of precious pain. He'd drugged me with his sexual skill. Made me an addict to his passion. A total slave to his love.

I was hopeless.

A fool.

Just like my fucking mother.

I hurled the pen back into my purse with a furious growl. "Goddamnit!"

At the same time, someone cleared their throat in front of me. I whipped my sights up to find John standing there again. A bewildered frown consumed his face, and he was wringing his hands like an Amish guy in a strip joint. "You...uhhh... okay?" Clearly, the guy wasn't comfortable around emotional females. At all.

"No," I barked. "I'm really not." But luckily, he didn't call me "hon" again. Probably saved himself from having to extract his balls from his spleen.

"Do you want to reschedule for next time? Really, Taylor, it's fine. You look a little...I don't know...frazzled?" He was choosing his words carefully, his voice soft as though talking to a child.

Which was getting on my nerves worse than "hon."

"God. Sorry, John." I punctuated it with a stiff exhalation. "It's been a really tough week at work. And I've got a lot on my mind. I was a million miles away." I faked yet another smile, gritting my teeth behind my closed lips. At this rate, I was going to need some damn veneers.

"I noticed that."

Forget the veneers. It'd be time for full-on dentures, because I was going to grind everything in my mouth down to stubs. But I had no choice and kept up the look through my prolonged stare. What exactly did he want me to say? His good ol' boy nature was working my last nerve, but I quickly reminded myself none of this was his fault.

"So. Are you ready for me?" I asked, patience as thin as my nerves.

"Yeah, we are." More of his weird hand-wringing thing. "But...uhhh...hey..."

"Yes?" I barely avoided dragging it out like a snake about to strike.

"Before we go inside, can I ask you something?"

I raised my eyebrows in expectation, not trusting my smart mouth not to go in twenty sideways directions if I opened it. This guy was cute but shit at reading a room.

"Well..."

"*John.*" I folded my arms. "Just spit it out."

He settled himself with a self-deprecating grin. "Well, I have my lunch break after your appointment. I was just thinking...maybe we could go grab something together? If... uhhh...you feel like it, I mean."

I pulled in another breath. His stammering was probably enticing to some girls, but not this one. John was the kind of man I'd chew up and spit out before the end of round one. He was kind enough and certainly good-looking—but a guy with a submissive streak this wide didn't call to the deeper desires in my blood, the primitive needs in the corners of my soul. Still, something had to be done about exorcising Mac Stone from my system. Maybe spending some time with someone else—besides the girls and their goo-goo eyes for their husbands—was the way to start that process.

The thought finally led to me throwing up a careless hand. "Ah, fuck it," I laughed out. "Sure. Why not?"

The hand I'd just held up became a stiff symbol of warning. "But, John, please understand that while I'm not involved with Dr. Stone, I have no interest in being anything other than friends with you, okay? I'm not ready for anything else." I owed the guy complete honesty.

"Hey, I get that," he returned. "But friends go out to lunch all the time, don't they? I mean, you probably should eat a little more, Taylor."

I rolled my eyes. It was better than my initial desire of booting him in the shin. "If you say that again, I will throat punch you. So if we are going to have any hope of a friendship, don't go down that road again. 'Kay? 'Kay."

My curtness set him back physically. I think I also freaked him out once more, because he simply turned and motioned for me to follow him into the Bloodmobile. But during all of that, I definitely caught the little smile tugging at the corner of his mouth as he went. Some guys just liked having their balls busted, I guess.

And the *other* kinds of guys? The kinds who rose to an insult like a moth to a flame, getting more and more excited until a frenzy swirled around them? The kind who incited similar energy in every molecule of air around them, literally changing the atmosphere with their presence?

That was the guy I yearned to be having lunch with. The alpha moth who could handle a girl like me.

Damn it to hell. Stop.

The blood draw went without incident, just like it had every other time before I knew the name Maclain Stone. Just invoking his name, even silently, was scrambling my brain while I sat there, but I managed to keep my shit together long enough not to pass out this time.

By the time I finished and had my snack, my thoughts were all clowned-out. I was ready for some fresh air in my lungs and some new human interaction to feed my mind. Wasn't a damn thing to be done for my aching libido, so I worked to ram it to a back burner while waiting outside at the table for John to wrap up and join me.

During those few minutes, I worried if I'd indeed made a mistake.

When he came out the door, all smiles and puffed-up chest, I was pretty certain I had.

"So where would you like to go, my lady?" His mock chivalrous tone already had my teeth all but wrestling each other again.

"Okay, really," I scoffed. "I'm no one's lady. And wherever is good. I can find something anywhere; I'm not picky."

"Well, I have a gluten allergy—and nuts and shellfish also. And eggs. Oh, and citrus too. We probably should go to this place I usually go. They have a great non-GMO menu."

"Yeah. Fine." Though it sounded like he was speaking another language. *Not* that I wanted to go there. At this point, I sensed simpler was going to be better. How the hell had I thought this would kill the damn moth? "Just get me some grub, and I'll be good. Probably best to take separate cars." Best—and wise. "I'll follow you. Where are you parked?"

John pouted. No, seriously. *Pouted.* "Oh, come on. Let's just drive together. The parking sucks everywhere in this town."

"Fine." I hated giving up the escape option if things got really awkward—not that they weren't already—but the guy had a point. "I'll drive, then. I'm right over here."

"Cool. My wheels are all the way over in the employee lot, anyway. Half my lunch hour would be over by the time we got there."

He laughed like he'd just told the best joke, and I attempted to join in. I was really going to try to give this my best effort—and in the end, I was glad I did.

Lunch wasn't too bad after all. I discovered the guy was very smart—probably overly so, for the job he had—and had a lot of interesting hobbies. I ended up telling him that I played chess, and he was eager to announce that while he wasn't very good, he'd love to play sometime. Of course, that sent my mind careening down the kinky Mac Stone path again, remembering the night the man had won himself a sleepover by beating me fair and square. On my own special antique board to boot!

Brilliant, arrogant jackass.

I hated him.

But there was the rub.

I didn't.

Not even close.

I could tell myself all the lies I wanted, but it wouldn't change the way my heart and libido betrayed me every time the man's soulful green eyes came into my thoughts. Or his insolent, inviting smirk. Or his sinfully sculpted body. Or everything he could do to me with it...

Damn it. There I went. *Again.*

John was being a good sport about it too. He caught me drifting off a few times—all right, maybe more than a few—but instead of being a jerk, he just waited patiently, picking at his falafel—or whatever the hell he was eating.

"What is that again?" I pointed toward his plate with my fork.

"It's quinoa, kale, beets, and goat cheese on a bed of mixed greens. It's pretty good, actually. You want to try a bite?"

I crinkled my nose. "Jesus Christ, man. Do you ever just jones for pizza? Or nachos?"

"Used to," he answered, his voice edged with notes I didn't recognize. "But I've been eating pretty clean for most of my adult life, so now that all that crap is out of my rotation, I don't really miss it." Ah. Superiority. *That* was the edge. I wasn't sure I appreciated it very much.

"Crap? Did you just call pizza crap?" I dramatically swept my hands up to clutch my heart, but John just scowled. "Dude, it's like the fifth food group." I laughed to emphasize the tease. "I'm going to go over and cry in the corner if you say that shit again."

Finally that got him laughing, and I beamed a smile in return. The guy was actually adorable when he relaxed a little. I had no doubt that he'd make the right girl very happy one day. I just wasn't going to be her.

After we settled in and had a few bites in silence, he murmured, "So, when you keep checking out into the stratosphere, is it the doctor?" He had the decency to look sheepish about the pry. "Did he hurt you?"

I took an evasive sip of my iced tea. "I really don't want to talk about it. Is that okay? I'm having a nice lunch here with my *friend*. Why spoil it?"

"You're right," he conceded right away. "I just want you to know you can confide in me, Taylor." But the capitulation didn't stop him from reaching for my hand. I quickly pulled back, occupying both my hands with a nervous fiddle at my napkin. "I'd like to be here for you. As your *friend*." He underlined the word by swiping up his hand, cutting off my interruption before it started. "That's what friends do for each other, right? I mean, who knows? Maybe some night *I'll* call *you* crying after some girl has broken *my* heart."

I let the comment hang in the air. I had no intention of giving John a single digit of my phone number when we parted today. He was nice, but that was *it*. There was nothing wrong with his friendliness and understanding, but there was nothing really right about it, either. I could get a dog and have as much fun—and maybe some great exercise, if he was one of those let's-go-running kind of pooches.

I weathered a twinge of guilt for thinking that way, but a truth was a truth. I had all the friends I needed with Claire, Margaux, and Talia. I didn't need some smothering guy who wanted to be my running pooch with benefits. We would never, and I meant never, graduate from the friend zone.

Finally resolved to that conclusion, I finished my lunch and was glad when John did the same, allowing us to head right back to the hospital. He was getting antsy because his lunch hour had ended ten minutes prior, and as much as I pushed Missy up Torrey Pines Hill, she would only go as fast as she wanted to go. I found a spot to park quicker than ever and got out to say goodbye to John—all the while wishing I could just stop and let him off in front of the Bloodmobile. But the dude and his lingering, all-too-tight hugging abilities had other ideas.

Ugh.

"I had a great time with you today, Taylor," he proclaimed. "Thank you for agreeing to have lunch with me."

"Hey, what are friends for?" I laughed, but it was a little too loud and a little too hard for the moment. My jig was up. I'd surrendered the dead giveaway—but the guy leaned in again, arms outstretched for another hug, causing me to start laughing for real.

His bewildered look was both priceless and heartbreaking. I was confident I hadn't sent any mixed signals throughout our meal. He must have sensed my ensuing bewilderment about that, because he sent over a sideways grin. "Friends hug one another, Taylor."

I tried to laugh again—not because I felt it but because he was right. I was acting like an uptight prude. Still, I gave him just one more hug—a swift one this time—and dodged out of his arms when he tried to peck my cheek. Okay, so friends did that too, right? Fine. Maybe I *was* a prude, then. At least when it came to guys suddenly looking at me like Labradors wanting to hit the beach trail.

"Yeah, uhh...okay," I muttered quickly. "See you around." I added a halfhearted wave as John headed for the RV and then rapidly spun back around to fast-track it to my car.

That was before I saw him.

Yes. *Him* as in...*him.*

Oh, *motherfucker.*

Especially because I was too damn late to prevent the inevitable. The hurricane named Mac was really going to happen. Dr. Stone, in all his incensed glory, was already at a full charge across the lawn, all but tearing the grass out by the roots with his pounding footsteps. His white coat flapped behind him like a superhero's cape.

He was furious. Unstoppable.

And so damn hot.

Meaning I was so fucked.

He finally stopped, chest pumping, hands fisted, and legs braced, on the median in front of my car. "That guy again?" He stabbed a finger at the Bloodmobile. "Really? Haven't we been down this road already, Taylor?"

He panted like an animal between the questions he hurled, and all I could think about was letting out the animal he called to in me. As in, tearing his clothes off. And then mine. And then fucking him like a rutting, wild thing at the mercy of my wildest, raunchiest instincts.

I tried battling the lust but recognized that fail at once. Instead, I shoved it all into another sensation. A rage to fully match his. "What I do is none of your damn concern." Unbelievably, I managed to seethe it out with a completely serene smile—and inwardly congratulated myself for it. Oh God, how it egged him on. And oh God, how I loved watching the twisted evidence of that across his carved, gorgeous features.

"Fuck. That," he gritted, prowling closer—and doubling the breaths in my lungs. "Everything about you is my concern, Taylor Mathews. Every. Thing."

He crowded farther into my personal space, forcing me to inhale his clean scent, to hear every nuance of his breaths, to feel every speck of his energy. He was finally so close, I had to tilt my head back to answer.

"Not anymore, Clown. You threw that all away—or are you conveniently forgetting that part too?"

His brows turned into umber slashes over his feral glare. "Forgetting *what*?"

"That—That stunt in Thermal," I spat. "We clear now? The seven hundred texts I haven't responded to weren't enough?" It was actually seven hundred and one as of this morning, but who was counting? "Not that smart for a brain surgeon. But I think we've been down that road before too."

His lips twisted. "I wouldn't have to be so persistent if you would just fucking answer me!"

I dropped my jaw. I had no other choice. "Are you really yelling at me about this? I mean, *really*?"

"I'm not yelling!"

"You need to check yourself. *Now*."

I turned on my heel and made a renewed beeline toward Missy, but Mac grabbed me by the crook of my arm. Yanked me back against his heaving chest. Secured me tight against him, my back to his front, using the position to dip in and growl directly in my ear.

"I'm not through with you, sassy girl." His deep voice vibrated down my spine, flooding my panties with freshly aroused cream. "I will *never* get you out of my system, Taylor."

When I went to pull away again, he locked his other forearm across my chest, holding me even tighter. I could feel his cock swelling and pressing into my ass, even before he ground that beautiful length against my trembling crack. The move was bold and lewd and—

"Not fair." I issued the last of it as the condemnation that it was. "So...*so* not fair." My voice was a low moan by now, thick with my abject need, my instantly insane arousal.

He didn't help a damn thing with his growly breath at my neck and those continued rolls of his hips. Oh dear *God*, his hips. "So much in life isn't fair, Sassy—but I refuse to watch you walk away a second time without fighting back."

"You...you had a second chance. I drove out to the damn desert to give it to you, and—"

"I can explain."

"Oh, bite me, Clown!"

The second it burst out, I identified the mistake it was. Or maybe the blessing.

At once, I was following the rebellion with a dark, low moan—as he sank his teeth into the flesh of my earlobe. He sent his tongue out, warm and generous, to soothe away the pain...

And to send a hundred shocks of awakening straight to my pussy.

"Mac. Stop," I finally—unbelievably—managed. "You have to stop. We're in the middle of a fucking parking lot!"

"And your point is..."

"Uh, parking lot?" I retorted. "And I'm not defiling Sally that way."

"I thought her name was Missy."

"Wh-Whatever."

I tried squirming away, but it was useless. And *he* was impossible.

"Come with me." Mac started tugging me away from the parking lot, toward the hospital's main building.

"No," I declared—but kept stumbling behind him, following like a desperate rat behind the Pied Piper. "Stop. Where are we going?"

He stopped long enough to swing back toward me—to impale my whole system with the hungry heat of his brilliant tiger eyes. "We're going to go settle this bullshit once and for all. If I have to cancel every appointment I have for the rest of the afternoon, so be it."

I let my jaw drop, spluttering at him. "You—You can't just—"

"Watch me, baby," he snarled. "Just. Fucking. Watch. Me." His stare flashed brighter. His hold clenched me harder. "I'll do it, and I won't think twice. Because I'm going to remind you why you can't be without me. And more than that, why I can't bear to be without you. Not for one more goddamned second."

CHAPTER FOUR

Mac

Rage.

Anger didn't quite cover the intensity of the emotion I was feeling. Rage summed it up fucking nicely, though. When I left the hospital to get some files in my car, I saw that damn blood bank truck across the campus and was drawn to it like a magnet. I had no idea if she would be there or if she would stay away just to ensure she didn't have to face me, but I started off in that direction without giving it much more thought.

Or maybe I'd been spurred by seven hundred unanswered texts.

Seven. Hundred.

Shitty thing was, it probably wasn't an exaggeration. Since my idiot-fest in Thermal, Taylor hadn't answered a single one of my text messages or phone calls. The next step was likely going to be showing up at her apartment, but I'd played that hand before. This woman deserved better than a fucking do-over. She deserved unique. She deserved extraordinary. She deserved everything outside my usual arsenal.

Then fate brought me the fresh approach, right in my lap. And I'd had nothing but pure intentions when I started toward the RV—okay, not true; it was rare that I had pure intentions about anything where she was concerned—but it had been a good start. But like I said, "pure" and I rarely got along when it came to this woman, and I was done apologizing for it. She craved me *because* of it. Now she just needed a reminder of what all that meant for her.

A fucking huge reminder, if I had my way about this.

And I fully intended to have my way.

My cock was steel between my legs. I was grateful I hadn't left my white coat in my office when I came outside. Storming across the hospital's lobby, all but dragging my woman by her hair with my hard-on leading the way, probably wouldn't sit well with the mostly senior crowd waiting for their appointments.

Flash of brilliance. Even with my swelling dick making me half-crazy, I remembered there was an outdoor entrance to the stairwell that led directly to the hallway to access my office. I just needed to guess which unmarked door took me there.

Tried the first one. Locked. I'd just come down that way a few minutes before and noticed a sign saying the door had to remain unlocked during business hours. *Fuck.*

"Mac!" Her exasperated burst made me realize I'd snarled the word out loud. By this point, her little puffs of exhaled air were washing over me every time she tried to break free—which was about every ten seconds. "Let go, damn it. I can walk myself."

"I don't trust you won't run off. And we really need to set some things straight."

I turned to emphasize that before trying the next door handle—and was nearly knocked off my fucking feet. There was an aroused glow, almost flame-like, in her deep-blue eyes. Her cheeks had delectable swatches of pink coloring them. Her lips were a slightly darker hue, freshly wetted and slightly parted. *Christ all-fucking-mighty.* I longed to yank her jeans to the ground and claim her right here. Yeah, *right here.*

And damn it, I almost did.

Instead, I pressed her back against the hard stucco wall, caging her with hands cupped to each side of her neck. I wasted no time taking her mouth in a brutal, possessive kiss. Her moan was swallowed by my desire, and I thrust my tongue in when her sexy sound escaped. I swept from side to side inside her lush mouth, tasting her intoxicating flavor, before wrapping my hand all the way around her throat. I pulled back from the kiss and waited for her to meet my stare.

"I've missed you so bad. So *fucking* bad," I grated out.

She swallowed hard, turning me on in a thousand more ways as her larynx undulated against my hand. "I...oh...I..."

I stopped her by kissing her again. Hard. And rough. And thoroughly. Finally, I pulled back. Not far. I only needed enough distance to husk out one vital question.

"What the *hell* are you doing to me?"

Her eyes flared wide. "What am *I* doing to—"

"I don't know how to control myself, Taylor. *Taylor.* I want to fuck you right here, out in the open, so every other man on this planet knows who you belong to."

She gulped again, such an unknowing tease against the light pressure of my palm. Her eyelids dropped lower, nostrils flared, as she tried—again, unsuccessfully—to form some sort of coherent comeback.

"Don't bother saying anything," I injected. "You can't deny this insanity any more than I can. Don't insult either of us by trying anymore." I leaned closer again, kissing the side of her jaw, trailing kisses toward her ear. I couldn't stop myself from adding tiny bites to that journey, craving to mark her creamy skin with my filthy intent. She wanted that possession too. I could feel it in every breath she took, in the movement of her facial bones under my teeth as she let out a sweet whimper. I reached up with my forefinger from where I held her throat and spread the saliva I left behind into her skin to soothe the bite.

"Oh, *Mac*," she finally pleaded, making my knees weak with the sweet sound. "Please!"

"What, baby? Tell me what you need. I'm your slave. Don't you understand that?" I pressed my forehead to hers, waiting with held breath to hear more of her sweet begging.

"Just..."

"Just what?"

"Take me somewhere and fuck me, Mac. I can't take another minute of not feeling you inside me."

Pride and lust swelled through my chest as I released my grip on her slender neck and grabbed her hand instead. I guided her trembling fingers directly to my cock and pushed into her hand through my slacks.

"You're going to still feel me a week from now by the time I'm done with you. Do you understand me?"

She sketched out a nod before I yanked away, tugging her toward the next door. I was thrilled when it instantly opened. The stairs led up to the medical offices, and if I could climb the flights with the woody I was sporting, it would be a physical feat for sure.

Time to make that feat happen.

Once we were on the next floor, I stuck my head out of the stairwell into the main hall leading to my office. The last thing I wanted to do was embarrass Taylor—or myself, for that matter. The coast was clear, so I hauled her behind me until we were halfway down the hall. I wasted no time in sliding my hospital identification through the reader, my pulse speeding up as soon as the lock disengaged.

I held the door open, letting Taylor hurry inside while I scanned the hall one more time. As soon as I'd followed her in, I rammed her against the wall. As soon as I had her right where I wanted her—as in, right now—I pressed in and then consumed her with my lips.

And sucked at her.

And devoured her.

And hungered for her.

With an eager mewl, she stripped my white coat from my arms, letting it fall to the floor where we stood. Simultaneously, I tugged her T-shirt from the waistband of her jeans and yanked it up over her head. I wasn't interested in savoring anything. Not right now. I needed her skin exposed and as quickly as possible. I was starving for her taste, for her smell, her sounds. I was obsessed with losing myself in the paradise of her. With forgetting the past month and a half and starting to rebuild our future. I needed *her*. It was that simple; it was that goddamned beautiful.

The button on her jeans was already open, and I pushed my hand into her panties without preamble. Her heated skin felt like fire as I skimmed over her mound and slid my forefinger into her wetness. Her sexy scent, getting stronger as I turned her on more, tickled my nose and made my mouth water.

Finally, I couldn't take the wait any longer. I felt like a kid in school, watching the clock through the last sixty seconds before summer break. Swear to God, I was as hard as a fucking teenager too. My dick pulsed even more as I broke away far enough to dictate, "Take these goddamned things off, woman.

Now."

I watched her getting tempted to fling back something saucy but quelled that bullshit at once with a dark and demanding look of my own. The tiny shiver she gave me in response, taking over her form from head to toe, robbed my breath more than going zero to sixty in three seconds. After that, my gorgeous girl had no trouble complying with my decree as fast as she could, shimmying out of the denim as quickly as the fabric would allow. But oh, how I noticed that she'd purposely left her cotton underthings right where they were. *Rebellious imp.* Did she think that'd be an issue for me, once all was said and done?

And done.

And done...

My desk was just beyond the small entranceway in which we were still crowded. There wasn't much on top of the thing since it was clinic day, so I finished the kiss by hoisting Taylor off her feet, growling in satisfaction as she wrapped her legs around my waist. She continued kissing my face and neck, nipping and licking and sucking, as I walked us over to where I sat to work on any other day.

After plopping her ass down on my desk, I fell back into my rolling chair. She looked at me and grinned, her imagination rapidly catching up with my plan. Her smart mouth had been unusually quiet, and I wasn't sure if that was a good thing or not. I didn't want her to get too caught up in her head the way she had a tendency to do, so I sat back in my chair and waited for her full attention.

"Yo, medicine man." Her adorable face scrunched up in mock panic. "You're not leaving me hanging here, are you?"

"Not a chance, baby. I'm just looking at you first. I want to commit this image to my memory."

"And what image would that be, exactly?" she quipped, taking my breath away as she let her knees fall open, blatantly teasing me to the point of pain. *Christ,* her pussy already smelled so good. "Me distracting you at work?"

"No," I growled. "You sitting in the middle of my desk like you belong there. Taunting me with your sexy skin and deep, thoughtful eyes. I want to make sure that every time I sit down here, I'm reminded of you exactly like this."

Her face pursed, betraying how she retreated to the exact place I didn't want her dwelling, before she seemed to snap out of the fast funk with another carefree grin. "You know I'd rather skip all this sentimental shit, right? Can't we just fuck?" She gave a careless shrug as she finished her thought.

Holy shit, how easy it would've been to simply accommodate her brazen little decree. But if I wanted easy, I could roam anywhere in this building and just crook my finger. I knew about the nursing staff's weekly pool, betting on who would be able to get me horizontal first. I wanted none of those women. I could barely *remember* those women—and I worked with many of them on a daily basis.

So, no. There wouldn't be any "just fucking" happening, no matter how delectable she looked while tossing out the offer. Oh, the woman *would* get her wish. Eventually. Just not yet.

Not right now.

Ohhhh, *especially* not right now.

"Ahhhh." I made sure my extended drawl communicated as much. "*There* she is."

"What?" With eyes gone wide as a cartoon nymph, Taylor snapped her legs together. She shot her stare to the door and then back to me. "Where? Who?"

I snickered. It couldn't be helped. "*You,* knucklehead," I chided. "The sassy girl I've missed. And adore." I sobered quickly, impaling her with the new intensity of my stare. "And love."

She swallowed hard. The movement emphasized the flush creeping up her neck. *So fucking lovely.* I longed to see that same rose hue extend all the way down her body.

"Yeah," I grated. "Her. The one who tells me to 'just fuck' her and then tries to shrug it off as humor. The one who hides every emotion she's feeling with smart-mouthed comebacks instead of the honesty she knows I'm going to ask for. To demand."

As I spoke, I pushed at her knees and spread her legs wide again. At the same time, I rolled my chair between them until I was flush up to the desk. She gasped and blushed deeper. I grinned—and then gripped her hips, hauling her to the edge of my desk, where her pussy was positioned right in front of me. Though I inhaled the heady, heavenly scent of her arousal, I didn't stop watching her face—even as I loosened and then freed my tie from the collar of my shirt. Taylor giggled when I chucked it carelessly over my shoulder.

Only then did I notice another perfect gift from fate herself. The scissors on my desk gleamed in the afternoon sun coming in through the tinted windows, catching my eye. At once, I reached over and snatched them from the little pencil holder they were in. I held them up, smirking as I clicked them a few times, clearly conveying what I planned.

"Mac!" she bit out. "No! Don't do it. What will I wear home? *Mac!*"

"Ssshhhh," I reproved. "You can wear your jeans. They're

right over there, Sassy. Safe and sound."

"But—"

"Sssshhh."

"But—"

"Sit still so I don't stab you."

"Oh, dear God."

"Sorry. He's unavailable right now. They've patched you through to his supervisor. How can I help you, ma'am?"

"You can start by not—"

"Sssshhh." I dotted that one with a waggle of my eyebrows, and she giggled again. Damn, that had to be the sweetest sound on the planet. If that's all I ever heard from now on, morning, noon, and night, I would die a happy man. Hearing joy in her voice was a medal of honor to my soul—though there'd be a dent in that thing forever, now that I knew how much pain I'd caused her. Weeks ago, I vowed to do whatever it took to make her happy again.

Now was the moment to activate that plan.

Snip. Snip.

A quick slice through each side of her panties' waistband, and the cotton fell away from her body—freeing her trimmed V to my view.

So. Fucking. Beautiful.

Pink. Glistening. Glorious. Exactly how I remembered.

No. Better.

Hastily, I yanked the ruined material from beneath her and dropped it to the floor. "Lean back on your elbows," I directed, barely keeping my shit together for a steady tone. Thank fuck she complied without hesitation or sarcasm, though maybe she already knew the move would push her shiny folds that much closer to me. Little minx. Not that I cared if she was playing with me as thoroughly as I baited her. We were good together, and we both fucking knew it. And soon, so very soon, we were going to be even better.

I reached down to cup her ankle with my corresponding hand. I lifted her leg, placing her foot on the arm of my chair, before repeating the motion on the other side. Every inch of every move was gentle but teasing, filled with all my little nips and caresses and strokes, until Taylor pushed out a frustrated huff at my deliberate dawdling.

"Mac! Jesus with the *fēng shui* already!"

Since I'd already anticipated such a line, I whipped my gaze back to her at once. Just as swiftly, she snapped her mouth shut with an audible *clack*.

I settled my posture in the chair.

Drawing her out. Making her wait.

And anticipate...

Once more, she groaned.

Once more, I grinned.

And then, not letting up on my deliberate moves, leaned forward and swiped my tongue up the inside of her thigh, just at the apex of her leg and pussy. I left an unusually wet trail behind, letting the air conditioning of my office cool every inch of that line...knowing the beautiful bumps it would bring out against her perfect flesh. I moved to the other side and did the same thing, holding her hips in place when she gyrated with a blatant invitation.

"Hmmm. Look how wet this pussy is." I slid the tip of my finger through her folds, spreading her open with my teasing touch. I ran my finger around her labia, barely contacting the juicy flesh, until a greedy, guttural moan escaped from deep in her throat.

"Please, Mac!" she all but shrieked. "Please, just do it!"

"Hmmm."

"No. *No.* No 'hmmmm.' Do it. Now!"

"I think I need some promises first, sassy girl."

"Y-Y-You...*what*?"

"Promises. I need them from you. And I'm just not sure you're ready to make them yet."

I pushed my finger into her but only up to the first knuckle. It was barely enough intrusion to ease her ache. My own resistance was faltering so fucking fast. I needed to taste her. I whispered my lips across her mound but held off on using my tongue. I wanted to drive her mad before I broke her.

"You're making me crazy, Clown. I can do this shit to myself. Put your mouth on me, goddamnit!"

She was going for imperious at the totally wrong time, considering the physical position we were in. I instinctively bit into her when she used that smart tone with me, and my teeth scored her outer pussy lip. I didn't bite hard, but it was so enticing to have that warm meaty flesh between my teeth. But as soon as she let out a high and breathy keen, the need to mark her deeper became a demanding drum in my psyche.

As soon as she stilled, I added a little more pressure. Testing her tolerance...her acceptance of the pain.

"Oh, my God. *Mac.* I'm...I'm going to come if you keep doing that. Uggghhh. Fuck! Ohhhh, what are you turning me into?" she moaned.

"A demon, clearly," I said against her soaked clit, letting my deep voice vibrate through her. My tongue took over on habit, licking the tight bud in slow circles, nudging her with just the tip before moving lower and thrusting inside her heat.

I went as deep as I could.

I tasted as much as I could.

And relished every delicious, creamy drop.

Her fingers sifted through my hair and then burned into my scalp while I buried my face between her thighs, lapping at her like a desert nomad who finally reached his oasis. Her sounds were sexy and low, a building storm about to break free.

"Is that good, baby? Do you like the way I feast on you?" Her body had already given her answer with trembling clarity, but I wanted to hear her words. I had to hear her sing my praises once more. Yeah, I was a selfish dick—and never prouder so than now. She'd worship me, goddamnit. She'd venerate me. She'd crave me so fucking badly, she'd never be able to face another day without me.

Nothing less than what she did to me.

"Yes. *Yes!* It's so good, Mac."

I released a long, low hum against her sensitive tissues. "Of course it is, baby."

She was lost too deeply to the desire to summon a word of sarcasm. Instead, she rasped, "I'm...I'm so close. I'm...I'm going to lose my mind if you don't finish me off. Please. *Please*, I'm begging you."

"Begging for what, beautiful girl? Come on, now. Let me hear you say it."

"Make me come. Holy *shit*! Please...make me..."

Her words faded, lost to taut and greedy gasps. She'd get the syllables back again, but they'd be a bunch of whiny, incoherent babbles—which would hit the softest spots of my being. They'd meant I'd gotten all the way through to her... showing me such a raw, real side of her. I craved that sound more than her laughter—and right now, I'd sell my fucking soul to have it.

Instead, I bit into her clit again. At the same time, I rammed two fingers high and deep into her pussy. She was so tight and warm, it was the best feeling in the world. Heaven, right here on my desk.

"Do it, girl. Fall apart for me. Then I'm going to fuck you so hard, you won't remember your name."

I pumped my fingers faster. Faster.

Her whole body stiffened. She arched her back, shoving her pussy harder against my face, sending me into a frenzy of licking and sucking and biting her flesh. "*Mac!*"

"That's good," I crooned. "So good, baby. Ride it out, love."

"D-D-Don't stop!"

"Not planning to." I curled my fingers up, ensuring I hit the perfect pad of nerves deep inside her, making her scream even louder. "Fuck. I could watch you come over and over again. Every time, I'd learn something new. You fascinate me, Taylor. You always will."

She wrapped her arms around my neck and pulled my face up to her thumping chest. Her breathing was fast, but her sigh was utterly content. I felt like a god when I made her unravel so thoroughly, reducing her to wordless nothingness.

But like every trip to paradise, it was over too damn soon—and finished with words as infuriating as they were cheeky.

"Okay, then." She all but chirped it, so obvious was her bid for nonchalance. "So...thanks for that. Guess I'll get out of your hair now." She gave me an even saucier smile while pushing me back. As soon as she was clear to move, she started scooting off the desk—

Until she wasn't.

Because I was grabbing her hips. Hard.

And then making her yelp, *loud*, as I stood with enough

fluid purpose to ram my chair backward. The thing shot all the way into the wall, and her endless blue eyes flared. She blinked them a few times as I inhaled through my nose, scenting the hot perfume of her sex all over my small office's air.

"Where the hell do you think you're going?"

She got in another blink. "You... It's the middle of your workday," she stammered. "I...I just thought—"

"Well, knock that shit off." I leaned down and consumed her soft, swollen lips. Our lovemaking always bordered on violent, and she bloomed in the best ways from the rough handling. "I'm not even close to being done with you."

As soon as I pulled away, a pretty smile slinked across her lips. "That your fancy way of saying you want to *do* me?"

My stare grew heavy, my cock and balls heavier, from her suggestive line. "And what if I said yes?"

"Then I'd say"—she worked my belt and slacks open with her thin fingers—"your wish is my command."

As she gave my cock room to expand, my mind added the implied finish onto her statement. Oh, *fuck*. What would it be like to hear my sexy sassy call me "master"? Just once. Okay, maybe twice...

My fantasies collided with my libido to send a long groan up my throat—just as Taylor dipped her hand inside my boxers and freed me entirely. To avoid spilling this quickly, I focused on unbuttoning my shirt the rest of the way.

Taylor shimmied to the edge of the desk, giving herself leverage to work my pants and boxers down around my thighs. The moment she wrapped her slender hand around my shaft, I felt it jump in her grip. *So fucking good.* I had held myself similarly so many times since we split up, fantasizing that it was her hand there instead, but none of my solo endeavors could compare to the real thing. She always knew just how I liked it, putting just the right amount of pressure on every thrumming inch of me before joining her other hand to the effort. As she slowly, attentively stroked me, her eyes never lowered. She locked my lusty gaze with the sapphire magic of hers, making the contact that much more intimate.

After a few wondrous minutes of that erotic torture, she used her right hand to pump my length harder while scratching her left down the inside of my thigh. My skin lit up like a brush fire. My blood rushed like those flames, finding new kindling. I let my head fall back as my senses absorbed every incredible sensation she was treating me to.

"Step back a little," she gently ordered, while pushing on my thighs so I would step back from the desk.

As soon as I complied, she slithered down to the floor in front of me.

"Dear *fuck*," I spat out—in all the best ways. My Sassy wasn't keen on giving head, but when she did, the experience was monumental. I sucked air through gritted teeth as I prepared for the initial heat of her mouth around my crown. She kept me guessing instead and just casually licked along the underside of my shaft, pumping one hand ahead of her tongue and reaching between my legs to cup my balls with the other.

At this rate, I'd be blowing my load down her throat instead of inside her tight pussy. *Not* acceptable. I pulled in a brutal breath, attempting to focus on details other than the sight of my red, swollen length penetrating deeper between her pink, full lips. The way her hair swung back and forth with her movements. The way her whole body followed her head with the fluid motion of a dancer. And the way she breathed through her nose, cooling the slickness her mouth left behind on my flesh.

So much for the bid for distraction.

I was going mad. No, this wasn't madness. It was insanity—and now it was damn near intolerable. I needed to feel her cunt around me. I couldn't wait another minute longer. All right, maybe a minute—but that was *it*.

I stretched down to take her hands, and she quickly pulled them from my reach. Always my little brat. I stepped back, pulling my cock from her mouth, whether she was on board or not. She looked up the plane of my body, her enormous blue eyes filled with lust.

"Stand up, girl." I helped her to her feet, steadying her by the hands she finally relented to my hold. I didn't waste any time in spinning her around to face the desk, pushing her torso down to meet the cool surface. She yelped a little but settled in, knowing what I was about to do. I couldn't help but tease her a little first, running my fingers through her wetness, wiping it as carelessly as finger paint across her ass and the backs of her thighs.

"My God. Your pussy is soaked." Another swipe through her sopping folds. Another couple of slicks across her gorgeous globes. "I'm going to fuck you so good, baby."

Taylor turned her face to the other side so she could see me better. There was a lazy smile across her well-used lips, which meant I was ten times harder inside three seconds. "So stop talking and do it already." She finished with a pert wiggle of her rear, which I promptly smacked with the flat of my hand. Her flesh jumped from the impact, but from those gorgeous lips, she simply emitted a long hum of pleasure.

"So good, Mac." She drifted her eyes shut. "I've missed this."

"You've missed *me*, you mean."

"Mmmmm. Not so much." Her eyes were still closed, but she tilted the grin a little higher.

"*Sassy*." I let my voice drop even lower, and she instantly shivered.

"I've missed your cock. I'll admit that much." She twitched her rear again, inviting a repeat of my spanking. I obliged with willing enthusiasm—right on top of the red handprint already blooming on her fine, firm ass.

"God, yes. Just keep doing it, Clown. Make me come, Mac! Do it with just your spanking!"

I let out another contemplative hum before growling, "I don't think so, Sassy."

"Whaaa?" she challenged. "Why?"

"Yeah. I'm right. You *definitely* deserve that. Going out with that loser blood jockey, right under my goddamn nose."

"Hey! That's not—"

Her scream pierced the air as I rammed my cock into her waiting cunt. With one thrust, I filled her channel with my erection.

"Fuck!"

Her eyes shot open from the sudden intrusion, but her body welcomed the invasion. Her heat surrounded me as I moved inside her, her body playing mine like a finely tuned instrument. For all I cared, the symphony could go on all night. She could use my cock forever.

"My fucking *God*." It grated out of me as brutal and bestial as I felt. "I've longed to be back here, Taylor." I slid slowly in and out of her body, watching as her slick entrance closed around me, fisting every searing, swollen inch of me.

"Sssshhhh," she reprimanded—which was real fucking

rich, given her current circumstances. "You're talking again."

Oh, yeah. She was pushing it, and I was ecstatic—to the point that without further thought, I grabbed a handful of her hair and pulled hard. I didn't let up until her body was flush against mine, both of us standing. The term being relative, of course. She was high up on her toes and I was squatting a bit behind her, but I was *not* about to lose our connection.

"That smart mouth of yours has gone too long without a lesson from me." I ground my hips tightly against her ass, renewing my grip on her hair.

"Mac!" She gasped. "Oh God, yes!" She broke out in an aroused sheen, her sweat turning her skin into a sight resembling fresh snow at dawn. She was literally glistening for me. "Punish me! Make me learn."

"Don't tempt me, girl." I leaned over and sank my teeth into her shoulder. "Not while I'm this deep inside you." The warmth of her skin filled my mouth, and I bit in deeper. I needed to mark her today more than any other. I hungered to remind her exactly who she belonged to. *Not* that moron out in the parking lot. Not any other guy in the whole fucking world.

Me.

I only realized I'd said it out loud when her skin pebbled beneath my lips, responding at once to my primal, carnal claim. But the single word wasn't enough. Would *anything* ever be enough with her? I wasn't sure I wanted to even know. "You're *mine,* Taylor Mathews. Understand?"

I didn't pull away from her until a full minute—or ten, or six hundred and twelve, like I was noticing—later, but when I did, it was to see I had actually broken her skin. I was so charged with passion, I'd gotten carried away. Tiny drops of blood filled the craters where my teeth had been.

Ah, fuck. Fuck, fuck, fuck!

I was a goddamned bastard.

Especially because the view of that mark only made my cock surge harder.

"Damn," I mumbled at last, causing Taylor to start.

"Wh-What? What is it?"

"You. You're...uh...bleeding."

"I shouldn't be. It's not the time for that."

"I mean...where I bit you."

"Oh?" A new energy stained her tone, though it was far from the horror I expected. It actually sounded like a mix of wonderment...and pleasure.

Which, fuck me sideways, did nothing to help my dilemma. The dirty truth she was forcing me to confess to her now. "You can hate me for saying it, Sassy...but that's making me harder than before."

"Hmmm." She reached back with her opposite hand and swiped across the bite, leaving a red smear across her shoulder and a matching stripe across her fingers. "I know."

"*Fuck.*" I shuttled deeper into her pussy, grinding my hips against her ass when I bottomed out. Then groaning from the depths of my being as Taylor glanced over her shoulder at me—and licked the coppery smudge from her hand.

"Fuck me harder, Mac," she whispered, staring into my soul. "Make me come."

"Goddamnit, girl. We were made for each other. I will spend the rest of my days winning you back completely."

With that, I threw my entire weight into slamming my hips against her ass. The force was so ruthless, she willingly sprawled across the desk to absorb the impact. Again and again I pounded her, each time feeling deeper than before. If I could crawl inside her, I would. I could not get enough of this little beast. I would never have my fill of Taylor Mathews. I needed to make her mine permanently.

Her moan ripped me from my own head, bringing me back to the thrashing woman I was inside of. She was clamping down on my cock with the walls of her pussy, milking my dick with her orgasm.

"You feel so good, love." I felt her tensing a little, as she always did when I used that endearment, but she caught the reaction in its infancy and relaxed at once for me. Damn good thing, too. At this point, I was sure a seven-plus on the Richter scale wasn't going to stop me from fucking her until we both went cataclysmic. "I need to fill you. Are you still on the pill?" We'd gotten over the condom tedium when we started seeing each other regularly, but since we hadn't been together in close to two months, I needed to be sure things were still safe.

"Yes," she answered at once. "Yes. Just do it. Let me feel you, Mac."

I pumped a few more times and let my release shower the inside of her channel. White light took over my vision for a few seconds, making me still behind her with enjoyment of the natural high. The mind-blowing drug of *her*.

My God.

This woman.

She would either be the death of me or the only thing that made my life worth living. This would go one way or the other now.

I leaned over her, arms braced on either side of her narrow frame on the flat of the desk. I was damn sure I'd never be able to fully focus in this room again. The walls would whisper with her moans; the air vents would tease with her scent. It was official. She'd successfully invaded every crevice of my being, and I was grinning like a new lottery winner because of it.

I slid from her pussy and then quickly pulled on my boxers. I needed to give her bite mark some attention, so I crossed into my bathroom to retrieve the small first-aid kit I kept there.

"Isn't that a bit much, Doc? I mean, you're good and all, but I don't actually require first aid." She slipped me a lazy grin. "Christ. Your ego really knows no bounds."

She was still strewn across my desk, and I wasn't arguing her choice one damn bit. As a matter of fact, I wondered if she'd agree to laze there like that every day—though a stiff breeze might blow *her* to the floor faster than my files and papers.

"Actually, smart mouth, you do," I drawled. I reached around her shoulder and poked my finger into the wound. The blood was dry, but I'd been mandated by the universe—no better way to qualify my heart, soul, and mind—to care for her in every way possible.

"Yowwww! That's a good one this time. I think your new nickname should be Jaws."

"Like the villain in James Bond?" I preened.

"No, like the giant fish." She laughed at her own joke, making me laugh in return.

"*Pfffft*. You loved it."

"True."

"Hop up." I smacked her bare ass. "Sit here in my chair, gorgeous girl, so I can clean it up. I'd feel terrible if it got infected."

"Infected?" While the word clearly startled her, she recovered quickly enough to mutter as she complied, "Yeah, who knows where your mouth has been lately."

Well, that did it.

I swiveled the chair around to make her face me and then leaned down until I was directly in her line of sight. "Just so we're clear, Miss Mathews: my mouth hasn't been anywhere since the last time it was on your delectable flesh. Do you understand me?" I dipped in even lower, until our mouths were just breaths apart. "It's you, Taylor. Just you. Now and always."

She swallowed, once more exposing her heart and then covering it right back up—as I fucking looked on. What the hell was I going to do about this? Perhaps what every good doctor could. Teach by example.

"Okay, okay," she finally groused, pushing hard on my shoulders—but I stood my ground, refusing to budge. "Come on, Mac. Let me up."

"Not on your fucking life."

She rolled her eyes, which damn near had me lifting her up to deliver more swats. But she saved her own backside—literally—by uttering, "Let's not be making hasty promises in the afterglow of sex. That's just bad form, and we both know it."

She tried to turn the chair away from me, but I stopped its progress with a commanding grip on one of the armrests. "There's nothing fucking 'hasty' about this, woman." With my other hand, I gripped her cheek. "I love you, Taylor."

Her lips parted as she fervently studied my face. "Mac—"

"Uh-uh," I butted in, tunneling my hand into her hair. "My turn. You *will* listen. I love you, damn it. And I realized, a moment too late, that I've loved you from the first time we met. At this point, I'm not convinced I didn't love you in another life too."

"*Mac!*"

"I'm not done yet. And yeah, I know this is the part where

you like to tuck tail and run, but I'm not letting you do that anymore either." I prodded at her scalp, making her head jog back to lock the oceans of her eyes with the resolution in mine. "We're done hiding from the hard stuff."

And still, the temptress summoned the cheek to roll out a seductive smile. "Well, thank God, because I love your hard stuff."

"*No,*" I ordered at once, catching her by the wrist of the hand she reached down with, aiming to snag me by the crotch. "No. Give me more."

She quirked a brow. "Greedy. You just had quite a lot of me."

"You know what I mean." I worked my thumb up, circling it into the middle of her palm. "Tell me you love me too. I know you do. *You* know you do. That pin dick you had lunch with even knows it."

At once, her other brow leapt up too. "Pin dick?" She laughed.

"I'd bet a Benji on it. Not that you'll be finding out, though. *Ever.*"

She returned her brows to normal, funneling my attention to the new lights in her eyes. The ones she didn't want me to see. Those sky-blue glints, betraying how deeply my caveman act truly touched her. Not that she'd let me on to that anytime soon.

"Shit." She pouted. "You can't just order me to tell you I love you and make it so."

I pushed my thumb in harder. "Why not?"

"Because it doesn't work like that!"

"Why not?"

"Oh, my *God.*" She swung her face to the side, as if expecting to find one of her gal-pals waiting to lend commiseration. How little she really knew. If Claire, Margaux, or Talia were really standing here, they'd be doing so with a tapping toe and a censuring glare for their friend. They liked me. At least I thought so. What wasn't there to like?

"All right, so what did I expect here?" she went on, half to herself. "I'm talking to a clown."

"You can try to cover this up with all the sarcasm in your sexy-as-fuck brain, baby—but it's not going to change this. It's not going to alter what's going on between us. I will *not* let you go again."

She huffed. Canted her head around enough to shoot me half a glance of vexation. "I heard you the first thousand times."

"Glad you finally listened. Now turn around and let me heal you."

"Oh, for fuck's sake." She smacked her forehead with a loud crack. "Did you really just say that?"

I let my silence be her answer for an extended minute. The better part of another. At last I murmured, "Doctors used to be called healers by their villagers, you know." I was almost done with my gentle cleaning of the blood, lingering longer than I actually needed to so I wouldn't have to face *my* fears now—and watch her walk out of my office. Always wondering if it would be the last time. Always holding my breath, thinking she might never come back.

Linger.

Linger.

I swallowed, attempting to regulate my staccato heartbeat, before asking conversationally, "So...what are you doing this weekend? Maybe we can do something." No way could I control the hopeful—dear fuck, even desperate—lilt to my tone.

When was the last time a woman made me feel this way?

The answer, from one of the secret corners of my soul, was terrifying.

Never.

"Let's...ummm...play it by ear." Taylor was being noncommittal, and I knew it was on purpose.

But I was much more determined to hold my ground, even if she was planning to drop the hammer on my dreams.

"Not good enough." I crossed my arms over my chest. I couldn't let down my guard against this woman and her power of determination once she set her fiery spirit on something.

"Well, it's the best I can do." And then she shrugged as if she didn't have a care in the world—even for me.

Crap.

"You can always make other plans, and I'd understand," she said. Another shrug—driving in her point worse than the first.

"Why are you doing this?" I applied some antibiotic ointment to her bite and then covered it with a large Band-Aid. The second I was finished, she pushed to her feet and then crossed to where her T-shirt lay on the floor.

"Why am I doing *what,* exactly?" With a couple of graceful swoops, she pulled the thing over her head.

"You seriously don't know?" I challenged. "Because you don't have this shit down to a fucking *science,* woman?"

She ran a hand through her hair, attempting to shake out the tangles. *Fucking goddess.* "You're the science man, Doc. Enlighten me."

"Playing hard to get?" I couldn't help but smack the desk in frustration. The action made her jump, and I instantly regretted the rash behavior, but I wasn't standing down from the point. "You were just here, damn it. You felt what we have, Taylor—just like I did." I copied her move, shoving a hand back through my own hair, albeit in frustration. "You're making me crazy!"

And she certainly didn't help my efforts otherwise with her quick snip of laughter. "I think you had some of that going on well before you met me, dude."

I had an answer for that, but it was clutched tight in my throat. Instead, I simply stared at her. Hard. Then harder, letting the quiet of the room thicken like a damn death pall. Holy fuck, maybe it was. At least it helped to punctuate the gravity of what I had to say, muttering it as I parked my ass where hers just had been. "Fuck it. Just fuck it. The truth is... I'm scared to death."

Well, at least that finally caught her whole attention. Taylor rushed back over, wasting no time in cradling my face in her hands. "*Why?*" she charged. "Why the hell would you say that?"

I raised my head. Formed my hands over hers, treasuring the feel of her skin against mine. "I'm petrified you'll walk away from this moment and freeze me out again. I don't think I can take another round of the Taylor Mathews Ice Age." I swallowed and didn't hide a single undulation of it. "I'm pretty fucking positive it's more than I can bear, actually."

"You're going to be fine." She rushed it out while pressing her fingers into my hairline. "*We* will be fine, Mac. But I can't just go headlong into the wall again. That's more than I can bear too, to use your words. We both really got hurt, and I don't want to feel that way again. Ever."

I turned my head, sliding my lips firmly against the center of her palm. Then the other. That was the most honest she'd ever been with me about her feelings. Taking the moment lightly wasn't an option. "Thank you," I finally whispered.

Her brows knit. "For what?"

"You know damn well what. And in return, I promise I'll do everything in my power to protect you from hurting. *Everything*, Taylor. If you are in pain—*any* kind of pain—I will heal you. If I don't do it with my hands, then with my heart. Let me be that for you, love. I'm on my knees here."

She reacted as I anticipated—by directing a sardonic stare down the length of my body. I indulged her the dramatic moment, mostly because I was still half-clothed with my dick hanging out, but before she could slide in a glib remark about the whole thing, I sealed my lips over hers again. The kiss was full and deep and passionate, and after a few mutual tongue rolls, we were both groaning hard and deep with skyrocketing lust.

But as much as I wanted to take things further—along with a thorough round two with her lady parts—I had to clean up and get downstairs. I pulled back and kissed her closed eyelids, consumed with obnoxious male pride while she swooned from our contact. God, I relished doing that to her. It sent *me* to the moon and back too. I loved every speck of the physical effect I had on her—and had no hesitation about using it against her if I had to.

"Hey. Sassy..."

"Mmmm...?" she replied with a misty glow in her eyes.

"Regrettably, I need to get downstairs. Like five minutes ago."

"Well, just tell Devon you were with me. She'll forgive you. She likes me."

"That she does. And who would blame her?" I quickly

finished getting dressed by snagging my tie and white coat from the floor.

"I can find my way out," she offered. "Get going so you're not late."

I shook my head. "I have to go down through the lobby anyway. Come on; I'll walk with you that far." I held the door open for her and made sure it locked behind us.

We held hands while we walked, just like we used to. We stole kisses in the elevator, groaning against one another's lips when other people came on board. I kissed her knuckles as we landed on the lobby floor and the elevator doors slid open. A quick walk across the foyer and it was time to say goodbye.

But before we did...

"Promise me, Sassy."

"Hmmm?" She looked up for an explanation.

"No Ice Age."

Her gaze sobered. The look was exhilarating and terrifying to the pulse I still couldn't regulate into normal territory. But at least she murmured, "I'll...I'll do my best."

I stepped in, looming over her, and pressed a little kiss to her temple. "That's all I'm asking for."

"Just don't hurt me again, Mac. We won't survive. *I* won't survive."

"I know." I took her lips beneath mine this time, with soft and committed purpose. "And I won't."

She pushed her head up toward me, seeking another kiss. I surrendered it with soaring elation—despite abhorring my job with a vengeance I never thought possible. Was this really *me*, resenting the crap out of the profession I loved so much? But I did, and I barely clamped back my raging roar.

But nothing mattered more in that moment than Taylor

Mathews. We were teetering on the edge of a turning point. It was real. It was imminent. It was goddamned awesome. A few more hours in one another's arms, and we'd truly be back on solid ground with each other.

"So...maybe I could come over tonight?" I just needed to be near her.

To my delight, her face lit up at the prospect—only to darken fast with disappointment. "Text me," she muttered. "I'm supposed to go to the fucking gym with Talia, but I don't know exactly what time yet. I swear, that wench is trying to kill me."

Quick chuckle. "Okay, baby. I'll talk to you later, then." I relinquished the laugh in favor of getting to buss her one last time. She pulled away with an adorable giggle.

I mouthed the words *I love you*, and she smiled before turning for the door. I stood watching her as she went through the sliding-glass panels, the sun glowing around her silhouette like it'd been lucky enough to capture an angel in its beams. But who was I to argue the point, when it was so beautifully close to right?

CHAPTER FIVE

Taylor

The sun blazed high in the sky when I came out of the hospital, warming my skin to match the temperature of my heart. I hadn't realized how badly I had missed Mac until I was in his arms. Well, maybe I knew deep inside, but I had a great way of denying what was right in front of me, even to my own detriment.

Searching through my bag for my sunglasses, I grabbed my phone and noticed the icons on the home screen.

"Sixteen messages... What the... That can't be right," I mumbled to myself as I crossed the lot to where Sally was parked. Thankfully the blood drive was over, so the Bloodmobile was no longer occupying a large part of the coveted spaces. The last thing I wanted was to do the walk of shame in front of John. I subconsciously reached for the bandage on my shoulder, grinning when I touched it through my T-shirt.

Fucking Maclain Stone. He was unraveling me, thread by thread, and I was pretty sure he wouldn't be content until I was nothing but a patch of threadbare material, transparent to all those around me. I wanted to trust him again and recommit my faith in us. And yes, I went ahead and openly admitted it: I craved to have something together similar to what my friends had with their husbands. But more than that, I wanted it with Mac.

Only with him.

Oh, dear hell. I was truly a goner. And for a guy who was bossy and egocentric and arrogant and impossible—but also gentle and caring and protective and generous. There were so many facets to him—and incredibly, *magically,* I loved all of those sides. Yes, even the side that had me walking out of our lovemaking session with a bandage on my skin...after he took me to the most pleasurable heights I'd ever experienced.

Yeah—I especially loved that side of him.

My car didn't have a fancy remote key, an alarm system, or even navigation. But Sally and I had a special bond, and after Mac came into our lives—and loved us both precisely for the girls we were—I felt even closer to her. Was it odd to be in a relationship with a vehicle? Not according to my favorite neurosurgeon—or Stephen King—but they probably shouldn't be mentioned in the same conversation.

I waited for the engine to warm up a bit before pulling out, giving me time to look at my messages again. If any of the messages were new, I predicted most would be from Mac. He had an odd habit of leaving me multiple short messages instead of one long one, but it made me smile because it was an honest reflection of the way his brilliant mind worked. Short bursts of inspiration, supernovas of emotion or concern, all relayed the exact moment he felt them. No protective shells for him.

Yet another reason why the man was so damn good for me.

More than I wanted to admit—at least on this front.

I'd been trying, though. Like crazy. Working to gain confidence and celebrate the independence I'd achieved.

Since the most recent "Save Janet" episode, I'd formed a new habit of always checking my caller ID first and had started letting her calls go to voicemail. Of course, I was still a Class A codependent, so I immediately listened to the message to make sure she wasn't in danger. Still, it seemed like a step in the right direction. Rome wasn't built in a day.

But really? *Sixteen* messages? And now I could see they were all from the same phone number. And it wasn't Mac's, unless he'd gotten a new line and had neglected to tell me before or after flying me to the orgasmic stars. The digits weren't identified as belonging to any police or fire department either, so with half a relieved breath, I dismissed any crisis involving Janet.

Half a breath.

I hit the arrow to play the first message, putting my phone on speaker so I could safely start backing out—

And slammed the brakes at once.

Sally and I both lurched forward on the recoil from the abrupt stop. I was beyond caring, as a pleasant and friendly voice drifted through the car—and sent shivers down the middle of my back.

And not the good kind.

"Hey, beautiful. It's John. I hope you don't mind me calling. I got your number off your paperwork. I figured you wouldn't mind, since we're friends and all."

"Excuse me?" I totally minded. It was such a breach of privacy, I could barely make my trembling body get the car back into motion to clear the way for the waiting car behind me.

"Anyway..." His voice trailed off for a few seconds, and then he seemed to remember he was still recording a message.

"Oh, sorry. Anyway, I just wanted to thank you for our lunch date today and tell you I really had a great time. I hope we can do it again sometime. Uh, okay, bye."

The message itself seemed harmless, despite how my nerves discernibly frayed at his use of "lunch *date*," but I massaged the steering wheel in a focused attempt to chill.

Before launching in on listening to the fifteen messages that still waited. All from John's number.

Screw *chill*. I went ahead and let my stomach turn.

This was definitely not good.

Not. Good.

I had been explicit with the guy. I'd said, over and over, that I wasn't interested in anything other than friendship with him.

Maybe they were butt dials?

Heartened, I pressed play again. The message was basically the same nonsense for the next two, all said in different ways. He had a great time at lunch. He was glad we were still friends. Blah blah blah. Now I was getting annoyed.

Then I played the fifth one.

And it was different.

Back to the painful stomach twist. And everything else in my body along with it.

There was a shift in his voice. Something that made my skin prickle, my blood freeze, and my limbs go numb. Something about his tone and the general vibe of his message. He'd changed, and it was eerie.

"Taylor, it's John again. Listen, I know you're just playing hard to get. I know you have feelings for me. Why else would you have gone out to lunch with me today? I know you said you aren't with Dr. Stone anymore, and that's good. It would be a shame if something happened to him and you had to mourn his loss. But I'd be there for you. You could count on me. You can always count on me, Taylor. I'm always right here. Waiting for you. Have a good night, my love. I'll see you soon."

I was waiting at a light, which gave me ample opportunity for a gawk of sheer shock. "My *love*?"

The word I always gave Mac such shit for was suddenly an ice pick in my gut. Holy shit. When had John decided to chug his crazy train into *my* fucking station? And honestly, why?

I dreaded listening to the other eleven messages, but morbid curiosity got the better of me. By the time I played the last of the guy's voicemails, I had to pull off to the shoulder of the 163 just to regain my composure. My hands were trembling too hard to drive safely.

"Taylor, my love. I must say before you lay your beautiful head down tonight, I hope you dream of me. Your lover. Dream of me showing your mind, your body, your very soul how much I adore you, how I'll care for you, cherish you. I can't wait to finally feel you around me in the most intimate ways. Sweetest dreams, my love."

I lowered my head to the steering wheel, though I contemplated dropping it all the way between my knees. Nausea clawed at me and swirled with terror welling in my throat. While John hadn't directly threatened me, his off-the-rails rambling and his veiled threat at Mac were enough to churn my gut and fire my rage. I'd known plenty of frustrated fury in my life, but John had just jabbed at depths I never knew existed. Worse, I felt helpless to do anything about them.

That was wrong.

There was plenty I could do.

And would.

I just couldn't decide what to do first. Go to the police station? Call Mac? Dial one of the girls? The somewhat normal human I'd lunched with had become a stage-five stalker in the span of sixteen phone calls. I checked the call log and did some quick math. John had left all sixteen messages within the two hours I had been with Mac in his office.

Two *beautiful* hours—getting my brains fucked out by the *actual* man I loved, not this loser. True as that was, and as desperately as I yearned to, Mac couldn't be my first phone call. The man was going to lose his mind when I told him what was going on, and I didn't want the man I loved being tossed in the slammer for murder.

I needed to calm down. Then I needed to decide the best course of action. That would only happen by calling in some backup.

I put my earbuds in and dialed Margaux's cell phone. I checked the passing traffic and eased back onto the freeway while her phone rang.

"Hello?"

"Hey, Mary Stone. How's your day?"

A heavy huff through the line. "Don't think I don't realize you only call me that when I can't physically harm you."

"Nice to hear your voice too." I laughed, but it was shaky and weak—not that I expected that to fly under the woman's radar. Margaux Asher-Stone-Pearson had mutant-level instincts when it came to hearing weakness in people, acquired while being raised by a woman who'd honed it into an art form. Thankfully for all of us, she'd chosen to use her superpower for good.

"Uh-oh," she muttered at once. "All right. What's going on, girl? Is it the doctor again? I'm seriously going to have a sit-down with that man, and—"

"No. No. It's not Mac. He's...well, he's great, actually." I sucked in a huge breath. "But that's not why I'm calling."

"Well then, tell me what I can do for you." She paused for a second, giving away her contemplation. "It's not like you to call for a chat when you're doing okay."

I sighed, attempting to add a laugh as well. I should've known better. "You know me too well."

"You're not as complicated as you think you are." Her tone was dry and honest, and that succeeded in getting me back to the realm of pissed-off. When did I become so transparent?

"Well...I saw Mac today."

"And?" Though her tone kicked up with worldly assurance at the end, practically voiding the question mark altogether.

"And we, uh...well..." Why was I beating around the bush with the world's most forward woman? "We spent some time together."

"Okay." There was distinct rustling, and I envisioned the woman in her office, leaning back and elegantly crossing her legs. "So you were fucking, and...?"

I laughed out loud. "You have such a way with words."

"It's a gift. What can I say?" I could picture her proud shrug now as well.

"So, when I got back in my car after leaving the hospital—"

"Okay, hold up."

"What?"

"You fucked him at the hospital?"

"Well, not in the lobby or anything."

"In an exam room?" I'd have to be sleeping to miss the hopeful lilt to her voice.

"Oh, God. *No!*" I spurted before even thinking to stop

myself. "In his office, if you really need to know."

"Niiiiiccce."

I rolled my eyes and shook my head. While I loved bantering with my dazzling friend—and would've loved nothing more than detailing her eager ears with another episode of *Sexcapades With Dr. Clown*—the issue at hand was too serious to brush off for another day.

"Okay, so after we...uumm—"

"Fucked in his office." She could have been standing at a coffee counter ordering her daily latte with the casual tone she used.

"Yeah, okay...so, when I checked my voicemail, I had sixteen messages."

"Whoa. Sister!" And just like that, the drawl was replaced by a yippy whoop. "Sixteen? After just leaving him?"

"Margaux."

"You totally have him by the balls. You must have done *all* the tricks I've taught you over the years!"

"*Margaux*."

"What?"

"They weren't from Mac."

"*Huh?*"

"They were from this guy John who works at the blood bank."

She rustled again. It was more a playing-with-her-hair thing this time. "John. Yeah, you've mentioned him. The nice one who gives you extra cookies after you donate."

"Right. *Nice*." I snorted.

"Well, *that* doesn't sound good."

"I had a moment of lonely weakness and gave in to a lunch invite from him."

"Before or after you bonked the clown in his office?"

"Before," I clarified. "It wasn't planned. Just a last-minute, friendly thing, you know? But he must have gotten the wrong idea—and sixteen messages later..."

What more did I need to say after the gravity of *that* doozy sank in? Fortunately, nothing. Margaux's heavy *whoosh* conveyed she'd gotten the message, loud and clear.

"Okay, so that's crazy with a capital C, but what is it that has you so upset? Did Mac find out? Is he mad?"

"No. No, it's not that. The guy—the messages—they started out all normal, friendly and all, and by the last one, he was acting psycho, telling me he loves me and can't wait to have sex with me."

"What the living fuck?"

"I know for sure I did not lead him on. But honestly, the whole thing is creeping me out." My voice cracked as I finished my sentence. Saying it out loud made it all sound even worse.

Her voice grew concerned. "I don't blame you. Where is Mac now?"

"At work. He wants to come over tonight, and I was going to hold him off, but honestly, I don't think I want to be alone after hearing this guy do a *Play Misty for Me*."

"A *what* for *who*?"

"Never mind." How could I forget that Margaux mentally jettisoned any film, TV, or pop-culture reference more than six months old? "To be honest, Margaux, my shit's getting more flipped about this by the second. If John pulled my phone number from my records at the blood bank, he'd be able to get my address too."

"So, not only is this creepy, I'm pretty sure it's a HIPAA violation on the blood bank's part." Her agreement, such a fast and unusual return to somberness, only torqued my tension higher. “Do you want me to come over until Mac gets there?” she offered.

Yes!

“No,” I compelled myself to say. “I’ll be fine. My neighbors are super nosy.” After her *hmph* of disbelief, I assured her, “If something bad were to happen, they’d know it in a heartbeat.”

“Fine,” she relented. “But promise you’ll call the second something seems weird. *Promise me*, Taylor.”

“Settle down, mama bear. I’ll call you, I promise.”

She still didn’t sound convinced—which again didn’t help one shred of my mounting anxiety. I knew her concern was meant to comfort me, but it was accomplishing the exact opposite. “So does Mac know you were out with this John guy?” she pressed.

“Yeah.”

“And?”

“And what do you think?”

“I think the clown probably turns into a caged lion when he’s jealous.”

I drummed my fingers on the steering wheel to at least take the edge off my nerves. “Oh, nice image,” I attempted to snark.

“But damn accurate, yes?”

“He...has a wide lion streak, yes.”

“Well, he *is* a Stone,” she drawled—which I cut off with a long groan.

“God,” I muttered. “He was furious when he saw me come back with the guy.”

“Holy shit.” A fresh rustle, followed by distinct high heel clacks. I’d driven Mary Stone to her feet in shock. “He was there when you got back?"

I groaned again. "That's how he and I ended up—well, never mind."

"Ohhhh!" From concerned to lewd inside three seconds. That had to be a record, even for Margaux. "Dirty hot jealousy sex. That's almost my favorite kind!"

"Stop." I slapped my forehead.

"Yes! I'm right, aren't I?" Satisfaction filled the phone line.

"Are you ever wrong?" I mumbled.

"Not often. But it does happen on occasion, and my sexy husband is usually the one to call me out when it—" A wail threatened to pierce my eardrum through the line. "*Shit*," Margaux spat. "It's Iris."

"No kidding." The excuse for a laugh felt damn good right now.

"She was down for a nap. Guess that's done now. So sorry, hon. I need to go. Remember, you *promised* to call if you need help."

"I did and I will. Give Iris a kiss from her favorite auntie."

My chuckling continued as we disconnected the call. Couldn't be helped, since I now imagined my friend rushing off to love on her baby girl—in the heels she'd never give up. If anyone was capable of the feat, it was definitely Margaux Pearson.

God, how I wished I was there at her and Michael's place. How I longed to be out on their patio holding that sweet baby instead of heading home to my quiet apartment. Still, the call had calmed me a great deal. I was feeling a little lonely, but I definitely wasn't *alone*.

I turned into my apartment complex and then circled

around the back to my parking space. I took particular care to notice everything around me as I walked to my apartment, deciding I was acting ridiculous and paranoid by the time I got inside. I always locked the door when I was home and quickly did that—both the deadbolt and the lock below it—before heading to my room for a shower.

I froze halfway across the floor when my phone dinged—signaling a text message.

Slowly, I lowered myself to the bed. I pulled a deep breath in and then out and then looked at the screen.

I miss you already.

Mac.

"Thank you, Jesus," I rasped, letting a stupidly teary smile spread across my lips. Suddenly, I yearned for the ability to fast-forward time. I wanted him—fuck it, I needed him—here, as in five minutes ago. The sensation wasn't just about the bullshit with John. Something was changing between Mac and me—something significant and special. I wanted to embrace every second of it with him. I wasn't sure where the usual me was hiding, but it was refreshing to simply feel the emotions as soon as they hit, no matter how scary and new they were.

I quickly texted him back.

What time will you be here tonight?

His response came immediately, and my heart beat a little faster.

Should be around seven.
Hope that's okay?

Yes, fine. It'll give me time to rest up from our earlier activities.

He texted back the little devil emoji, and I giggled. Yeah. *Giggled.* What the hell was he doing to me? I was acting like every other silly girl I knew, yet nothing about it felt wrong. Just the opposite.

Everything about Maclain Stone felt amazingly, incredibly *right.*

After quickly showering, I got into bed for some much-needed downtime. I pulled the covers up to my waist and then grabbed my e-reader for some old-fashioned escape fiction. I had tons of chores I could do around the apartment, but I just wanted to exist in the happy little place that had formed in my heart. It was peaceful and comfortable, and I wanted to enjoy the beautiful dream while it lasted.

Because beautiful dreams were never the lasting kind.

Life had made sure I knew *that* one real well.

The sound of my phone woke me from a dead sleep. Judging by the size of the drool mark on my pillow, I'd been asleep for hours. The sun was low on the horizon when I peeked out my window, and I realized I had slept close to three hours. I felt around in the covers and found my phone, trying to clear my sleepy eyes to see the screen.

"*Shit.*"

More messages from John. Four voicemails, to be exact. But I also had two texts, from Margaux and Mac respectively, balancing out the panic that wanted to take root in my gut again. Margaux was in full mama-hen mode—for which I was truly grateful—checking in to make sure I was okay and that Mac was still coming over. And speak of the devil—or in this case, my sexy-as-hell guardian angel... Mac wanted to know if I was up for takeout or venturing up to Hillcrest to find something new we hadn't tried.

I sent a reply to him first. Shrimp and lobster sauce sounded like paradise in paper boxes, and best of all, the local Chinese place delivered. He wouldn't have to make an extra stop—and he'd be back here in my arms that much sooner.

I refused to listen to the voicemails from John. With a determined set of my shoulders, I decided to tell Mac what was going on here. *All* of it. He'd likely go über-scary clown on me, complete with red eyes and raging teeth, but after that, he'd have some practical advice on how to handle this guy—and my own whirling feelings around the whole thing.

Like every good little codependent, I mentally scoured my memories of the lunch with John, wondering if I'd said or done a single thing to lead him on. The answer was a huge, fat *no*. Even my clothes were modest, since I'd been ready to head out to the beach for the afternoon.

Another quick text, to Margaux this time. I assured her I was fine and that Mac would be at my place in a couple of hours. I received a thumbs-up and a kissy-face in response.

There was still time to kill before my man got here, so I freshened up before finding a cute little sundress in the deep recesses of my closet. After ironing out the wrinkles from it, I put on some eyeliner and lipstick. Mac would be leaving work any minute, so I sat down to play a few turns of chess while I waited.

I had no idea how much time had passed, I was so deep into my game. When Mac knocked on my door, I was so engrossed in my strategy, it was a complete surprise. I didn't even hear his car pull into the complex. That little white number of his had a very distinctive purr, and I used to know the moment he was near.

Just to be safe, I looked through the peephole before opening the door.

And almost fainted.

It wasn't Mac.

John. He was *here*, waiting expectantly on the other side of my door. He was dressed in a white button-down shirt and a shockingly trendy sport coat, and he carried a huge bouquet of flowers.

"Shit!" I hissed. "Shit, shit, *shiiiiit*!"

What the hell *now*? Ignoring him wouldn't solve the problem. The lunatic had probably left his chainsaw in the back seat of his car. He'd buzz his way in if he had to—literally.

I could dash and grab my phone, either texting Margaux or even dialing the police, but again—chainsaw. My door would be particle board sushi by the time any help arrived.

I stepped back, flattening my hands into vertical push-ups on the air. "You've got to get a fucking grip," I ordered myself. "And you've got to handle this whack job like the piece of crap he really is."

After forcing down one more long breath, I opened the door to the point where the metal chain stopped the progress. And yeah, I knew I was all but asking to be made into a Stephen King teaser blurb with the move, but desperate times called for desperate measures.

"What are you doing here?" My tone was complete ice.

"Hello to you too, beautiful."

At once, I wanted to smack the boyish smile off his face.

"That's not my name, John."

He dipped his head a little, looking at me over the top of

the flowers. "It is now."

I was sure I left grooves in the wood from where I clutched it. "Listen. I'm not sure where our wires got crossed, but you have to leave. I don't want to see you again. All those messages? That was creepy, dude."

His face crunched into angles I'd never seen on it before. Angry, ugly angles. "I like it better when you call me my real name, Taylor."

"You *really* need to leave. *Now*. My boyfriend will be here any minute, and he won't take kindly to you on my doorstep."

"I thought you said he wasn't your boyfriend?" Even in the dim porch light, I could tell he was getting flushed. Whether from anger or embarrassment, I wasn't sure.

"Well, things changed. He's definitely my boyfriend again."

"*No.*" His skin got darker, and the kind gaze faded. "You don't know what you want!" His tone was already shifting back to borderline John Hinckley Jr., and I dashed a glance to my phone on the table, thinking the 9-1-1 idea might have been the smarter way to go here. "You need a good man like me."

"What I need is for you to leave." I pronounced all of it at extra-loud volume, hoping the next-door neighbor was peeking through her curtains like the dutiful busybody she was.

"Is there a problem here?"

As soon as the low, sexy rumble of my own white knight came from beyond the light of the overhead bulb, I almost lost my emotional shit. I had no idea how thoroughly I'd been pretending to be brave...until I no longer had to be. Now I was just tempted to be a whimpering fool, but I held composure as Mac sauntered up, having quietly come up the walk and finally overhearing our exchange.

"Oh, hey. You're that fuckstick from the Bloodmobile, right?" He chuckled his insult, clueless to John's reddening face.

"And you're the infamous Dr. Stone." John glared at Mac, challenging him already.

Mac just shrugged. "Yeah, maybe. But how do you know my name?"

"I work in the lab at the hospital when I'm not volunteering at the blood bank. Everyone there knows who the new cocky asshole in Neuro is. And these days, I only volunteer out at the van on the days Taylor has an appointment—so guess who's at the hospital as often as you are?"

"Ursula at the lobby coffee stand?" Mac rejoined. "Because really, she's one of the few I give half a fuck about." He paused for half a second to let John get in a good fume over that before cocking his brows and stating, "Now, I'm only going to say this once, junior." With the deliberation of the lion Margaux had compared him to, he shifted into John's personal space. Not far, but just enough. "I distinctly heard Miss Mathews ask you to leave—and I suggest you do just that."

"Or what?"

John crossed his arms over his chest, trying to intimidate Mac away. Mac merely laughed. "Or I'll escort you to your car myself. And I promise you, you will wish you hadn't chosen that option."

For another long second, John looked like he would really push the point. But with a mocking laugh that sounded like a twelve-year-old scoffing off a video game loss, he used the balls of his toes to bounce backward and scoot away. From over his shoulder, he called, "I'll see you soon, my love. I'll call you tomorrow."

"Oh, dear God." I groaned. *Really?* Was he fucking insane? First of all, with the pet names. Second, right in front of Mac. I shot my stare to Mac—and watched him grow about two inches taller before my eyes.

"I'm not going to repeat this, John-Boy. Run along. And don't ever come back here again." His voice sounded lethal. I was surprised John didn't piss himself right then and there. I would have.

But at last, the asshole got the message enough to get in his car and drive away.

Mac shook his head, picked up the bag of takeout he had set down on the concrete, and came in.

I laughed, but it was an awkward and nervous sound. I knew this night was about to go in the complete opposite direction of what I'd truly hoped.

Mac quietly closed the door and locked it behind us. He casually strolled to the kitchen, set the takeout food on the counter, and then got plates from the cupboard.

I busied myself with getting the food out and putting it on the table. Neither one of us said a word while we moved around each other. I was worried this was the calm before the storm. The quiet before Hurricane Maclain made landfall.

We took our seats and began to dig in, but before his first forkful met his lips, he looked up at me in an eerily quiet way. "Are you going to tell me what happened?"

"Yes," I answered, trying to borrow some of his calm-that-wasn't-really-calm. "But I don't want to ruin our night. And you're going to be very mad. Very. Mad. And what happened to the agreement about just having this all delivered?"

"I was starving and didn't want to wait until we ordered and then the time they'd take to get here with it. And I'm already very mad. But not at you." He stabbed at his food with the vengeance of a modern Van Helsing. "I'm furious at that stupid fucker who can't seem to respect another man's belongings."

"Belongings?" My eyebrows shot to my hairline.

"What do you want me to say? Another man's *woman*. My *property*? You'd balk at those terms too. Don't beat around the actual issue here, Taylor. How the hell did he know where you live?"

"I'm...I'm not sure." I let my fork slide from my fingers, my appetite suddenly gone, before dropping my head into my hands. "Okay, that's not true, either."

This whole situation was fucked up, but I'd promised him no more ice-outs. And in this case especially, he deserved the whole truth, no matter how wickedly uncomfortable it was to give up.

"I...I think he looked at my records at the blood bank. When I left the hospital today, there were sixteen messages on my cell phone from him."

Mac said nothing. At first. "I see."

I wasn't sure he did, but I forced myself to go on. "When I got home this afternoon, I took a nap. During that time, he called four times."

Silence.

Too much of it.

Filled with too much of me, appetite completely gone, watching Mac steadily chew the bite he had just taken, perfect manners and decorum in place. He wiped his mouth with the paper napkin from the restaurant before standing and walking into my living room.

"Mac, I *swear*...I didn't lead him on. I told him explicitly that I was only interested in being his *friend*. When he asked me to go to lunch today, I thought it would be a harmless thing." *To keep myself from mooning over* you, *dipshit.* I already thanked my tongue for not going *that* far.

He stopped. Didn't turn around. For that matter, he barely moved. "But you knew he had a crush on you."

"I knew he—" I shoved to my feet now too, the wind crushed in my throat. "What are you saying? That I asked for this? You don't even know the whole story yet, and you're already blaming me?"

I couldn't believe that much had come out of me coherently. But damn it, I was hell-bent for leather on this. No way would I stand for him blaming *me* for that lunatic's behavior.

"Baby." The way he *whoosh*ed it out was an apology in itself, and I allowed myself to breathe again. "I'm not blaming you—not in the slightest." Though he'd turned to face me again, he stopped in his tracks for a second time. I could all but paint a lightbulb of comprehension in the air over his head. "And hold up. What do you mean, I don't know the whole story? What aren't you telling me? I told you I wouldn't let you put walls up between us anymore."

I held up my hands. "And I'm not. But you need to calm down."

"I'm calm."

And the sun would rise tomorrow in the west instead of the east, but I wasn't about to let *him* in on the insight.

"Taylor? *Hey*." He waited until I met his penetrating stare with my own. "This guy seems like a nutburger. You going to tell me what else happened?"

The marketing honchos at Stone Global always harped

at us with a key phrase. *Show, don't tell.* Instinct told me that might be the best tack here, so I walked over to my kitchen counter and grabbed my cell. "Maybe it's best that you just hear this," I told him.

I hit Play, letting John's messages play out in their entirety. Their increasing yuck factor filled my tiny apartment, and I could feel the air around Mac getting colder and colder—until I began to wonder if *he* was invoking a new Ice Age, in a quiet and unsettling way.

The last message had barely begun, but as soon as John waxed on about being inside me, Mac jabbed at the screen with a ferocity that made me jump. I looked down, bewildered he hadn't cracked the device's screen. He stood up and scrubbed a hand across his face and around to the back of his neck. I felt terrible. Surgery days were always long and trying for him, and it had been my intention to treat us both to an amazing, sex-filled night. Instead, we were dealing with this tangled mess.

"I'll deal with this guy. He won't bother you again." His words were a declaration. A statement of finality, not to be discussed further.

"Mac. What are you going to do? You can't beat him up."

"I won't touch him. And what do you care what happens to him? Should we just sit here and think he's a harmless guy until he corners you in a dark parking lot or behind some random building? Do I wait until he rapes you, Taylor?" His breathing was furious and rushed. His calm facade was faltering, dissolving. "Or fucking worse?"

"Worse?"

"I'll handle it!" he barked, and I tried not to recoil. "It won't be an issue again."

"Mac." My own voice was small and timid in response.

"You're scaring me."

He cursed beneath his breath. Then lunged over, closing the space between us and hauling me against his chest. He held me there for a few minutes while we both worked to calm down. "I'm sorry," he husked, pressing his lips into my hair. "I'm so damn sorry. I didn't mean to scare you. I just get fucking *crazy*, thinking of someone harming you."

"I know." I stroked a hand across his hammering heartbeat. "I *do* know."

"I will never let anyone hurt you," he vowed, his voice still trembling. "As long as I live, you will be safe with me."

"Thank you."

What else could I say? Though apparently, it was all I *had* to say—because the man broke out in a long, savoring chuckle that had me jerking back, peering harder for an explanation.

"What?" he flung, addressing my frown. "No smart remark? No trading sass for intimacy? And hold the phones... Not one single clown reference?" He mellowed the laugh to a grin, trying to bring some levity to the very heavy air that had settled over the room—and us.

I helped him out—a little—by dealing a playful bop to his shoulder. "*Hey.* I'm trying to turn over a new leaf here."

Mac cupped my cheek, lifting my face for his soft kiss. "I can tell."

"I said *trying*," I qualified. "I can't say my bullshit still won't sneak out, so don't get too used to the emotionally healthy fun."

I smacked his arm again. This time, he caught my hand and swooped it up to his lips, smacking all of my knuckles. "I'd be sad to see it all go, actually."

I side-eyed him. "Hold up. Let me just grab my phone

again so I can record this for posterity."

"Not necessary." He turned my hands over, sweeping incredibly hot lips across the insides of my wrists. "I'll say it anytime you want, baby." Then he ran his thumb up the inside of one of my arms while following the same path on the other with his amazing, adoring lips. "I don't want to change *all* your leaves, Taylor. I love your firecracker side as much as I love your quiet and thoughtful self." He lifted his gaze, regarding me with that leonine side of him once again. "And oh yeah...that sexy, naughty side had better not go *anywhere*." As I giggled, he stressed in a murmur, "I love *all* of you, woman."

So much for giggling. I was all sighs as he pressed in, kissing the tip of my nose and then pecking me quickly on the mouth. "Let's get this food put away. Then...I want dessert."

"Oh, shit," I blurted.

"Hmmm? What is it?"

"Dessert." I blinked big, flirty eyes at him—already sensing where he was going with his suggestion. "I'm just not sure I have anything suitable here, Dr. Stone. Maybe there's some ice cream?"

He growled. Dragged my hand down to his stiffening cock and pressing that hot and hypnotizing length into my palm. "I'm not talking about ice cream, Miss Mathews."

If we were in a restaurant, I would've been screaming for the check.

Instead, with my lust-driven breaths matching his, I curled a devious little smile full of kittenish intent—and used my advantageous leverage on his body to tug him out of the kitchen. "Why don't we just leave the food right there?"

Mac groaned, his crotch swelling against my palm, as we laced the fingers of our free hands on our way to the living room. "What food?"

I pulled him down onto the ratty sofa he hated so much, though I was pretty sure the worn cushions could've been splintered boards and wouldn't have mattered less to him. When I pressed him down, straddled his lap, and pulled my little sundress up to my hips to give him a quick peek at my panties, I knew I had won the debate.

"I like the way you think." His slow grin matched the slide of his hands traveling up my thighs.

"I thought you might," I answered before covering his mouth with mine.

CHAPTER SIX

Mac

I wasn't exactly the brand-new guy at Scripps Green anymore, but I hadn't had many chances to veer off my normal beaten path. The places I usually ventured in the hospital numbered in the single digits—which was why today felt like being behind the scenes on a movie-studio tour. Things didn't look the way I'd expected, doubling the difficulty of my mission.

But ohhh, I *would* succeed.

Come hell or fucking high water, I was going to find the goddamned lab.

Where that loser worked.

Oh *yes,* John the whack job and I were going to have a nice little come-to-your-savior regarding his obsession with my girlfriend. Maybe not so little. And maybe I wasn't going to save his ass for shit. But the gist was there, burning in my psyche, and I was ready to hand down the fire and brimstone.

But at the moment, the savior had taken a wrong turn somewhere. Somehow, I'd ended up in the facility next door to the actual hospital, which turned out to be a test facility for all kinds of strange things. I wasn't sure I even wanted to know all exactly what.

Eventually, I found a door that exited to the outside parking lot. I regained my bearings and decided to start all over again.

That probably meant the front desk and actually talking to one of the senior volunteers. Every morning, after grabbing my caffeine from Ursula at the little cart, I strode right by the small station without as much as a glance in that direction. The cotton-swab-headed crowd that milled around it was there to help incoming patients find their way around the campus, not suction suture sites for me.

But today was different.

Today, I'd be Prince fucking Charming to whomever I had to, in whatever *way* I had to, just to find the right access to the asshole at the top of my fire-and-brimstone list.

I straightened my jacket, straightened my shoulders until they were as square as a linebacker's, and then plastered my finest, most charming grin onto my lips. Within a few seconds, I set my sights on one of the spritelier looking ladies at the wide counter.

"Good morning, Dr. Stone. Can I help you? You look a bit...might I be bold and say...lost?" She had a mischievous grin, and I couldn't help but think of Taylor. She was going to be a saucy little granny like this one day, wearing a little jewel angel on her collar but flashing a daring devil in her eyes. And I was going to be the dirty old man who fucked her to paradise every night.

Oh yeah, I'd really just gone there.

And I'd loved every second of the dream.

The dream I swore to make a reality with her. *Only* her.

I was more sure of it now than ever before. Somehow, we'd come through our crap and emerged in a brighter, better place. We'd reconfirmed it to each other for most of last night, lavishing each other's bodies with attention and affection before falling asleep in her nest on the floor until the alarm went off this morning, blessedly late. I had surgery rotation today but didn't have to scrub in until nine.

"Actually, I *am* a bit turned around." I added a new smile to my sheepish tone, and she ate the shit up with a fork and spoon. "But only if you have a minute?"

"Well, that *is* what I'm here for." She waggled her brows, and I swam in confusion for a minute. Aside from my mother, I didn't interact with older people who weren't patients of mine. Was she being friendly or flirty? Where was the damn line?

Soldiering on was probably the best option. "I'm sorry." I injected what I hoped looked like an embarrassed smile. "I didn't catch your name?"

"It's Helen." A more robust brow wiggle. "And aren't you just as charming as you are handsome?"

I think I may have actually blushed. *Fuck*. I mean, *fudge*. That was the proper stand-in word, right? Oh, fuck it. I was so out of my element, there was no salvaging the effort. "Well, uh, thank you, Helen. I'm simply looking for the lab. In-patient, I think. To be honest, I'm looking for an employee who works there."

"Oh? Hmmm." She strolled over to a simple computer and started typing in her login. When the hunt-and-peck session was done and the screen flickered to life, she looked up at me expectantly.

Holy shit. Was it going to be this easy?

Just to be safe, I cocked my head, cranking up the feigned aw-shucks stuff. I'd likely have to take three showers after this, but it'd be worth it.

Taylor, and her safety, were worth everything. "I...umm... only know the guy's first name," I admitted. "It's John. I only know he works in the lab. We ended up playing a pickup game the other day at the gym, and he left his, uh, sunglasses—yeah, his *sunglasses*—behind." Yet another beam of the charm. "I just wanted to return them to him."

"Well, that's awfully nice of you. Too bad your gym didn't just have a lost and found." Was this her way of letting me know she didn't believe a word I was saying? Or was that my guilty conscience talking?

"I...well...just wanted to be a pal, you know? Do right by a buddy."

After deliberately working in the Captain America speech, I went for it. The full wattage, slay-the-ladies-every-time smile. Sure enough, Helen blushed all the way to her stylish white hairline.

"Well, let's just see what we can find. I'll do a search by the laboratory department and the first name John, and we'll go from there."

I went around the desk and leaned over her shoulder while she tapped on the keyboard. Seven Johns appeared in the search for the lab department, and five of those seven worked in the same division, so I asked her how I got to that area of the hospital.

"You've been so helpful, Helen." With a gallant turn and then a knightly bow, I bent and brought the back of her hand to my lips. "I really appreciate you taking the extra time this morning."

And there went that completely bad-girl gleam in her gaze again. "Anytime, Dr. Stone," she drawled, making it clear she probably had some wild child tattoos hidden beneath her prim blouse and slacks. "That's precisely what we're here for." She smiled widely too, and her sweet features wrinkled even more.

On my way to the area Helen had shown me on the

directory map, I checked my phone for email. There were no issues that couldn't wait, so I rode the elevator to the floor below the lobby.

The doors parted.

Jackpot.

There was my favorite whack job in the whole wide world, *entering* my elevator car.

Best of all, the fucker didn't even notice me. John's attention was buried in his phone, so all I had to do was wait until the doors slid shut and we started moving again. Calmly and steadily, I stepped over to the panel. Without any noise, I pressed the stop button.

As soon as he looked up and noticed he and I were the only ones in the elevator, his jaw plummeted. His day was about to get really bad, and he knew it.

"Good morning, asshole." That was all I could muster in the way of a greeting.

"Uhhh. Dr. Stone." And then he blinked. Then again. "Wh-What can I do—"

"Shut up." I took a defined step toward him. The pussy physically shrank, backing up into the corner of the lift. "We need to have a little chat, John-Boy. Well, more like I'm going to tell you what's on my mind, and you're going to listen."

I gave him props—not many, but a few—for straightening his stance and jogging out his round jaw. "I don't want to hear anything you have to say unless it's professional hospital business. Need I remind you, we are at *work*."

Yeah. So he had a bit in the way of balls. Not intelligence, but definitely some balls.

"You don't need to remind me of anything, dipshit."

"You *cannot* legally say that to me!"

"Yeah? And you can't legally misuse a patient's private information to stalk her. A woman who has no interest in you, I might add—as she's apparently told you on numerous occasions. So let's just be clear, right here and now. She. Isn't. Interested. To the tune of *zero,* man. So as of this fucking second, Taylor Mathews is officially on your no-fly list. You don't speak to her. You don't call her or text her. And you sure as fuck don't show up at her apartment. *Ever* again."

Ten seconds passed.

Ten seconds more.

The dipshit just stared.

Fine by me.

"We clear so far, John-Boy?" I didn't wait for him to respond. "Good. Let me give you a stern warning while I have your attention. If anything happens to that woman—as in, the woman I love to the point of crazy—you'll regret the day you ever met either one of us. She is *mine.* She will always be mine. And my report card has always said *doesn't share well with others.*" I stepped all the way up to him now, my forward leg almost between his, securing us chest-to-chest. "So you need to move your stupid ass on to your next stalking victim. Don't fuck with me on this. If you do, you'll wake up dead somewhere. And my guess? No one will give two shits about it."

I backed up but didn't waver my view on him except to jab the button for the floor I needed. The elevator started moving again. I kept my eyes on the asshole. The elevator car was only big enough for one dumbshit, and he'd already checked that box with resounding glory.

"Oh, and John?" I said, just as the elevator slowed to a stop at my floor. "Have a great day."

The doors opened. I stepped out, leaving John fuming in

his pathetic corner. He flipped me the bird before the people waiting entered the small space, and the sight of him was quickly blocked as the elevator filled up.

I took a deep, calming breath and strolled across the lobby and toward the surgery department so I could get ready for my first case.

Time to save some lives.

It was the mantra that drove me. The cause that made the grind worth it. Now more than ever.

Because now, I knew how precious life could really be.

Between my first and second surgeries of the day, I went up to my office to grab some lunch and call Taylor. As fulfilling as the day had already been, it was all eclipsed by the chance to speak with the pale goddess who'd gotten way the hell under my skin. Honestly, I was all but crawling in that skin by now—and being here in this room, which was now redecorated in wall-to-wall memories of the woman, I was obsessed by thoughts of her. I was so tempted to type up a resignation letter and just leave—strictly for the chance to get out of here and love her. Fuck her. Explore every detail of all the things that would make her happy. There was so much I already knew but so much I still had no idea about.

Not enough time.

Never *enough time...*

I pulled out my phone to call her, only to be confronted by an email from Scripps Human Resources. The subject line glared at me, stilling my movements as I read.

Disciplinary Action

My heart rate picked up while I waited for the entire message to load. My nervous system didn't cooperate any further as I continued reading the message.

Dr. Stone,

The purpose of this letter is to advise you of the decision to suspend you without pay for ten (10) working days from your position as a surgeon with the Department of Neurology and Neurosurgery. The reason for this suspension is your unacceptable conduct, particularly pertaining to unprofessional and offensive behavior as outlined in a recently filed complaint by another hospital employee. In addition, this letter shall serve as notice that any further neglect of duty or any other infractions will be viewed as unwillingness, rather than inability, to comply with reasonable expectations, and shall result in further disciplinary action, up to and including dismissal.

Your suspension will begin on the third day of business after acknowledgment of this action is received and end at the close of business ten working days following. You are expected to return to duty at the time of your regularly scheduled shift. This personnel action is in accordance with subsection 12.3 of the Administrative Rule of the California Division of Personnel, CODE *R. §143-1-1 et seq., and provides for a three (3) working day written notice.*

During the period of suspension, you are restricted from all areas of the Scripps Green campus except the Human Resources Department. Further, you are not to remotely access employee technology resources (email, database, etc.) or otherwise perform work for the Scripps Healthcare Network. If it is necessary for you to come to the campus, an appointment must be arranged in advance, and security will meet you in the lobby. You may arrange such a meeting by contacting Human Resources.

Please sign and date this notice and return it to the email listed below.

Mother. Fucker.

I already knew who was behind this. A certain lab minion. I wish I could say I was shocked that he would get the hospital involved and this became a personnel situation, but I wasn't. I was sure he wasn't forthcoming with the stalker bullshit that caused me to threaten him in the first place, either. I doubt the human resources team would be thrilled with that sort of behavior.

I'd been on this job for about seven months, and word around the department had been that I was being considered for department head. That would all be thrown out the window with a black mark in my employee jacket like this. That bastard was going to pay for this. Naturally never again on the hospital's grounds, but I could easily find out where he lived and pay him a visit there. Why the fuck not, since he clearly had no trouble with that kind of shit, right? John-Boy had picked the wrong guy's career—and woman—to fuck around with.

But I still had work to do. And for the next three days, I would be a model employee and then have an unexpected ten-day vacation. Maybe I could persuade Taylor to go away with me. Other than Thermal, we hadn't taken a trip together, and she always talked about traveling with wistful longing. Maybe I would contact Killian—so maybe it *was* awesome to be cousins with my girlfriend's boss—and arrange for Taylor to get some time off. *Hell, yeah.* A surprise holiday. If I had to take time off from work, might as well make the best of it.

Lemonade out of fucking lemons.

My second surgical case of the day turned out to be a nightmare. Everything that could have gone wrong did. From the point when I reviewed the procedure with the patient and his family in the pre-op area to the readiness of the OR team to the anesthesiologist strolling in just as the patient was about to leave because his nerves had gotten the better of him.

By the time we got him calmed down and began the procedure, we were fifty minutes behind schedule. But I refused to be rushed just to turn the room in time for the next patient. I was steady and sure, and I did my job the only way I'd ever known how—carefully and methodically, regardless of any external distractions.

On my way home from the hospital, I finally got a chance to call Taylor.

"Hey, beautiful. How was your day?" I was unable to keep the exhaustion from seeping into my voice.

"Oh, same shit, different day," she laughed out. "You know how it goes."

"Yeah." I could barely muster much more in the way of a reply.

"How about you?" Her voice was like my balm. "Save some lives today?" Hell, yeah. My sassy, sexy balm.

I rewarded her for it with a laugh because she loved teasing me about the whole God complex, and she wasn't too far off the mark most of the time.

"Same clown, different circus," I responded. "Same old same old."

No way on earth was I going to tell her about the real shitstorm of the day. Not while we were both rushing and preoccupied and I was still pretty well soaked from that downpour. Dropping a nuke like the drama with John would be like tucking a goodbye note on her windshield again.

"Hey. Listen." I deliberately went low and velvety with my tone. "Can I convince you to drive up to Oceanside? I'd really love to spend the night inside you."

"Well, when you put it like that..." Her breathy exhale made my cock ache for attention.

"I'll be waiting. I love you, Taylor."

"Bye, Mac."

It was not going unnoticed that she still hadn't told me she loved me. I held out hope that this vacation would be her vital turning point. If we spent ten full days with each other, she'd start seeing I wasn't waning in this commitment to her. To *us*. I had no intention of letting her go, and this escape would be the ideal chance to prove it.

The sun was low on the horizon when I went out onto my deck off the third floor. I loved this home more than any other I'd ever lived in. Although the waterfront homes here were close to one another, the view was priceless and the sounds of the ocean were healing for the soul. Especially mine. Especially right now.

Taylor had a key to the front door, so I left her a note in the kitchen to come up when she got here. I sat on the modern deck chair for about thirty minutes, watching two seagulls play tag on the salty breeze, diving and soaring without a care in the world.

"Mac?" My perfect girl's musical voice drifted out to the deck as she walked through the master suite.

"Out here, babe." I stood and held my arms out, greeting her with an intense hug.

"Hey." Her voice was soft and feminine, matching the

flowing skirt she wore with a simple tank top. A studded brown leather belt wrapped around her tiny waist in two loops, the second settling low on her hips.

Crushing as my embrace already was, I wrapped my arms around her even tighter. “Mmmm, just what the doctor ordered. My very own prescription for happiness.” I buried my nose in her hair and breathed in her light, earthy scent. It had rapidly become my favorite in the whole world.

“Do you want a beer? How about some dinner?” An unexplainable desire to take care of her consumed me.

“I'd love a beer, but I don't want you to have to go all the way down to the kitchen.” She looked up at me, squinting her eyes as the sun peeked over my shoulder.

“I have a few in the refrigerator in the game room. You get comfortable, and I'll get you one.” It was difficult to release her so soon when she felt so right in my arms.

“You're spoiling me.” She leaned back again so she could look into my eyes—and as she did, hers narrowed by a fraction. “Hey.”

“Hmmm?”

“Are you okay?”

“Long day. I'll tell you all about it.” I kissed her forehead and then nudged her toward the deck chair. “Sit. I'll be right back. Are you warm enough? Do you want me to bring a throw?”

“You really do know me well, don't you?” She smiled sweetly, and my chest swelled. This interaction was so healthy and domestic, and I wanted to beg her to never leave me again, right here on the spot.

I returned with two beers and the chunky throw she loved from my bedroom. I considered buying her one for her place, but I'd instead lure her here with things she liked. Plus, if I had my way—and I usually did—she'd be here with me full-time. Naturally, what was mine would become hers too.

"Let me sit with you." I tugged her to stand and sat down on the lounge chair first, spreading my legs so she could nestle in the space between them. As soon as she was settled in again, I covered her with the blanket. I opened one of the beers and handed it to her, keeping the other for myself.

We sat there for a long while, just enjoying each other and the fresh ocean breeze. The sun was almost down, turning the horizon into a blend of lavender sea spray and pink sky. Far ahead on the peach-shaded sand, a family walked along with their two dogs, looking like six happy ants. In the odd way that the ocean winds carried sound, we were pinged every few seconds with their bright, carefree laughter.

I wanted to be them.

With more burning desire than I'd ever felt for any goal in my life.

Nothing had felt this important before. *Nothing.* The sky could've opened up and shone a blinding beam down at me, and I couldn't be more clear. It was as if every other decision in my life had been meant to supplement this one. Where to go to college. What specialty to focus on. Where to live. *How* to live.

All of it had brought me to this. To her.

But now we had to get through the rest of the process. To *us.*

That began right now. This second.

"I ran into John today." Okay, so maybe I should've led in with something else, but I was always a rip-the-Band-Aid-off kind of guy.

"Oh no." Taylor laughed for a second, not surprised at all

by the ambush, likely because she was used to them by now. And damn it, even that recognition felt wonderful. "Do I dare ask if he's still alive?"

"Of course he is." I fought to keep the mild irritation from my tone. This mess wasn't hers. I'd gotten myself here, fair and square, all on my own. She didn't deserve to have her head bitten off for it. "I'm not an animal, Taylor."

"Well." Her voice was still as light as the soft brushes of her fingertips through the springy hairs along my forearm. "Only when I tell you to be."

I yearned to lurch up, drag her into the bedroom, and show her exactly what kind of "animal" her closeness could unleash, but I took a long pull from my beer instead, ordering the alcohol to do its thing to my nervous system. It kept my voice to a calmer rumble as I assured her, "Yeah, he's fine. Although I'd still love to teach that fuckstick a clearer lesson."

"So, what *did* happen?" she finally asked.

"Well, I was heading downstairs to see if I could find him in the lab—"

"Wait." She dug in a few fingertips. "You were actually on the prowl for him?"

Her surprise was laced with indictment, but no way was her "animal" biting on that fight. Which wasn't really a fight. Which I was happy to elucidate again for her. "I told you I'd handle it, Sassy."

She relaxed her grapple, leaving behind cute little half-moons in my forearms. "Fine."

The grumble was the closest thing to "Yes, sir" that I'd get. I accepted it and moved on. "When I got on the elevator, the lunatic conveniently hopped on with me. He was glued to his phone at first, so he didn't see me. That changed as soon as I stopped the elevator."

She tensed and pressed her fingernails into my arm again, though she didn't go for the full-on claw thing this time. "So what happened? What did he say? Was he still being so over the top?" She turned a bit in my lap now, making me miss the full contact with her body. Probably for the best. Thoughts of hauling her inside and doing caveman things to her wasn't the best influence on my self-control.

"Well, he was scared." I compelled myself to stay all-business instead of gloating god. "I could see him shaking."

"Well, no shit."

"But I didn't hit him, baby. I didn't even touch him."

"Okay." Her stare was as serious as the sea stretching behind her. "I believe you."

I brushed some of the white-gold strands away from her face. "I know. And thank you."

"So what did you say to him?"

"I let him know it would *not* be okay to ever speak to you again. And to never show up at your apartment. Ever."

"That's hilarious. I bet he pissed himself." She pressed an elegant hand to my chest. Christ, how I loved the sight of her touch on my body. *Anywhere* on my body. "Well, thank you for being my awesome white knight. For protecting my honor."

I lifted her hand and kissed those pretty polished fingertips. "As I always will."

Her gaze softened, and I could tell *she* was thinking about some bedroom caveman fun too, but she clearly ordered the inclination aside, growing thoughtful once more. "He hasn't called or texted me anymore."

A gruff snort. "Maybe he isn't as dumb as I thought he was."

My whole body hummed, since my instincts expected her let's-go-to-the-cave-and-fuck look to return. Instead, her expression darkened, opting for deeper contemplation. And a much harder examination—of me.

"But there's more to this, isn't there?" she charged. "Your mood is way off for just getting to strut your macho stuff around another guy. Normally, that gives you a serious contact high."

I chuffed again. "'Macho stuff?'" I narrowed my eyes while taking another gulp from my bottle.

"You know what I mean." She waved a dismissive hand. "You'd usually be all pumped up and shit after that."

As she took a drink from her bottle, I got in a deep breath. I let it out in a sigh. I had to tell her what happened, despite the fears it would spoil our night. There'd be plenty more nights we could make perfect. I just had to write off the loss now and hope she'd help with the "moving on" part of the equation.

"I left John-Boy trembling in the elevator, and I scrubbed in for my first case. By the time I was finished in the OR, I had an email from human resources."

Taylor's voice audibly snagged. "About what?"

"Well..." I was stunned, but happily so, by the sardonicism that sneaked into my tone. Yeah, I could appreciate my own levity, especially at a time like this. "Our friendly neighborhood shithead filed a complaint against me for inciting a hostile work environment."

"And they reprimanded you without hearing your side of the story?" she spewed, instantly enraged on my behalf. My little spitfire. Fuck, I loved her. "I'm not sure that's how that's supposed to be handled."

"It's a hospital, baby," I stressed. "I guarantee, in a place like that, every law is followed to the letter. We live in a litigious world, and hospitals are always ripe for the picking."

"You have a point," she conceded. "But still..." She trailed off in thought for a moment and then quickly rebounded. "It doesn't seem fair. Would they be okay if they knew he was stalking me? That he used medical records to find my personal address and showed up on my doorstep? Uninvited?"

She was getting riled up and fast. While her distress was the last thing I'd intended or liked, I was increasingly touched by watching her turn into Firestarter in my defense. I enjoyed the feeling for a few seconds more before launching into the point that would likely switch it off.

"I think you should consider filing a police report, Taylor." I'd been thinking about it all afternoon, and I finally decided to push the point.

As predicted, her reaction was a pout that stretched down to tight brackets at the corners of her lips.

"*Listen to me.* This way, if he starts really acting stupid, it'll be on record from the beginning."

She waved her hand again. "I really don't want to get involved in all that." She made a sour face. "I've had to deal with the police more times than I want to admit. You know that, Mac."

"Yeah." I took a heavy breath. "I do."

"So why are you push—"

"They put me on a ten-day suspension without pay as disciplinary action."

Maybe dropping *that* bomb would change her mind. For several seconds, it looked like it would. She popped tall, sitting straight between my legs, though remained unusually still and quiet.

"You've got to be kidding me."

"Wish I was, love."

Finally, she turned to face me. Then said with a shaky voice, "I'm so sorry. This is all my fault. I should've never had lunch with him. Even though I know with certainty that I didn't lead him on, I just should never have gone in the first place."

"Okay, now you're really going to listen." I scooped one of her hands into mine. "It's not your fault, baby. It's my own. I'm the one who threatened him in the elevator. I could've just left last night be where our interaction ended. But I just didn't feel like he really got the message, that he was taking me as seriously as he needed to be. But confronting him at work was stupid. I've ruined my chances for department head for sure, but I have no one to blame but myself."

I drained my beer while the gravity of the situation sank in. What a fucking mess.

"Such a load of bullshit. He's getting away with everything he did." Her voice wobbled as she ducked her head back in against my chest. "It's not fucking right." She even mewled a little as I tucked a heartfelt kiss against her temple, still crimped with frustration. And there it was. Yet another thing I loved about my streetwise, sassy girl. She believed in justice. But justice for all.

"Hey. I have an idea. Hear me out before you say no." It was well past time to explore the silver lining in these storm clouds.

"I hate when you start conversations with conditions. It makes me nervous." Her skeptical look was as adorable as her contemplative look.

"Not conditions." I bussed her forehead again. "Necessities."

"Excuse me?"

"I know you, lady. In some ways, better than you know yourself. You're always ready with the contrary." I was only half teasing. She definitely was a professional devil's advocate.

"I am not," she protested. Adorably, I might add. And I could've sat there all night, basking in the fun of bantering with her—but I *was* getting to a point here.

"So seriously...I was thinking."

"Always a dangerous thing," she quipped. I let her have the win, knowing I might need to collect on the other side of the tally.

"Why not take these lemons and make lemonade?"

"I'm not following." She squinted her eyes in suspicion.

"I have ten workdays off."

"So you...what? Want to open a lemonade stand?"

Again, I let her have her fun with the banter. "Ten days off," I emphasized. "That never happens, even when I take a scheduled vacation. They said I can't even log in to the hospital's computer system while I'm suspended, so I won't even be able to catch up on case notes or anything."

"Oh shit. They're really making an example out of you, huh? I am so sorry, Mac."

"Stop apologizing. You have zero blame here. But yeah, there is a zero-tolerance policy on violence in the workplace." I put my hand up, already stopping the regret in which she wanted to keep wallowing. "But here's my proposal." With my other hand still wrapped in hers, I tightened my hold. "Let's take a vacation."

Her mouth slowly parted. Clearly, she'd expected me to really proposition something like a lemonade stand. "Uuhhh..."

"Just you and me," I rushed on. "Maybe somewhere adventurous. Or exotic. Somewhere you've always wanted to go." I stiffened the hand I already had in the air, knowing her first obstacle before she uttered a word of it. "All expenses paid, baby. My treat. *Stop.*" I extended the "stop" hand right into her face. "I won't hear of it any other way. You know I have the money. I make an excellent living fixing brains, and I inherited a shit ton from Killian's father when he passed. So don't stress about it." I added my most dashing grin, the one I'd used to twist Helen's panties this morning, for the perfect linchpin of persuasion. "Let's just get up and go somewhere."

She slowly shook her head. "I...can't just drop everything and leave, Mac. I have a job. It may not be as important as fixing brains"—she mimicked my voice, making it impossible not to chuckle—"but I have bills to pay. No work, no money."

"Yes, but don't you get vacation days? If I had to wager a guess, I'd bet you have a ton accrued and probably donate days to other people who need them instead of taking them yourself." I tilted my head, daring her to deny my assessment.

She looked sheepish when she answered. "Well, not every time, but yes, I've done that."

"Do you have at least ten days?" I really wanted—needed—her to say yes. I hadn't even realized how much until this second.

Gradually, a smile spread across her lips. "I do."

"See? This sounds like a good idea, doesn't it? Where do you want to go? Tahiti? Hawaii? Where?" I pressed as soon as she let her grin brighten every inch of her doll-like face. "Come on. Tell me."

I dug my fingers into her sides, making her squeal with laughter. As soon as I relented, she bit one edge of her lip and then murmured, "Well..."

"Yeah?" I prodded.

"I *have* been watching the Travel Channel a lot lately. So don't think I'm just stark crazy."

"I already *know* you're crazy, girl."

She giggled. The sound resonated through my chest like a fucking angel had landed there. And maybe she had.

At last, she ventured, "If you're serious..."

I kissed her. Not for long but definitely for impression. "I've never been more fucking serious in my life."

A new giggle. Another angel in my chest. "Well. I'd...love to go to the Dominican Republic."

"Done."

My one-word answer made her smile even more prominent. "Just like that?" she practically stammered. "That easy?"

"Of course. I asked you where you wanted to go, and if my baby wants to go to the DR, then we go to the DR. *Wait.*" I flung out a mocking glower. "They have indoor plumbing, right?" Not that I wouldn't piss in the jungle for a week alone with her. Of course, that meant she had to wear a seashell bra. And I'd find the smallest damn shells on the beach...

"In most places." She giggled while I tickled her again.

"Okay. The Dominican Republic it is."

"Well, let's not get too excited. I have to check in with Killian."

"Ahhh, of course. My cousin. The puppet master of all San Diego." I rolled my eyes at the thought of having to ask his permission for anything. We'd been getting along better since I moved to San Diego, but my natural instinct was still to bust the man's arrogant-as-fuck balls. Then again, maybe it just took one to know one.

Taylor smacked my chest and then rolled her eyes. I

grabbed her little hand so fast she didn't have a second to pull back.

"Did you just smack me?" I widened my eyes.

"It was a knee-jerk reaction. *Maaaccc.*" Her whining came from her lips at a downward angle across my lap as I pulled up the yards and yards of material of her skirt.

"Jesus Christ," I spewed.

"Hold on. I'll go page him."

"Fuck that. Where the hell is your ass in all this? You need a spanking, woman. If I could find some flesh first!"

"No!" she exclaimed. "No, I do *not*!" But then she stilled and said with a sexier-than-sexy husk, "Okay, maybe I do. But really, I need to call my boss first if your wild off-to-the-DR plan is going to fly." She barked out a laugh. "Ha! See how I did that?"

"Oh, dear fuck," I muttered. "But you have a point. So up you go. But remember, I'm keeping track, sassy girl."

"Of course you are. My phone is downstairs in my bag. I'll be right back."

I watched her until she disappeared from view. Looking back out over the white caps on the breaking waves, I felt like the luckiest bastard alive. Forced to take a break, getting to share it with the woman I loved, and more happiness in my heart than one man deserved.

Life was good.

And only getting better.

CHAPTER SEVEN

Taylor

We had one stop in Atlanta with a pretty short layover, and then we were on our way to our final destination. So despite the nearly twelve-hour journey, we were both wide awake when we arrived in Punta Cana.

I was more excited than I ever remembered being in my life.

I had traveled around the United States for my work with Stone Global, but the international experience was completely different. My passport was brand-new and now had its lone stamp proudly emblazoned on the first page. Mac explained we would have to go through customs again on the way back into the United States, regardless of the fact we were citizens, and I realized how little I knew about life outside my own little bubble in San Diego.

He had been to twelve other countries outside the US, but he had never been to the Dominican Republic. I was even more thrilled that my first time would be his as well. I'd packed a lot on the agenda, everything from lounging on the beach to snorkeling and jeep excursions, and I wanted to start it all as soon as possible. I'd barely slept on the plane, and I wasn't convinced I'd be able to sleep once we got to the hotel either. I felt like a kid on Christmas morning.

No. Better.

In the world of Janet Mathews, Christmas was never much to look forward to.

Our hotel was the best Mac could find, and we were fortunate to be able to book something on such short notice. Since so much of the country was unknown to us, the only thing Mac insisted on was a top-of-the-line hotel. The rest of the trip was all my planning—and there was *a lot* on the schedule. I wasn't sure we'd really get to see it all.

The bellman wheeled his cart ahead of us along the winding outdoor path, finally stopping when we got to the end of the building. Our room occupied the entire corner of the top floor, and when he opened the door to the suite with a grand flourish, it was...

Breathtaking.

"Wow." I probably repeated it twenty times before switching up to my next favorite.

"Oh, my God!"

I rushed over to the window and pulled the heavy drapes back as far as they'd go. "This *view*!" Such paltry words for an experience I could only describe as a miracle. Our room overlooked a small piece of paradise, complete with flowers and streams and swimming pools, with the sparkling Atlantic just beyond. The staff members at the registration desk had said we would be especially impressed in the morning as the sun rose over our balcony.

A special energy in the air inspired me to turn back around. There was the man of my dreams, looking rugged and stubbled and carved and perfect, gazing at me with glittering adoration in his eyes.

"Fuck. Me," he growled with low appreciation.

I flashed back a coy smirk. Murmured only for his ears, "In what position, exactly?"

Though his gaze gained the smoke of pure lust, he went on. "You are the most beautiful thing when you are this excited. There is life in your eyes like I've never seen before. Remind me to whisk you off on impromptu vacations more often."

I crossed to him, wrapped my arms around his neck, and stood on my tiptoes to kiss him. And then deeper, darting my tongue between his lips. And then—

"Hold that thought, baby," he husked. After tipping the bellman and sending him on his way, he came back over. I'd moved back to the window again, needing another hit of my gawking awe of the view.

"I'm thrilled we did this." He pressed up behind me, snaking his arms around my waist. "I may have to thank John personally when I get back to the hospital."

"No!" I snapped. "You stay far, far away from that loser!" I wrapped my hands atop his and leaned back into the solid strength of his broad chest. "But I'm glad we did this too. Thank you so much for making all of this possible. It's literally a dream come true. I...I seriously don't know how to thank you enough."

He ground his swelling crotch into my backside and then leaned down to kiss my ear. "Oh, I can think of a few ways."

"Really?" I teased him by pressing my ass back into his cock.

His rapidly surging cock...

"Definitely." His voice was dark with promise, and his scruff tickled my neck.

"*Wait.*"

"Huh?"

I turned in his arms and ran my fingertips through his spiky stubble. “I need to freshen up. Way too many hours in the same clothes. I’m going to shower, and then maybe we could go exploring the property?”

“I’d like to explore you first.” The tigerlike gleam in his greens matched the primitive power in his growl. “But if you insist. Showers and then exploring. We’ll see whose version of that comes out on top.”

The smoldering grin with which he finished made my stomach flip more wildly than the stunning surf against the beach. I tamped down my ensuing flood of lust while deepening my caress along his jaw. After I did that for a good minute, studying him in earnest, Mac finally laughed out, “What?”

As he raked that intense stare across my face, I framed both sides of his. “I kind of like all this. Have you ever had a beard?”

“I have a few times. It gets freezing in Chicago in the winter. Sometimes a beard serves a purpose higher than racking up hipster points.”

“You are the furthest thing from a hipster, Dr. Stone,” I drawled. “I think you’re safe, even with a bit of facial hair.”

★ ★ ★ ★

A shower had never felt so glorious. I had barely slept the night before. My excitement and nervousness about the trip had me tossing and turning most of the night. Now, after standing under the warm spray for much longer than necessary, exhaustion crept in. The high of the travel buzz had worn off, and my arms and legs felt like lead weights hanging from my body.

I strolled out of the bathroom and wound through the

suite to the bedroom. Soft snores came from Mac, asleep in the huge bed. The warmest feeling spread through my chest as I climbed in beside him, leaving the plush, white, spa-like robe thrown on the bench at the foot of the bed. I tugged the covers up over the both of us and settled in against his side. Within minutes I was asleep, the day's activities taking their toll on my consciousness.

The next morning came quicker than my sleep-deprived body would've liked—but since my "alarm clock" was Mac's mouth calling my senses to attention, I was cured of any desire to sleep in further.

My eyes fluttered open to see the top of his head on a downward trail over my body. I spread my fingers through his damp hair and realized I must've slept through him getting up and taking a shower. The suite was large enough that I'd been insulated from his noises.

"Hmmmm. What a lovely wake-up call, Dr. Stone. You on morning rounds?"

He grinned up at me after nibbling the soft flesh of my belly. "Glad you approve, Miss Mathews." He licked a taunting circle around my navel before adding, "You know, you could wake up this way every morning."

"Don't get ahead of yourself, Clown. We just revived this circus."

"I still think you should move in with me." He kissed a very wet path toward the apex of my thighs as I wondered where the *hell* that proposition had just come from. Was this just the vacation high talking, or had he been rolling the thought around for a while? How serious *was* he?

And despite my staunchest effort not to give in to the mental dodge-and-duck, I did. Dodged. Ducked. As fast as I could.

"Less talking," I decreed, though I sighed more than spoke the words. "More licking."

He grinned wider before sinking his teeth into my thigh. He stayed that way, clamping deeply into my trembling flesh until I dropped my head back and moaned.

"*Maaaac.*"

"Hmmmm?"

"Please!"

He pressed his tongue to the abused area after releasing his jaws, spreading the pain into a wildfire that ignited every damn nerve in my pussy. When I felt the bed dip under his weight, I lifted my head and watched him shed the towel that had been wrapped around his waist. His long, swollen cock bobbed out in front of him.

"I don't think I'll ever get tired of looking at you," he growled.

I smirked as a light blush warmed my whole body. "That's a good thing to hear at the start of a ten-day vacation, mister."

"Spread your legs." His voice was deep and gravelly, fuel to the fire that replaced the flush. That burned, torrid and tormenting, inside me. "Let me see what's mine."

"Actually, it's mine. I just let you borrow it on occasion." But I still obeyed, for two great reasons. One, I always came out on top when he got bossy. And two, I knew my cheeky attitude spurred *his* desire.

"Is that right?" He tilted his head to one side with a sexy smirk. "I see it quite differently."

"And why am I not surprised?" I purred it while reaching between my legs and then sliding my middle finger slowly through my feminine folds. "And what do you see?" Holy shit. I was already so damn wet for him. No way could I could deny it or hide it with sassy remarks. This man lit my fuse like no other had before. The combination of his commanding ways, his demanding sexual hunger, and his open adoration of me set my system ablaze every time we were together.

"Already wet for me?"

Unbelievably, I screwed up the nerve to shrug. "Eh. It could be for anyone, really. It's a normal female reaction. You should know that, Doc."

"You like teasing me, don't you?"

I just slowly nodded—already seeing that my tender admission stoked his inferno even more.

"Come back over here," I pleaded. "And taste me."

"In time," Mac assured. "First, I want to watch you touch yourself. Show me how you get yourself off when I'm not there to do it for you."

Oh yes, Doctor!

But I kept the outburst to myself. I had to get busy here.

While spreading my legs wider, I settled back on the pillow. I loved watching Mac's features go taut, including the sexy-as-hell tic that vibrated in his bold jaw. His arousal ramped my own. Exponentially. My pulse throbbed in my clit as the blood rushed to supply the tissue.

Mac gulped. Hard.

And guess what happened to my clit in direct proportion?

I kept going. A little faster but not harder. With my index finger, I swirled around the bud, barely giving myself enough pressure to get off. I wanted this to last. I wanted to see how dark, dangerous, and hard-up I could get my beautiful, erect boyfriend.

"Don't hold back!" he snarled out. "You like it harder than that, girl. Give yourself what you need. You're going to come for me, and you're going to do it hard. You're going to be so wet and creamy, and then I'm going to bury my face in that gorgeous cunt and lick every sweet drop from you."

I moaned—but swiftly pitched it into a whine. "But you're so much better at it than I am."

"I doubt that. Who knows your body better than you?" He leaned in for a better view.

"I think you might." Oh, hell. I probably should never have admitted that. It just powered his ego more. But right now, I was baring more than just my flesh to him. I knew it, and he definitely knew it. I watched the comprehension in his eyes. The gratitude he gave me for exposing as much as I could to him. More than I had to any other lover—any other *person*—in my life.

I was terrified.

But I'd never been so damn turned on.

"Slide your fingers up inside," Mac grated. "Feel how warm you are inside there. *Fuck.*" He swallowed hard again and fisted his erection. He only pumped once, but it was enough to bring a magnificent milky drop to the top of his beautiful crown. "My cock is so ready to feel you."

I shifted my weight and slid my heels up to my ass. I dropped my knees wide and moaned as pleasure seeped through me, brought on by my thrusting fingers. "Mac, *please.* Just...just put your mouth on me. Eat me until I scream. I'll get off in seconds, and then you will have what you want."

His gaze turned to emerald fire. His jaw clenched harder. "Close your eyes." As soon as I complied, acting all too eagerly because of the thick lust in his voice, he dictated, "You'll keep them shut, no matter what. Is that clear? *Tell me,* Taylor," he bit out when all I did was nod. "In words. Tell me now."

"Yes," I whispered. "Th-That's clear."

"Good. Now use this." He yanked my hand away from my pussy, only to wrap my fingers around a heavy, rubbery object. I ran my touch along the thing, quickly deducing it was a firm rubber dildo, similar in size to his cock.

"What the— Did you just find this lying around?"

"I brought it with me in my luggage," he explained. "Now no more talking. Fuck yourself with it, Taylor. Let me watch it move in and out of your body."

"Aahhh, the kinky clown is in the big top this morning, I see."

"*Do it.*"

I was *not* going to argue the point. With my heartbeat doubling and my pussy tingling, I slid the thick toy through my folds, running its tip across my clit to get that part lubricated for penetration. When I pressed the dildo to my opening, it slid right in.

"Ohhhh." A huff of air escaped my throat. It felt so good to be so full, even if it wasn't Mac inside me.

"Does it feel good, baby?"

"Yeeesssss." I moaned from low in my throat.

"You look so sexy. All pink and juicy, full of that cock in your hand. Press it in farther. Fuck, yesssss."

His hiss had my eyes popping back open. I watched as he took his cock back in hand, stroking himself with intent purpose. "Can't you just do it?" I whined. "It would feel so much better."

His resolve must've finally caved, because quicker than I could track, he was between my legs and taking over the handling of the dildo.

"Will you let me put this in your ass?" His sexy growl had

gone to schoolboy hopefulness.

"Will you let me put it in yours?" We hadn't explored much regarding the end zone up to that point.

"Probably not. Although we could discuss some other options. Your tongue? Yes. Finger? Maybe. If the moment was right." He said it all very matter-of-factly.

"So, you should be able to stick something the size of a cucumber in my rear, but I can't do it to you? How is that fair?" I continued toying with my clit while we bargained nonchalantly. This was so surreal. I'd never done this kind of shit with any man before—nor had I ever felt this carefree and comfortable. I could talk about anything with this gorgeous, outrageous genius. The only man on the planet—in *history*—who could handle all my crazy quirks, bold humor, and voracious erotic needs.

"Well, life isn't fair, my love. And your body was meant to take things into it." He put his face between my legs and licked the inside of my thigh while continuing to shuttle the rubber cock in and out of my clenching tunnel. Soon, he was making a path of small bites toward my clit. I hated when he bit me there, but I loved it even more. That anticipation built as he made a lazy circuit around my pussy.

"Mac. Please. Just—"

"Patience, my sassy girl. I know what you need," he lectured between nibbles.

Tremors surged through my legs, so I tightened my thighs against Mac's shoulders to try to disguise the way he was unraveling me. But his soft chuckle against my skin told me he knew just what effect he was having on my will to stay calm. He pressed his tongue firmly against my clit and swiped up, over and over again, until I clawed desperately at his scalp. A low keening noise escaped from my pressed lips, and it only seemed to add to his enthusiasm.

"Let it out, baby. Your beautiful cries. Your perfect passion. Come for me. Let me feel you fall apart, Taylor. I'm right here. Always right here." He pulled the dildo out, and the quick loss of fullness was my undoing. Arching my back off the bed, I pressed my pussy into his mouth as hard as I possibly could. As I came with the most powerful climax of my life, the man lapped and sucked my clit, slurping and licking the juice that ran freely from my body for him.

Because of him.

The white sheets stuck to my damp skin when I sat up, my bedhead hair in a wild tangle from thrashing about in coital bliss. And I do mean *bliss*. Mac's green eyes glowed with satisfaction, even though his erection still swelled between his thighs, his balls drawn tightly to his body. The usual tame style of his hair had been traded for a wild shock of every-which-way-ness, making him look just a tad unhinged. And ohhhh yes, even sexier than before.

"Whatever shall we do with you now, Miss Mathews?" The sex appeal of the man multiplied every time we touched.

"Me?" I mouthed the word with feigned innocence, watching Mac stand up and prowl around the bed toward me.

"Hmm. This week is going to be quite the challenge." He sat down right beside me, crowding his large frame into my personal space. I couldn't take my eyes off his erection for more than a few seconds at a time, as if I'd never seen it before—or any other erect penis, for that matter. It just looked so virile, proud, capable.

So...beautiful.

I licked my lips and shot my eyes back to his when I

realized he was waiting for me to answer a question. A query I hadn't heard.

"Hmm? What?" My voice broke with embarrassment.

"What has gotten into you, girl?" His chuckle was more admiration than jest.

"I... It's just... I... Well, never mind." Regardless, I felt awkward about my feelings in front of anyone.

"No, tell me." His deep resonance shot straight to my pussy, flooding more moisture to the already swollen tissue.

"It's silly." I looked down at the bedding surrounding us. What was I going to tell him?

"Tell me, Taylor. No more Ice Age, woman." He was definitely going to make sure I stuck to that promise.

"It's just—you're so beautiful. So, just so...such a...man. See? That sounds dumb when I say it. It was better in here." I tapped on my temple. "Sometimes you should just let me keep some things to myself."

"I like to know what's going on in there." He settled a whisper-soft kiss on my temple. "You are amazing, and brilliant and beautiful. Thank you for sharing that. But now"—he waggled his eyebrows in a silly way but immediately grew serious before issuing his instructions—"lie on your back with your head right here, hanging over the edge of the bed."

Ohhhh, my.

Unbelievably, my sex already thrummed with more anticipation as I hurried to arrange myself the way he directed. I scooted down and then flattened out, lying across the bed sideways with my neck extending over the edge. My head was supported enough so I could gaze up at the fan making a lazy circle overhead—

Until Mac leaned over, his carved nudity invading my

field of view.

"Perfect, baby. Are you comfortable?" he asked, looming over me.

I nodded yes, only to meet his disapproval. "I thought we'd been over this already today, Taylor. You know the rules in my bed."

"Yes, I'm comfortable, Clown, Sir," I answered out loud, resisting the bratty urge to mock his tone of voice.

He tried to look stern, but I didn't miss the twinkle in his eye. "Tilt your chin up to the ceiling...and then open your mouth." He pressed two fingers under my chin to illustrate the position he was looking for.

I kept my eyes fixed on his, maintaining the position he asked. Slowly I opened my mouth, and he stepped closer to the bed, gripping his cock like he was holding back a Doberman on a choke chain.

Oh, shit.

This was going to be good.

Really. Damn. Good.

I licked my lips, already anticipating his swollen flesh meeting my lips. We locked eyes, holding each other's stare. His greens turned damn near black as he dipped in and pressed the tip of his cock to my anxious mouth. I parted for him eagerly, licking the salty tip before sucking the head wholly inside. As he hissed, I eagerly did it again. Then again. With every new pull, I watched Mac's eyes slide closed with abject pleasure, and I inwardly preened. It felt so damn good to give this to him. To indulge him this exquisite pleasure.

"Don't stop," he snarled out. "For the love of *fuck,* don't stop."

I didn't stop.

I teased the underside of the crown with the tip of my tongue a few times before opening again to let Mac invade me deeper. I flattened my tongue to let his cock glide to the back of my throat, anticipating the gag and calming myself by swallowing against it. In the process, I took him even deeper.

"Fucking *God,* woman. So good. You're so...fucking... good."

He threaded his fingers into my hair just past my ear, cradling my head at the base of my skull in his large hand. I moaned around his dick, coating him in my saliva. It all started running down my cheeks, since I was basically hanging upside down, making everything slick and slippery for his movement.

"Relax, baby. I need to move. Let me fuck you like this. Put that sassy mouth to good use." His rough voice and rude words made my pussy vibrate even harder.

"Mmmmmm." It was all I could respond with, but I rubbed my legs together before letting them fall wide open, imagining Mac was between them instead of halfway down my throat.

He pulled back from me, but only by a fraction, before sliding back in. He did it over and over, sometimes going a bit deeper, gagging me and making the pathway slicker with my saliva. My eyes watered, the tears running back into my hairline. As soon as Mac looked on, his erection throbbed even harder.

"That's right, my beautiful. Cry for me, baby." He started thumbing the drops away, alternately feeding them to me along with his cock or sucking them off his own thumb. "More. Deeper. *More.*"

Dear freaking God. I was so turned on, I wanted to explode. Craved it. Needed it. I was writhing around, trying to find some sort of relief, something to gain friction from, but Mac held the better part of my body in place with the grip on my head and cock down my throat.

Abruptly he withdrew from my face and flipped me onto my stomach. Because the man was so much bigger than me, he could literally toss me around without much effort. I scurried onto my hands and knees and did a quick 180-degree turn, offering my aching pussy for his use. And dear fuck, how I needed to be used. To be screwed until I forgot all the chaos in my head and all the worries of my world. Filled with him until every feeling and every sensation was nothing but him. To be nothing but his perfect, wet little toy.

He rolled his hips, notching his cockhead to my heat. But he paused, growling through a second that felt like a decade, before ordering, "Tell me." Another hitch of his hips, taunting my weeping entrance with his huge, velvety heat. "Beg me."

"Yes," I answered at once. "Take me. Fuck me. *Please*."

I was drenched, and he was ready. Mac slammed into me, pushing my face down into the bedding as he hauled my hips back up in the air against his. It was feral. It was harsh. It was perfect.

"Okay, baby?" he asked roughly.

"Yes. Just fuck me!" Madness had set into my system. My skin crawled with need. My pussy clamored with desire. My spirit eagerly wrapped around the sound of his primal growl...

As he unleashed himself completely.

He pounded into me without stopping. Without tenderness. Without mercy. We traveled halfway across the bed before we burst into tandem orgasms that had us panting and collapsing, one on top of the other, in breathless wonder.

"Jesus fucking Christ, woman." He panted. "Fuck." Mac

slung his arm over his face and sprawled across the bed.

I just grinned. Goofy and high on endorphins, I really didn't have much to add. I just snuggled into his overheated side, rubbing my nose against his skin and feeling like all was right in the world.

We lay there for a little while until finally one of our bellies announced, without grace, just how long it had been since we'd had a decent meal.

"Didn't they say something about a breakfast buffet when we checked in?" I asked but made no motion toward getting up.

"Yes, and if we hurry, we can still get in on that." But of course the man in the room was a burst of motion at the mention of food. "We better shower again, though. I'm pretty sure we both smell like sex."

I followed his example and rolled off the side of the bed and walked toward the bathroom. Food was definitely sounding like a good idea. "Agreed. I'll hop in really fast."

"Excuse me?" He put his impossibly long arm out, blocking my path. "We'll do it together. That way you can wash my hard-to-reach spots, and I can do yours."

His grin was irresistible. Nevertheless, I protested, "Do you *ever* want to get out of this room?"

"No. I mean yes. Are there other choices for answers, professor?"

I smacked at the meat of his shoulder. "You're impossible."

"And *you're* gorgeous after I've invaded you for an hour. But right now, I'm serious. Shower first and then food. That's it. No more dick for you until later. You're killing me. Fiend!"

"Me?" I stood and stared at him in mock disbelief.

"Come on." He pulled on my arm. "Let's go or there won't

be any good stuff left."

We showered together and, wonder of all wonders, did not have sex. After we washed, rinsed, and toweled off, I put some product in my hair and decided to go for a messy beachy look. Since I'd only packed casual sundresses and shorts, I randomly grabbed something from the closet, and off we went.

"So, what do you want to do today?" Mac asked, covering his eggs in hot sauce—though he suspiciously eyed the activities list I'd made on the plane while he'd slept. "What's that?"

"I made a list." I beamed, mighty proud of my preparedness. When he only grinned, looking ten years younger than his ordinary surgeon self, I giggled. "What? No remark about over-planning? About how you prefer to live life 'on the edge'?"

"Nope." He smiled again, totally oblivious to the gaggle of females eyeing him from two tables over. I felt petty but vindicated as he scooped up my hand and nuzzled the inside of my wrist. "I like your list making. You're adorable when you're in get-the-most-out-of-every-experience mode."

I still looked at him skeptically but decided to press on with my list. I'd put serious thought into making it, after all. "Well, according to the resort's website, we can do all kinds of things right here on the property, or we can take an excursion into town just a few miles away. They will even take us in their vehicle," I said authoritatively.

"Okay, what kind of things can we do here? I think for the first day, staying here sounds better. I'm still a little beat from the trip."

"I agree. Sooooo..."

I took a big breath before rattling off a bunch of options. By the time I got done, especially now that I could see his energetic reactions to each new suggestion, I was beyond excited and nearly bouncing in my seat.

Okay, maybe not "nearly."

As I did about my tenth happy dance, fists pumping and head swinging, I looked up to find Mac simply staring at me. A half-eaten piece of toast dangled from his fingers while a half-loopy smirk teased at his lips. Great. He was so damn gorgeous like that, I swore I'd never look at another piece of toast the same way again.

"What?" Still, I was immediately self-conscious. I couldn't interpret this new look of his, and it was damned unnerving.

"I swear, if there weren't other people here, I'd fuck you on this table."

And *there's* where he was going with things. "*Mac.*" I blushed and didn't even hide it.

"What?" he countered. "You're so fucking sexy when you're this excited and happy. I don't think I've ever seen this much pure joy in another human." He growled, and the sound vibrated straight to my pussy. "It's addicting, is all. *You're* addicting, Taylor Mathews."

"Oh..." was all I could manage. The look on his face was so intense, my heartbeat stuttered.

But the spell was broken when the waiter came to refill our drink glasses. He didn't notice, or maybe just didn't care, that we were in the middle of thoroughly eye fucking each other. "Is everything to your liking?" he asked with a droll sneer.

"Yes, thank you." I smiled, confident my cheeks were red as a drunk Santa by this point. But this giddiness didn't have a thing to do with booze. It was all the intoxication of Maclain Stone—who took my breath away with a new grin as the server walked away.

"So," he said. "Parasailing it is, then?"

"Really?" My excitement picked right back up where it had been when I finished reading the list. "You would do that?"

"Sure. Why not? When we're done here, let's walk down to the shack on the beach and make reservations. Maybe we'll have enough time for a quickie before they take us out." He casually took a drink from his glass.

"Oh, my God."

"What?"

"You're a sex maniac."

"And there's something wrong with that...why?"

"There are rehab groups for that, you know." I said the whole sentence while smearing butter on the most delicious-looking blueberry muffin, never taking my eyes off the task—so when he swept in his large hand and suddenly captured my wrist, I dropped my knife with a startled yip. The clatter of the silver against the white stoneware caused a few of the other resort guests to turn and see what had caused the commotion, though they turned away once Mac got busy again.

Oh, yeah.

Very busy.

He leaned across the table as far as he could without leaving his seat, which with his large frame was nearly halfway, and said in a very low rumble, "If wanting to fuck you every second of my day is an illness, I never want to be cured. Ever." He turned my wrist over, once more lifting it to his mouth. To anyone else, he was delivering a kiss on the inside of my wrist—but it was actually a bite, so long and hard and deep that I had to stifle a moan behind my free hand.

Mac lavished the mark with his warm tongue before releasing me. All I could do was stare at him, my mouth slightly parted, eyes drooping with arousal. He was slowly killing me with his passion. I had no idea a person could die this way, but it was definitely happening.

One incident at a time, I was falling in deeper.

One heartbeat at a time, he was winning me over.

One day at a time, I was becoming more and more...

His.

God help me.

CHAPTER EIGHT

Mac

One by one, we ticked off every item on Taylor's list. We swam with dolphins, snorkeled, parasailed, and even learned how to make our own sushi. I think I'd leave that to the professionals moving forward, but it was fun giving it a try. Indulging my beautiful girl and every single whim she dreamed up was becoming my second favorite pastime. Top billing would forever be making her scream my name while I was balls deep inside her heat.

Fuck, yeah.

Forever number one.

Every day we spent together, I learned something new about her. I'd dated models and managers and more than my fair share of doctors too, but she was easily the most fascinating person I'd ever known. Her curiosity and intelligence were so pure and sincere, it was a secret treasure not many were privileged enough to experience. She made me unreasonably happy, but I wasn't about to question or pick apart the feeling. For once in my life, I just wanted to accept it all at face value for what it really was. For what *she* really was.

My destiny.

I was supremely giddy about seeing parts of her that very few did. I would venture to guess, albeit cockily, that there wasn't another guy out there who'd unlocked what I had. She was a woman who took time. Patience. Insight. Most morons out there likely ran out of one, let alone all three, once they found out she was more complicated than her gorgeous face and possessed a huge heart inside that sexy, creamy body.

But I was in this for the long haul. I took the time to find things out about her, dig deeper where the assholes just gave up. But when I saw her little threads hanging loose, I had to pull and see what I could unravel. Best of all, I was never disappointed. It was more than just all the movies we liked, the places we wanted to see, and our sick sense of humor when people-watching throughout our adventures. It came down to intrinsic shit about her humanity, like the way she carefully thought about all sides of an issue before making judgment and her kindness to everyone we met, no matter what their station in life. From local kids to housekeepers to vacationing magnates, nobody was better or worse in her view, and they all fell in love with her for it.

But none of them as deeply as me.

And still, I craved to learn more. To discover more. There was so much hidden beneath the surface of this woman, an entire lifetime wouldn't be enough to uncover it all. But I wanted to try. Damn it, I wanted that lifetime.

Yeah. I just said that.

I wanted to spend my life with her.

But first, I still needed to hear her say she loved me.

So many moments—fuck, *so many*—when I sensed the words were right there on her lips. When she'd been so *damn* close. But then she'd shake herself free of some thrall in which she kept imagining I had her and recall them back into the depths of herself. The places I hadn't yet uncovered in her.

The places where the little girl in her still existed, alone and let down and wounded—and vowing never to be hurt like that again.

In a word, I was stuck. I didn't know what else she needed from me at this point, other than time. But I could give her that too. I'd give her whatever she needed. I was hooked on this woman like a user on crack. She wasn't joking when she said I needed rehab. I'd never had it this bad for a woman.

About the eighth day of our trip, we were lying by the pool after she had given me a mind-blowing suck on our private balcony, and my cell phone rang. I hadn't heard that annoying sound in almost a week and hadn't missed it in the least. I almost let the fucker go to voicemail, since Taylor was looking fine enough in her bikini for me to consider an early retreat back to the room, but when I recognized a San Diego prefix, I decided to pick up.

"Maclain Stone." My tone was curt as usual.

"Hey, Mac. It's Killian."

"Uhhh...hey, Kil." I shrugged when Taylor shot me a curious stare. My cousin was the last person I'd expected on the other end of the line.

"Sorry to bother you on your vacation."

"It's all good." I made an effort to sound a bit warmer. He had, after all, been the one to sign off on Taylor dropping everything at work to do the Dominican with me. "What's going on? Everything okay?"

"I'm guessing Taylor is there with you?"

Gruff snort. "You remember saying she could come with me, right?"

"I mean right there with you." His tone was a mix of affection and tension. I'd never really gotten the strange nuance, but Taylor was teaching me to read more subtleties in people, so I rolled with it. "I was hoping you could put me on speaker. This really involves her."

"Oh. Well, why didn't you just say so?"

The line went rough with his harsh exhalation. "I. Just. Did."

I gestured for Taylor to scoot closer while setting the phone on the little table between our two lounge chairs. After pressing the icon to put the call on speaker, I called out to Killian, "Okay, you've got us both."

"Good day, Mr. Stone," Taylor respectfully intoned. I just rolled my eyes. The almighty Killian always got the formal treatment. *Whatever.*

"Taylor, please, call me Killian. You're practically family."

Double eye roll for his ass-kissing response.

"Hey, Taylor." Claire's gentle voice joined the conversation.

"Hey, Mama!" Taylor brightened at once, her voice filling with the warmth she reserved for her sister-close girlfriends. "How you doing? And how's my gorgeous baby girl?"

"Regan's fine. Little crazy girl, cruising around like she owns the place." Claire laughed.

"I love it! You're in so much trouble now," Taylor teased.

"You have no idea," Killian mumbled. Fatherhood suited him. Secretly, I envied the bastard even more.

"So what's this all about? I can't imagine you called us in the DR to talk about your daughter's milestones."

Taylor smacked my chest with the back of her hand, and I couldn't say I blamed her. My dry tone seemed like a buzzkill, even to my own ears. Still, I glared for good measure. Taylor glared right back. She'd definitely be getting a swat of her own for that later. I held up one finger to let her know I was counting. She just rolled her eyes, and I added a second finger. Her response was a proud single finger of her own. *Beautiful brat.*

"There's no easy way to say this, so I'm just going to say it." Killian huffed. "Taylor, your apartment was broken into and vandalized last night."

Taylor sat up straighter. "Excuse me?"

"I'm so sorry, honey." Claire's sympathy was underlined by the sound of a giggling child.

Kil jumped back in. "San Diego Police called us here, since this is your place of employment. And with your next of kin being, well—"

"Janet," Taylor supplied when he hesitated. "And useless."

"Well, I didn't want to say that, but okay," Killian finished.

"Why would someone want to break into my apartment? I literally have nothing that matters. Mac won't even sit on my sofa, it's that old. This doesn't make sense." She stopped, sensing the tension from the other end of the line at the same moment I did. "What?" She loomed closer over the phone. "Come on, you two. *What gives?*"

Kil cleared his throat with purpose. "Apparently it wasn't really theft," he finally relayed. "It was more—"

"Personal." Claire completed the play this time.

"Shit," I growled beneath my breath.

"Do you have any idea who may have an ax to grind with you?" Claire questioned. "I mean, you and Mac have been seeing each other for quite a while now, but there were... uummm...some things written on your walls."

"*Shit.*" I took no pains to mute the word now.

"Written?" Taylor pressed. "On my walls?"

Killian took his turn at bat again. "I'm not going to candy-coat this, Taylor. They were pretty insulting things."

Taylor's face had gone ghostly white. She'd picked up a nice bit of sun on our holiday, but in the course of this one phone call, the color was totally gone. "For fuck's sake. Just spit it out. What did that motherfucker write on my wall? I know who did it. And when I see him again, I'm going to rip his tiny little dick off and shove it down his throat."

"Okay, so she's taking this better than I thought." Killian's tone left no room for guessing how sensitive the conversation was about to get. "Mac? Can you pick up the phone, buddy?"

I held the phone to my ear and held Taylor's trembling hand with my other hand.

"Hi."

"So you know who it was?" he asked.

"We have a pretty good idea, yeah," I answered quietly.

"He wrote some pretty graphic stuff. Whoever it is, he's one sick fucker. And I don't mean like you and me sick. I mean like, he-should-be-in-prison sick," Killian supplied.

"Hey, speak for yourself, man. I'm not sick in any form of the word." I laughed, trying to make light of a horrible situation.

"When are you coming back?"

He didn't sugarcoat that inflection, either. The intention was crystal clear. Vacation time was over.

"Apparently on the next flight we can arrange," I answered, attempting to disguise my disappointment.

"I was hoping you'd say that."

"Why?"

"Because I can help."

"Huh?"

"I've got a jet."

Now I was the one rolling my eyes. "Oh, yeah. How could I forget?"

"The plane is in Chicago right now. Margaux's there, along with Claire's father. The saga of Andrea Asher continues. The woman is making both their lives a complete hell, but when I spoke to her last, there wasn't a lot more they could do to help the authorities. She told me they were planning on coming home. I'm sure they won't mind rerouting to grab the two of you."

I abandoned the eye roll. Even felt a little guilty about it now. "Shit. That's one hell of a detour, man." To be honest, I was even bordering on uncomfortable. That was a lot of people changing their plans just for us. "Seriously, I can call the airline, and—"

"The fuck you'll call the airline," he retorted.

"Kil—"

"You're family, Mac. It's time we both started acting like it. So shut up." He said it as though it were as good as done. "Margaux and Colin will be happy to make the change, given the circumstances. I'll let the crew know to make the necessary arrangements and will call or text with the details."

Again, he left no room for argument. He clicked off, and the line was dead before I could say thank you or goodbye.

I set my phone down. Shoved it and the table out of the way. I reached over, attempting to yank Taylor over to my chaise and into my arms, but she resisted with equal force.

"Hey."

"What?" she snapped.

"Come here. This is crazy shit. Let me hold you for a second."

"I've been through 'crazy shit' before, Mac. And I don't

need to be *held* through it. I'm not a child."

"Then stop acting like one. Who said it was for your benefit?" I pulled her toward me again. This time she let me, although I still wouldn't say it was with enthusiasm. Or even compliance. She was begrudging at best, but I refused to let her get away with it. "Goddamnit, Taylor. Don't put a wall up between us because of that fuckstick. Not after the amazing week we've had." I said the last of it into her hair, rubbing my cheek against the side of her head.

"I'm sorry." Finally, her voice cracked. Her shoulder shook. "I'm just so...sorry. Everything's ruined." She sniffed hard and finally, *finally*, burrowed into my neck. I hated that it had taken this horror to make her crack this far open for me, but part of me surged and swelled with hope. And she thought *she* was the fucked-up lost one?

"Only if you let it be." I held her tighter. Funneled every particle of my courage and strength into her, around her. As much as she would take. As much as she'd give me the blessing to give. "Don't let him win, damn it."

She leaned back, letting me see the rage and frustration twisting across her face. "How can you say that? Only if *I* let it? He was in my apartment! My fucking home, Mac!"

Jesus. I *was* a sick fuck. Here came the fireworks I had expected—and perhaps even needed. The vulnerability I craved from her. The reality and honesty.

"I know, honey." I gathered her back against me. "I know."

She started shaking with rage, and I couldn't blame her. I let her indulge as much of the emotion as she needed until she calmed herself with a huge breath in.

Eventually she asked, "What's the plan now? I mean, what are we doing? Was that what you and Killian were talking about?" She pushed away and lurched up before starting to pace back and forth. "Are we going home? I don't want to go there now. But what about my stuff? My clothing and my stuff?" She stopped, slamming a hand to her forehead. "My chessboard!" she wailed. "Oh, fuck. Did he ruin it? Do you know? Did Mr. St—Killian—did he say anything about it? And where am I supposed to go now? I can't afford another security deposit. I'll never get that one back with writing on the walls. Oh, my God! This is a fucking nightmare, and he's a fucking bastard. Are the police looking for him? We're going to have to tell them now, Mac. There's no other choice."

She was rambling a mile a minute. I thought about cutting in...for about half a second. She needed to get this out, and I let her. When anyone around us gave her the stink eye for her rant, I stabbed them with a dirtier glower in return.

Finally, after thoroughly running herself out, she stopped and just looked at me.

"Fucking say something!" she shouted.

I rose slowly. Kept my arms at my sides, neutralizing my stance. "First of all, remember I'm on your side, Sassy. Yell *to* me all you want, but don't yell *at* me."

"Sorry," she mumbled.

"Nothing to be sorry for. You're upset. I am too." I did the calm-head-in-a-crisis thing for a living. Those skills kicked in naturally, just as hers did to freak out. "Killian is sending his jet to pick us up here. He said he's going to give me more details as soon as he has them. That's all I can tell you on that end. We should probably get back to the room, pack up, and then be somewhat ready to go. Since the police are already involved, we need to tell them everything we know."

I paused, needing the break to lay all my thoughts in an

orderly row. "That includes the lunch date, the messages, the texts, and him showing up at your apartment—the first time." I hesitated to include the last part, thinking John hadn't been fully confirmed as the guilty party, but unless my girlfriend had another stalker romping around in the background of her life, the statement was a sure thing. "And yeah, we'll probably have to talk about me threatening him at the hospital and him lying to Scripps HR."

She came back to where I still sat on the lounge chair and crawled into my lap. Looping her arms around my neck, she pressed her forehead to mine. "I *am* sorry I yelled at you," she whispered. "None of this is your fault. I'm just so mad. And sad."

"Sad? Don't be sad, baby." I leaned back to look at her. Mad I could understand, but the last thing I could stand was for her to be sad. I'd move heaven and earth to see the radiant joy on her face that was there just an hour ago.

"Our trip has to end. I never wanted it to end." Tears filled her eyes, and one lonely drop escaped and rolled down her cheek. I felt like someone had just stabbed me in the fucking heart.

"*Baby*. We can take another trip just as soon as everything settles down again. I promise. I'll take you anywhere you want to go."

"Promise?"

"I promise." And I meant it, with every speck of my heart and soul. It was so rare to see Taylor cry from sadness. I would do everything in my power to keep that level of pain from her life as long as she let me.

At last, while I still stroked the back of her head, I murmured, "Let's go upstairs and get packed. We may still have a long day ahead of us."

"Wait." When she pulled back, it was to palm away her tears and then blink at me with newly lucid eyes. "Is Killian really just going to send his jet down here for us? That's so crazy." She sounded as amazed as I felt about the gesture.

"Apparently Margaux is in Chicago with the jet. There's some guy with her too—but not Michael." For the first time, I realized the impact of that. And for the second time, Taylor looked as stunned as I felt.

"Huh?" she charged. "*What* guy who isn't Michael? And *Chicago*?"

I frowned. "I'm sure that's what Killian said."

"That makes no sense." Her gaze drifted toward the large swimming pool, where people were seated at the swim-up bar, chatting in the afternoon breeze. The halcyon scene contrasted greatly with the vexation in her eyes. "I spoke to her right before we left on the trip," she stated. "She didn't mention a thing about going to Chicago. Besides, she wouldn't just randomly pick up and go *there*."

"Why not?"

"Because she hates that city now. Too many shitty memories."

"Ah. Right. Because of all the crap that went down with her mother, right?"

"Andrea Asher is *not* her mother—especially not now. The woman's a first-rate criminal and a creepy fugitive who's fled the country. And she did so with—"

"The cousin who won't be named," I filled in. Piece by piece, the memories started coming back. I'd always been too busy and filled with self-importance to notice anything that happened with my three cousins, even when Killian was outed as the Stone-who-really-wasn't-and-then-was-again, but the notoriety of Trey's actions had penetrated even my sanctum of saving the world, one hunk of brain tissue at a time. After a list of scandals a mile long, including attempting to blackmail Margaux, he'd slipped past the feds and disappeared somewhere beyond the States, taking his cougar lover with him. The woman had left her husband for the tryst—

Ding, ding, ding.

"The husband," I said out loud.

Taylor scowled. "The *what*?"

"Asher's husband. I think he's also Claire's dad?" *And who the hell's on first?* This was why I never paid attention when the nurses clucked like hens, talking about the latest happenings on their favorite nighttime dramas. Actually, I also didn't listen when they discussed other shit, but crap like this was the biggest trigger for my Mute button.

"Colin?"

"Yeah." I jabbed a finger into the air. "That was it."

"So Margaux's in Chicago...with Colin?" She rubbed her forehead, deep in thought. "I wonder what *that's* all about..."

"Sounds like you'll have a chance to find out." A new shrug. "He made it seem like the new flight plan was no big deal. I guess when you own a few jets and a bunch of people who sit around waiting for you to tell them what to do, it's just that." I rubbed my head too. The whole idea was such a foreign notion. I mean, I grew up within a wealthy family, but Killian was on a whole other level.

We walked on the meandering path through the resort for one last time, my arm around her slender shoulders, holding her close to my body.

"It's nice to see you and Killian getting along a little bit better?" She worded it more as a question, inquiring about the way our phone conversation went after I took the call from the speaker.

"I guess so. He made a comment about us treating each other like family, being there for each other more. I'm not really familiar with the concept, to be honest with you. I wasn't really tight with any family growing up because my mother is so hideous to everyone."

"*Mac.*"

"Well, she is. You know it. I know it. Everyone who knows her knows it. No sense sugarcoating the issue. We never had relationships with anyone for very long because she would get into a fight with them and cut them out of her life when they disagreed with her. Of course, it was always their fault, never hers." As we walked up the stairs instead of taking the elevator, doing anything to prolong our respite in paradise, I muttered, "I don't know why it took me so long to recognize the pattern."

"Well, I think as children, even as adult children, we want to see the best in our parents. It's easy to turn a blind eye to their shortcomings, you know?" Her soft voice was warm with understanding, even after everything her own mother had put her through over the years.

"You're an amazing woman, Taylor Mathews." We stopped in front of our door, and I turned her to face me. "I love you with all my heart. We're going to get through this storm, just like we will get through any other storm life puts in our path."

"You're a pretty amazing man yourself, Maclain Stone." She smiled up at me. "I'm very fortunate to have stumbled into your circus." She stretched up and kissed me one last time before our world would be turned upside down.

CHAPTER NINE

Taylor

While being chauffeured home on a private jet should've been an experience of a lifetime, especially considering I was in the company of some wonderful friends and my extremely sexy lover, the oppressive weight of the disaster that awaited us in San Diego hung over my head like a guillotine. I considered taking advantage of the drinks repeatedly offered to me by the jet's overattentive staff, but Mac put a stop to that plan before it gained wings.

"I don't think you're going to want to be nursing a hangover on top of everything else when we get home," he said stoically, taking the third drink from my hand.

"Oh, don't be a party pooper." I tried to reach around his large torso to grab the drink off the small table where he had just placed it. He took my hand and held it in his, kissing my knuckles with his typical breath-stealing adoration.

"Just think about it," he softly exhorted. The past week in nirvana had turned my taciturn boss man into a loving hunk. In my mind, I replayed everything he'd done to me on the sheets, the beach, the balcony, even under the waterfall during our hiking trip.

His quiet voice shook me from my musings, though, dumping me right back into the mess we were dealing with.

"We really have no idea what's in store for us when we get home."

"What's all this *we*? That jackass didn't break into *your* place, just *mine*," I cracked.

"Hold up." His auburn brows crunched over the newly sharpened shards of his green eyes. "Do you really think I'd let you deal with this alone?" Gone was the quiet, calm, serene version of the man, and as he spat his response, Colin Montgomery conveniently feigned interest in the same clouds we'd been cruising over for an hour. "When is it going to sink into that head of yours, Taylor? I love you, goddamnit. Part of loving someone is helping them through crappy situations like this. It's not just the good stuff. It's the bad stuff too."

Thank God for Margaux, who came out of the restroom at that exact moment, saving me from having to further the discussion about *love* and *feelings*.

She plopped down in the seat across from me. "So what happened between the day you called me from the side of the freeway and this guy spray painting love notes inside your apartment?" She opened the bottle of water waiting for her beside her seat and chugged back about half. "God, I get so dehydrated when I travel." Setting the bottle down, she stared at me and waited for me to fill her in on the details about John.

"I don't know." I rubbed my temples. "He's a nutcase. Mac had words with him at the hospital."

"Words with him?" she interrupted. "Is that a euphemism for argued with him? Threatened him? What? I mean, you ended up having to take an unscheduled vacation."

Mac laughed. "Nothing slips by you, does it?"

Margaux slid out a sly smile. "That's why they pay me the big bucks. So, do you work with him? Did you know him before all this started? Is this a grudge thing on top of him crushing on our girl?"

"Jesus, slow down with the questions, Sherlock. And your girl is sitting right here, need I remind you?" I hated when people talked about me like I was a child and couldn't handle what was going on.

"Take it easy, Sassy." Mac turned and addressed Margaux. "I never saw the douchebag before this all started. I didn't even know where the hospital lab was when I went looking for him. As a matter of fact..." He stopped himself, going unnaturally quiet. Finally, he murmured, "Fuck. Why didn't I remember that before now?"

"What?" I straightened. "Remember *what*, Mac?"

"The day we faced off in the elevator..." His gaze grew unfocused as he recalled what had happened. "The whack job said something, but it didn't really faze me at the time. Only now do I realize how creepy it was." He stopped *again*, causing Margaux and me to burst with tandem groans.

"Okay, Stephen King," Margaux teased. "Way to build suspense."

"Right?" I added.

"I'm just trying to remember the context," Mac explained. "John said he only volunteered with the Bloodmobile when he knew Taylor would be donating." He turned to me again. "How long have you been donating blood? Did you do it on a regular basis? Like something he could keep track of? Did you have to schedule an appointment, or could you just walk up?"

I shrugged. "I don't know, really. I've been donating for a few years. They keep records of that. You can schedule an appointment online or just walk up to the Bloodmobile when you see it parked somewhere. They try to make it convenient for people to encourage more donations. I have an online account. I can look at my history."

Margaux stood up and went over to where her carry-on had been stowed for takeoff. She whisked her laptop out of the front of the bag. "Here. We can just check. We should be at cruising altitude and have Wi-Fi by now."

"Was he there every time you donated blood?" Mac asked.

"Maybe not every single time, but often. I don't know. It's not like I was keeping track of it in my diary at night."

He grinned. "You have a diary?"

"Wouldn't you like to know?" I taunted.

He leaned closer. "Do you write about me in it?"

"Wouldn't you like to know?" I repeated in the same tone before standing to join Margaux at the small table where she was setting up her laptop. Mac quickly snaked his arm across my waist and pulled me into his lap, a little yelp escaping me from the surprise of the movement.

"I have ways of making you talk, Ms. Mathews." His voice was heavy with promise just before he sank his teeth into my shoulder.

"Stop. Don't need to hear *or see* all this." Margaux playfully plugged her ears and then switched to covering her eyes but widened space between two fingers to peek through.

"Wow. You've embarrassed Mary Stone. The impossible has been done." I beamed up into his handsome face and his eyes on fire with desire.

"Oh, don't get too full of yourself over there," Margaux chided. "Come log in to your account so we can see just how long McCreepy has been creepy."

Just like that, the sexy mood was gone. I sighed and pulled myself off Mac's lap with leverage from the armrest. As soon as

I was next to Margaux, she swiveled her laptop to face me. I quickly typed in my credentials on the blood bank's homepage.

In a low whisper, her eyes glittering with intrigue, "Was he biting you?" she asked.

I giggled as quietly as I could. "It's his...thing."

She made a swoony face. "Holy shit."

A new giggle. "And now I like it too."

"*Nice*." She gave her head a quick shake to get back to the matter at hand.

Mac came and joined us at the small table, all three of us bending our heads over Margaux's laptop.

"So, it looks like you gave blood every two and a half or three months? Does that seem about right?" Mac asked.

"Well, here," Margaux said, pointing to the screen. "The time in between appointments gets longer. These are the most recent dates. So why did the time in between get longer? Were you picking up on a strange vibe from John?" she prodded. "Did that make you not want to go anymore?"

"No," I answered timidly. "That wasn't why."

"Well, then why?" she pressed.

I pointed at Mac.

"What does he have to do with anything?" she asked, not realizing she was treading in sensitive territory.

"I've been a little...preoccupied," I said defensively and then quickly followed that with: "I mean, before, I didn't have a lot happening on my social calendar. Sometimes just going out and donating blood was something to do—a reason to get out of the house. Something other than work or rescuing Janet." Having to admit that out loud made me realize how pathetic my life actually was before I met Mac.

"Well, maybe the psychopath picked up on the change in

your routine too," Margaux mused aloud.

"It probably didn't help that the last couple times I was there, *he* showed up." I jabbed a finger Mac's way again.

"That was just a coincidence." This time Mac was doing the defending.

"Well, yes and no." I scoffed with open skepticism.

"Yeah, but McCreepy didn't know that," Mac argued.

"I guess not. But there was more than enough posturing going on between the two of you."

"I don't like being challenged." Caveman Mac didn't bother apologizing for it. "The second time, when I saw you hugging him, I literally saw red. If he hadn't gone back inside that bus by the time I got across the parking lot, I don't know what I would've done to him."

"And at the time, I would've thought he was harmless." I shook my head in disbelief.

"And look where we are now." He sat back in his seat, cocking a smug smirk.

I pushed to my feet. "I never said I was a good judge of character."

"Present company excluded," Margaux quipped.

"Still debatable." I arched a new brow Mac's direction.

He held up his first finger like he was counting.

I scoffed. "I'm going to snap that finger off and hand it to you." But as soon as I was done with the threat, he grabbed me around the waist again. At once, I batted at his hands—for what little good it did me. I ended up planted in his lap just like before.

"Does he always just toss you around at will?" Margaux stared at the two of us piled together in one chair.

"Pretty much." I stiffened my pout in matching degrees to

my limbs in his lap.

"But if you weighed more than a piece of paper, you could fight back." The interjection came from Colin, who'd been observing our banter with a twinkle in his eyes and a small smile across his handsome face. I was struck by how much Claire resembled her dad, and I already knew that little Regan was going to grow up as a gorgeous mix of the Montgomery and Stone genes. Poor Killian was going to be fighting off the boys with pretty huge sticks.

Margaux closed her laptop with an efficient snap. "I'm going to go call home," she declared. "I miss my little monster. Maybe if she's not napping, Caroline can put her on FaceTime."

She trotted off toward the back of the plane. When she was out of earshot, Mac said, "Maybe this is all my fault."

What the hell?

Maybe I just hadn't heard him right. I twisted in his arms so I could look directly into his face. "Why would you say that?"

"I don't know," Mac uttered, stabbing a hand through his hair. "Maybe I did egg him on, like you said. With all my 'posturing.'"

"No." I pressed my hands to both sides of his worried face. "That wasn't my point, Mac. Not in the least. This guy is messed up in the head. Neither one of us brought this on. We can't start thinking like that. If that were the case, then I'm to blame too. I egged him on by going out to lunch with him. Are you okay with me saying that now? Blaming myself for *his* obsessive behavior?"

"Absolutely not." His growl was rough and immediate.

"Then there's no way any of this is your fault either. Not one little bit."

He nodded, clearly accepting my assurance in every spirit I gave it. Being acknowledged like this was...nice. Really nice. So why wasn't I able to give him the same thing? To trust the words and feelings *he* gave *me* as the complete truth?

His sultry snarl brought me out of my ruminations. "You know, Sassy..." And then he ground his impressive cock up against the sensitive crack of my ass. "You're really fucking sexy when you're defending me. I think I like it. A lot."

"You're impossible, Clown. Insatiable and impossible."

"Guilty as charged." He grinned, and I pressed my forehead to his.

"And on *that* note..." Colin got up as well. "I think I'm going to find a more comfortable place to get some much-needed sleep. Our visit to Chicago has, regrettably, tapped me out."

I watched the man disappear into the back of the plane as well and made a mental note to check in with Claire about what was going on with all that. Since the feds had yet to locate Andrea and Trey, the subject of their heinousness had been, out of respect to Margaux, back-burnered by our tight little group. Seemed like it was all about to hit the front flames once more.

But first things first. We had to put this crazy man, John, in his place.

"I really don't want to deal with all this bullshit. It's so unfair. We had the best trip ever, and now I don't even know where I'm going to live." I closed my eyes and wished it were all some sort of terrible nightmare I could wake up from.

"With me. *Duh.*" He said it so casually, making me open up to meet his gaze again.

"Mac, I'm serious. I'm not talking about a one-night sleepover. I truly don't have money for a security deposit on a new place, so I need something that'll be for a while."

"How about forever?"

But he'd muttered it so quietly, and like he had marbles in his mouth, that he could have just as well been saying *now or for never*.

"*What?*" I demanded. "What did you just say?"

"Just that we'd work out something for the better." His lips quirked, all but blaring his bold lie, but I had bigger issues to work through here. Huge things to think about.

"Well, I've got to figure this out," I went on. "From what Killian was saying, I won't be getting the money back that I put down on the apartment. I will *not* go stay with my mother in her double-wide. Claire and Margaux have babies now, and as for Talia and the guys..." I shook my head. "They're doing everything in their power to make a baby, and I just don't want to be around all that."

I was working myself up into a new lather. His darkened glare said as much.

"Taylor. For the love of fuck. I said *stay with me*. I'm very serious about this. Move into my house in Oceanside. You love it there."

I bit my lip. "You're right. I do."

"And there's more than enough room for the two of us, so what's the problem?" His tone shifted to the "hurt" range, and I knew I needed to try to explain.

"It's not the way it's supposed to be." I leaned my head back on his shoulder, wanting him to understand my thoughts more than anything.

"What does that mean?"

"You're not asking me because you want me to be there."

"Why am I asking you, then?" He huffed. "Honestly,

Taylor Mathews, you're the most confusing human I know. Please, explain this to me. Why did I just ask you to move in with me if I don't want you there?"

"You're asking me because I *need* a place to go." Christ, it was so obvious. Why did it seem so clear to me, yet he didn't get it at all?

I turned in his lap so I could face him. He just stared back, utter bewilderment twisting his handsome face. "What does that mean?" he growled. "Because you *need* a place to go? This is a normal course of events. You need a place to live, I say, 'Yes, I have a wonderful place we can share; come live with me.' And normally, you would say, 'Thank you, Mac. I'd love that, Mac.'"

I took a deep breath, doing my very best to hang on to whatever shred of patience I had left. "Try to follow me on this. It's not like we reached a place in our relationship where we decided we should move in together. No. I just had some psychopath break into my apartment, and now I have no money to move into a new place. Our hand is forced to make a decision we weren't ready to make. See?"

Something clicked into place, and he finally followed my line of thinking. "Okay. I see what you're saying. And I completely disagree. Just because we didn't have the conversation before John decided to redecorate for you doesn't mean we aren't ready to live together." He paused for a few seconds, letting me absorb my semi-victory. "Do you feel like you're ready to live with me? Because I feel like I'm ready to live with you. Hell, I feel like I'm ready to marry you, but you won't even say you love me."

The blood drained from my face.

Hell. Did the plane just freeze in midair too?

Oh, shit. Oh, shit. Oh, shit.

I couldn't breathe. I wasn't even sure if that was a good thing or a bad thing.

I moved to stand up, but Mac held me tighter.

"Let me up." I tugged on his hands that were clasped around my middle.

"No."

"Yes."

"*No*, goddamnit. You always run. As soon as the L-word comes up, you take off. Physically or mentally, you depart." He released his arms from around me, and I stood up, just like he predicted I would. But I didn't walk away. I just needed to be standing. I needed to deal with the extra energy coursing through my body. So many things were going on. I wasn't sure we needed to add this to the pile of complications.

So I stood there. Not knowing what to say. Not knowing what to do.

I just stood there.

But then, something happened.

Something deep inside me...

just...

cracked.

All the years of holding my shit together, keeping my life in line while mopping up after my addict mother's follies, containing all the emotions deep down in a safe place where they didn't have to be felt... And then it all just burst out, rushing free from me in a tsunami of hysterics and a torrent of tears. Whether that's what Mac actually intended—or even expected or hoped to ever have to deal with in his life—that was what arrived. The fucking storm.

Of me.

Right at his feet.

Literally.

In a sad, messy heap of sniveling, sobbing, snotty, gasping-for-air, chest-heaving wails, I collapsed in a ball at Maclain Stone's feet, utterly inconsolable for what seemed like a millennium.

When I became somewhat aware of my surroundings, Mac was on the floor, cradling me in his strong arms like he'd found an injured animal. He rocked me gently while stroking the hair back from my tear-dampened face, softly whispering words to me that didn't quite reach my ears above the humming in my head. I clutched the sleeve of his shirt in one hand and the placket of his button-down in the other, holding on for my very survival. Not the physical kind. This was worse.

Whatever had just happened was so far beyond my own explanation, I decided to take comfort in his physical nearness instead. I reached up to touch his face, the scratchy stubble of his unshaven beard, just to feel the roughness under my fingers. The careful concern I saw in his beautiful green eyes when he looked down into my face made the emotion well up again but this time for a reason I fully recognized.

He loves me.

The thought gonged through me like the revelation it was. Like the sun finally breaking through my storm. Like the miracle I could finally embrace, in all its magical and beautiful intensity.

He truly loves me.

It was in his heart and in his soul. He showed me all the time—but he really showed me right this moment with the way he gazed upon me. Adoring me, even in my snot-nosed messiness. Lifting me up, though I was really and truly at my lowest.

Loving me...no matter what I'd thrown at him so far or could ever dream of subjecting him to in the future.

Loving me.

And I loved him.

I was no longer lost. He was my everything. My beacon home. My grounding wire. My safe haven. My heart knew it, and it had known for some time. It was my head that was having trouble getting on board with the plan. But now, even my stubborn head realized I was at risk of losing him, or at the very least, hurting him, if I didn't return the sentiment. And soon. If there was one thing I could be sure of after the past week I'd spent with this amazing man, losing him would be the hardest thing I'd ever have to endure.

"Are you back with me?" he murmured, careful not to kick off another rush of emotion.

"I'm so sorry." I really didn't know what else to say after all that had just happened.

"Don't you dare apologize. You've been under an enormous amount of stress, baby. You don't ever have to apologize for feeling your emotions around me. It proves you're alive in here." He touched the center of my chest, just above my heart.

"I have no idea what that was about. One minute I was standing there"—I pointed to the spot where I had been upright—"the next thing I know, I'm here in your lap again, feeling like I've aged about ten years and have had the wind knocked out of me. Did we lose cabin pressure? Maybe it was hypoxia? That's a real thing. I've read about it."

He smiled, eyes scrunching up, knowing I was looking for every excuse I could come up with rather than admitting I just had a Grade A emotional meltdown.

"If the offer is still open, I'd like to come stay at your place when we get home." There. I said it. Baby steps, right?

"Of course the offer still stands. Why would I retract it?" he said gently, still stroking my hair back.

"Well, we're sitting on the floor of a private jet when there are plenty of perfectly good seats available because I just proved what a basket case I really am. Just for starters."

"Do you remember what I said about the good times and the bad times? Love doesn't stop and start like a trendy fashion statement. This is the real deal, Taylor. I love you. I'm in it for the long haul. You can't get rid of me, Sassy." He kissed the tip of my nose, and I sniffled, realizing what a mess I must look like.

"Okay," I whispered. I just wanted to close my eyes and sleep in his arms, but I knew he had to be terribly uncomfortable. His big frame was folded up to cradle me between a row of cabinets and the seats we'd sat in for takeoff. I also knew if I fell asleep here, he wouldn't say a word. He'd just sit here and hold me until I woke up, even if that meant he had a stiff back for the next week.

"I'm going to go freshen up. I must be a sight." I stretched up to meet his lips, savoring his warmth when I pressed mine to his. I wanted to tell him I loved him. I wanted to just blurt the words out and make the whole ordeal final. But I wanted it to be more special than with me sitting in a heap on the floor of an airplane after I'd just gone to pieces at his feet. I would come up with a perfect time and place, and it would be something neither one of us would ever forget.

CHAPTER TEN

Mac

We touched down at Montgomery Field in the early evening thanks to an accommodating tail wind. A Stone Global car waited to take us back to Lindbergh Field so we could get my car from the parking lot there. Unfortunately, it was too late to go by the police station and answer their questions about our dealings with John, but I couldn't say that I was overly disappointed. I was exhausted from the trip and was looking forward to getting Taylor settled at my house before she changed her mind.

"Boy, my cousin sure lives the life, doesn't he?" I toyed with the ends of Taylor's hair while she rested against my shoulder. The back of the luxurious car had more than enough room, but we sat side by side regardless.

"It was very nice of him to do all of this for us," she answered quietly.

"Yes, it was." I would give the guy credit where it was due. We would probably still be sitting in an airport somewhere if it wasn't for him.

"I need to go by my apartment and get some things," she said, staring out the window.

"I don't think that's a good idea. Not tonight." It was like pulling the pin out of a hand grenade and then counting down the seconds until the explosion occurred.

Three.

Two.

One.

"What am I supposed to wear to work? This?" She looked down at the gauzy sundress she was wearing, flipping the hem up with a feisty hand gesture.

"Killian said the police have the whole place sealed off because it's a crime scene. You won't be able to go in there without a police escort anyway. Why don't we go by the mall and you can just pick a few things up?"

Three.

Two.

One.

"A few things. Of course. Because I have an endless supply of money, Mac. Because I grow the stuff on a plant on my windowsill at the office. And hey, why not just buy a whole new wardrobe while I'm at it?" She pulled out of my arms and scooted a few inches away on the seat before I could react.

"You don't have to be difficult, baby." I was tempted to just stop the car, drag her over my lap, and spank the reprimand into her. But we were both goddamned tired, and the shopping couldn't wait. "I'd be happy to buy you what you need."

I didn't even have a chance to count down after that one. "I'm not being *difficult*," she retorted, mocking my voice. "I'm being realistic."

"Well, so am I. We can stop somewhere on the way home and get you some things to hold you over until we can get into your apartment." I could tell she wasn't happy about the plan, but surprisingly she didn't argue further.

The driver dropped us off at my car and helped me load

our luggage into my trunk before driving away. The poor guy looked like he wanted to get back in the car as quickly as possible before he did or said something to cross my sassy little queen.

"Where to, my lady?" I glanced at the woman pouting in the passenger seat, attempting to be bright with my tone. Yeah, *me*, being "bright." I was really whipped for this woman. "I'm... uh...sure you know the shopping haunts in this town way better than I do. I know there's a mall downtown here somewhere, and I know there's one in Carlsbad closer to the house, but that's about it." She could grumble all she wanted. We were *not* going to her apartment until the police cleared us to do so.

"But I have a perfectly fine wardrobe at my apartment. This is just wasting money." She crossed her arms over her chest and sighed.

"Taylor, please. Most women would jump at the chance to go shopping with someone else's credit card."

"I'm not like most women, am I?" she snapped, and for some reason, her nasty attitude was doing weird things to my cock. Sexy good things.

"No, my love, you most definitely are not. And for that, I am ever thankful." I leaned over and kissed her, softly at first, but hunger quickly built, and I deepened the kiss, tangling my tongue with hers until a soft moan came from low in her throat. I pulled back to see her eyes still closed, her lips parted on a sigh.

"Death by clown," she murmured, touching her lips with her fingertips.

"What?" I chuckled.

"Death by clown—that's what my obituary will read," she said, finally opening her eyes. Then she randomly blurted,

"Fashion Valley will be fine." She was referring to the mall where she wanted to stop.

"That's the center off Friars Road?" I asked to confirm I had my bearings. I still got confused at times with the different parts of the city.

"Yeah." She sighed again, looking out the window as we eased onto Harbor Drive. "This has always been one of my favorite views in San Diego. This strip right here." She motioned to the view out the window to our right and shrugged. "It's just so, I don't know... San Diego."

"I agree. You get a perfect vibe of the city just in this one vignette." It gave me an excellent gift idea for her upcoming birthday in the next few months. I stored the notion away with a few others I had come up with.

The mall was pretty crowded with after-work shoppers and people out for dinner. We stuck to the larger department stores and ended up leaving with at least a week's worth of work clothes, lingerie, pajamas, and some casual clothes for around the house. My suggestion for her to walk around naked while at home seemed to fall on deaf ears.

"See? That wasn't so bad, was it?" I asked when we got back in the car. I had piled all the shopping bags in the back seat since the trunk was packed to its limit with our luggage.

"I'm paying you back for all of this," she stated matter-of-factly while checking her lipstick in the mirror of the visor.

"We'll see," I humored her while easing the car out of the parking space.

"I'm serious, Mac. I said I would move in with you. I didn't say I was looking for a sugar daddy."

"There's a difference between me wanting to buy things for you and me being your *sugar daddy*." I spat the comeback, not regretting a single syllable. "Jesus Christ, woman. Why is it so hard for you to accept things from me? If you bought me something, I wouldn't think there were strings attached. I would just think you saw something and you thought of me or you just wanted to do something nice for me. Where did this twisted quid pro quo thing come from?" I looked back and forth from the road to her, genuinely wanting to hear her answer.

She sat quietly for a while as we drove north toward Oceanside. Just when I thought she wasn't going to answer at all, she finally said, "It's because of Janet."

"What is?" I asked to clarify.

"My screwed-up rationale."

"About receiving gifts?"

"Yeah. Think about it. For as long as I can remember, when a man bought her something, she was either sleeping with him or selling drugs for him. Whatever the case, she always owed him something afterward. Nothing was free and clear. There were always strings attached. That's all I've ever known." She put her hand up to stop me from talking, even though I hadn't made a move to interrupt her. "It's not fair to put that baggage on you," she stated. "I know that. But I hope you can see that I'm trying. I mean, do you see that? How I'm trying?"

The sun was setting, but the way the car was lit, I could see her eyes were welling with tears. I took her hand and held it to my lips, kissing her soft skin several times before answering. "I do. I see it, Sassy. You're so amazing. So brave and beautiful. I see it."

When I wrote that letter to her—the letter I now know broke her heart—I said she needed to change things about herself. That she needed to live *her* life and stop paying penance for her mother's mistakes. I knew, even when I was writing the words, that they were harsh. But I also knew she needed to hear them. Needed to move beyond that phase of her life. It was necessary, if the two of us had any hope of building a life of our own. So even though those times were so painful for both of us, I knew now that I'd still write that letter and let her go. All that agony had led us to this moment. She was growing, and therefore *we* were growing.

★ ★ ★ ★

I slept like the dead that night. The combination of the travel, the time difference, and having my sassy girl in my arms were a lethal blow to my consciousness. The alarm woke both Taylor and me in what seemed like minutes after our heads hit the pillows.

While my master bathroom was enormous, sharing the space was going to take some getting accustomed to. We were both used to functioning on our own, so having to be considerate of someone else was something that took conscious effort. Nothing I minded, though, for the trade-off of being able to wrap my arms around her anytime it struck my fancy.

Setting a second cup of coffee beside her on the countertop, I waited for her to turn off the hair dryer before I spoke. "I'm going to go call the detective and see what time he wants us to come down to the station. Since I still can't go to the hospital, I can just drop you off at your office and then come back and get you. Then we can go to the station together. If that's what you want?"

She drank from the mug before answering, "This is

so good. You could always be a barista if the brain doctor thing falls through." She gave me a bratty wink before taking another sip. "Are you sure you wouldn't mind? That's a lot of backtracking. We could just run by my apartment, and I could get my—"

She froze midsentence, setting down the coffee with a hard *thunk*.

"What's wrong, baby?" The look on her face instantly made me worry.

"Oh, my God. Do you think he—" All the color drained from her face, and her hands were trembling. "I—I didn't even think of it until now. Oh, my God. Did he trash my car? Did he vandalize Sally too?"

"Hey. *Hey*. Come here." I pulled her against my chest and held her there. "It's okay. We'll find out. It's *okay*," I murmured.

"It's not okay!" Suddenly, she was shoving herself out of my arms. I mentally strapped myself in for her blowup. "I hate him, Mac. I hate him for doing this to me! If that loser even *touched* that car..." She looked up at me with tear-streaked cheeks, her bottom lip trembling.

Fucking trembling.

"I know she isn't much, but I love her. Especially since you—I mean, since you love her too. So now I love her more." She cut in on herself with a watery laugh. "That sounds silly, huh?"

"That's not silly at all." I caught a couple of her tears with my thumbs before pulling her close again. When she sagged willingly against me, my world was complete. "I love hearing that. But baby, I really don't think we should go near your apartment. Let's talk to the detective first. We can ask him about Sally then."

I refrained from vocalizing my biggest fear about going anywhere near her place—the horror I'd been fighting since Killian first called us. Was John still lurking out there? If they'd nabbed the motherfucker, they would have told us, right? Or maybe not. I hadn't had the chance to ask Kil if they'd taken John into custody, and the issue was nagging me constantly. Until I knew for sure, I didn't dare let Taylor get anywhere near that place. I needed to keep her safe, above all things, until we knew exactly where that jackass was.

I held her for as long as she would let me—which, of course, wasn't nearly long enough—before she pulled away to finish with her hair. "I'm going to be late if I don't get moving. I'll be ready to go in about ten minutes. You should go get dressed so we can leave."

"Yes, ma'am." I gave a mock salute and headed off toward my closet.

We met by the door that led to the garage, where I always did a quick run-through to make sure I had everything. I was going over my mental checklist, and Taylor stood and stared.

"What are you doing?" she asked while laughing.

"I always go through a checklist in my head to make sure I don't forget anything. It's a silly habit I started in grade school, and I still do it every day. But at least I never forget anything."

She stretched up on her toes to quickly kiss me. "Sometimes you are the most adorable clown in the entire circus."

I didn't miss the chance to wrap my arms around her, holding her in place for another kiss. A *much* longer one. "Hmmmm. I really like starting my day this way. I'm adding kissing you to my checklist."

Her smile sobered. "Checklist or not, you know this day is

going to suck, right?"

"Pretty much." My expression changed to match hers.

"I'm glad I don't have to face it alone. So, if I haven't said it lately, thank you."

"I wouldn't be anywhere else. And you're welcome. I love you. Now let's go. I hear your boss is a real asshole."

She smacked my arm as we went out to the car. I flashed a stern look in return. When I slid into one of my favorite places, behind the wheel of my M2, I looked over to Taylor. "Have you really not learned your lesson about striking me?"

She grinned before answering. "Maybe. Maybe not."

"Or maybe you just need a refresher lesson, Ms. Mathews." I pressed the ignition button. The engine roared to life inside the garage, the sound bouncing off the concrete walls, making it seem exponentially louder. I couldn't hold back the grin it brought about every time.

"Like a little boy with a really loud toy," she shouted around her own grin.

"It appears to have the same effect on little girls as well." I winked.

"Yeah, I guess it does," she conceded. "I'm getting very spoiled with these fancy cars you drive me around in, though. Poor Missy is getting an inferiority complex."

"Well, maybe we should look at something new for you. That old car, as much as we both love her, may not be reliable enough now that your commute is going to be twice as far."

She scowled. "Ugh. I hadn't even thought of that. Shit. I can't afford a new car. Well, technically, I can. I mean, I can get something sensible. Nothing like this, obviously." She motioned around the inside of my little M2.

"But you won't have rent or utilities anymore. So that

should free up quite a bit of your monthly budget." I couldn't help but play devil's advocate.

"True. But that isn't very sensible to spend the majority of my salary on a car, Mac."

"And I'm guessing if you came unglued about me buying you a few new outfits, a car would—"

"Absolutely not." She cut me off before I could even finish my sentence. "Don't even think about it. I'm serious. *Don't.* You'll be taking it back if you do."

"You can't return a car, baby. It doesn't work that way." She could be so adorably naïve at times.

"Well, you'd have to find a way. Or it would sit in your driveway and never be driven. I'm serious as a heart attack about this."

"All right, all right. No car. Got it."

"So, when are we meeting the detective? Did you contact him?" She changed the subject quickly, but my gears were still turning on the new car topic.

"He wants us at the station at ten. I think I'll just hang out at that little café around the corner from your office. No sense going too far. How about an SAV, then? A little X3?"

"Clown, I said no."

"Technically, you said no car. I'm talking about an SAV. It's different."

"No. Vehicle. Period. I swear we will not have sex in any way, shape, or form ever again if you buy me any sort of motorized vehicle. How's that? Are we completely clear now?"

"You wouldn't..." I gripped at my chest.

"Oh, I would," she assured. "It would be miserable, but I can be very stubborn when trying to prove a point."

"Good to know. Good to know." But inside, my message

was different. *I already know, baby. I already know.*

And I wouldn't change it about her for all the BMWs in Munich.

We filled the rest of the drive with chitchat. Memories of our trip, sharing our favorite activities, our favorite meal, and how bummed we both were to have cut the trip short. We were downtown before I knew it, and I was pulling up at the impressive entrance to Stone Global Corporation. It was ripping me apart to say goodbye to her, but knowing I'd be back in less than three hours helped ease the disappointment.

"Okay, I'll meet you back here at nine forty-five?"

"Sounds like a plan. See you soon. Try to stay out of trouble until then." She kissed me quickly and hopped out, giving me a stellar view of her fine, *fine* ass as she walked through the front doors of her office. If it wasn't for the jackass beeping his horn behind me, I would've stayed here and watched her until she disappeared from view altogether.

A quick flip of the bird to the dick in the rearview and I pulled out into traffic again. I drove down the block, trying to find a parking space near the trendy little café. I'd hung out at the place a lot after Taylor and I separated, hoping to catch her on a break or lunch, but she never came in. After I saw how much thinner she had gotten when I ran into her at Drake and Fletcher's place for the first time after our split, I realized she had probably skipped a lot of lunches altogether. That guilt was still a burden I carried. I hated that I'd done that to her. Her health had been compromised because her heart was ruling her head.

That made me think about her car situation again. I needed to find a way to convince her to let me help her buy a new car. As much as I loved her 240sx, the best possible outcome of today's appointment at the police station would be finding out that John-Boy had vandalized her car too. I knew how much she loved driving Sally, but the car was old and unsuitable for the miles required of a daily Oceanside-to-downtown commute.

Lightning strike.

Well, that was what my idea felt like. Why hadn't I thought of it before? Part of what Taylor loved so much about Sally was driving her. If she got behind the wheel of something else—something like my M2—she'd fall hard and never look back. I was sure of it.

It was brilliant.

I was fucking brilliant.

She wouldn't need any more convincing. The car would do the selling on its own.

I wanted to reach around and pat myself on the back. I almost did—but my ringing cell interrupted my self-appreciation fest.

"Mac Stone."

"Hey, cousin. It's Killian."

"Hey. How's it going? Listen, man. Before we get into anything else, thank you again for the flight home yesterday and the car at the airport. It was all really appreciated. I don't know how I can repay you." I felt like an idiot after saying that, but what *was* proper protocol for thanking a guy for a ride in their private jet? A little note with flowers and butterflies?

"No worries. Really, it's all good. Remember when you helped me out with Fletcher? I didn't know how to thank you for that. We just can help each other out when we can. Cool?"

His relaxed tone made it all seem so damn normal. *Hey, you fix my buddy's brain; I'll fly you across the world. No problem.*

"Definitely. Sure." I was stammering, but this family-takes-care-of-each-other stuff was brand-new territory. "So what's going on? Is Taylor okay?" I actually started to panic. I hadn't even thought he might be calling because something was wrong at the office.

"Uhhh, I guess so. I mean, I don't work directly with her on a daily basis. I haven't even seen her this morning." He trailed off with a chuckle.

"Sorry," I muttered. "I'm a little edgy with this idiot still out there somewhere."

"And I don't blame you. I'd be out of my mind if this kind of shit happened to Claire."

"Did they apprehend the whack job? I guess I should've asked that the other day from the DR. I didn't even think of it until we got back into town. Somehow, being back is making all this worse."

Killian snorted. "You don't say."

"Her safety is all I can concentrate on."

"That's actually what I wanted to talk to you about. I know how your temper can run...shall we say...on the hotter side?"

I laughed, knowing it was true. "Yeah, I'm feeling a little possessive these days, on top of everything else. I can't help it. She's—I don't know how to say it—under my skin. Like in a big way. You know?"

"You're in love, idiot," my barely older cousin answered with the sagacity of fucking Yoda.

"Yeah. That."

He turned his snort into a laugh. "Like the song goes, it's a 'many-splendored thing.' But it's a serious bitch too. I feel you, man. Wait until you throw a kid into the mix."

"Oh, whoa there, chief. She won't even let me buy her a

damn car. Let's not get ahead of ourselves." I laughed again, only this time it was forced.

"Hmmm. Let's come back to that," he said thoughtfully.

"Or not," I added dryly.

"Seriously though, the reason I called. The police didn't pick that douche canoe, John, up yet."

"Are you kidding?" My volume climbed so hard and so fast, several café patrons turned to look in my direction. "Why the *fuck* not?"

"And this is why I wanted to tell you before you got to the station. You need to keep your cool in there, Mac. More importantly, in front of Taylor. Apparently the asshole has an alibi."

"A—" I was too stunned to say anything else.

"Yeah. Someone's vouched for him, and they've already checked out. The only hope of tying him to the crime scene in her apartment is going to be the evidence they collect there."

"Fuck. Me," I groaned, scrubbing my hand down my face.

"Exactly. So we have to hope against all hope they don't fuck anything up."

"So who *is* this police department, then?" I could focus on my rage or on attempting to gather as much information as I could before picking up Taylor. "Keystone Cops or the next *CSI* hopefuls?"

Killian's steady voice helped calm me. "Not sure. I haven't had any dealings with them, but Margaux has. Michael's mother was roughed up really badly a while back, and they've dealt with the police on some other events. I'm going to pick her brain and see if she remembers anyone at the station who was top-notch. We'll see if we can get them on the case."

Curiosity got the better of me, even though I knew it

would just add to the rage burning just under my surface. "So where does the fucker say he was?"

Killian snickered. "You're going to love this."

"Great. Let's hear it."

"Cheetahs."

"What the hell is that? Sounds like a strip joint."

"Bingo. It's up in Kearny Mesa. You've probably seen it off the freeway." His landmark references helped me identify where I'd seen the seedy joint.

"Oh, sort of by Miramar, right?"

"That's the one. And one of the dancers there says she gave him a lap dance and he gave her a huge tip. That's why she remembers him being there."

"Did they pull security tapes? Can they prove he was there? I mean, he could've paid the stripper to say that. That's not really an airtight alibi, in my opinion." My voice was gaining volume again, and talking about strippers and alibis had a few stray eavesdroppers hanging on to my every comment. I decided to head outside to finish the conversation.

"I thought the same thing," Killian said, bringing my attention back to the phone. "Maybe we can have someone dig a little deeper into that if the police don't give it the attention we think it deserves."

"Hey, Kil. Don't take this the wrong way, man. But why are you so invested in this? Again, I'm really grateful, believe me. But I just don't get it." I wasn't used to someone having my back to the degree he was, and it was in my nature to question his motive. I wasn't nearly as suspicious as Taylor would be, but he was really getting into the nitty-gritty of our situation.

"Taylor is like family to Claire. They've been best friends for a long time. She's been there for my wife repeatedly. So when my fairy said to help this girl, I jumped to it. And further, as I told you when you were in the DR, we're family. Family helps each other out. Now stop giving me shit, or I'll fuck you up like I used to when we were little." His lighthearted finish made me laugh, and the whole speech made perfect sense. Killian and Claire were just good people. It was that simple.

"Oh, you wish. I used to kick your ass, and you know it! On and off the basketball court."

"Now who's dreaming?"

We both laughed for a bit before his assistant, Brita, interrupted to remind him of a meeting he had scheduled for nine thirty. That gave me precisely fifteen minutes to kill before I needed to be back out front to pick up Taylor.

With my cup of espresso in hand, I walked back to where I parked my car. I scrolled through my email on the way, deleting most of the messages as I went. One from the hospital needed attention, but it mostly reminded me that I needed to check with the detective to see if the hospital had been made aware of John's involvement in the investigation. There was no way that sonofabitch wasn't the guilty party. Proving it was going to be the sticky part.

Strangely, I had missed a call while talking to my cousin. It was from a number in Chicago. I scrolled to the voicemail screen and played the message over the speaker on my car while letting the engine rumble to life.

"Maclain, it's your mother."

Fuck. Just the sound of her voice made the hairs on my neck prickle—and not in a fun, tingly, oh-goody way. I hadn't spoken to her since the morning we had breakfast together. We had a monumental fight when she disrespected Taylor and I stood up to her. The only reason she would call now was that she needed something from me.

"We need to talk, son. There are things I need to say to you, and it can't be done over the phone. Call me back at this number. It's urgent."

And then the call was disconnected. Not a single "please." Definitely not an "I'm sorry" or "I was wrong." God fucking forbid those words would ever spill from my mother's mouth.

Tension I didn't need today. In any way, shape, or form.

I deleted the call and her message as fast as I could. After that, it was a pleasure to focus on much better things—namely, the sight of one sassy, sexy Taylor Mathews strutting toward my car at exactly nine forty-five a.m. when I pulled up in front of SGC.

Damn it, I was a lucky man.

I hopped out and scooted around the front of the car to the passenger side in time to open the door for her.

"Hey, gorgeous," she said, kissing me on the lips. "Going my way?"

"I will go anywhere you want me to, beautiful."

She slithered into the leather seat, and I closed the door. I jogged around the rear of the car this time and got back into the driver's seat. "How was work?" I asked while checking my mirrors and looking over my shoulder before pulling out into traffic.

"It pays the bills." She shrugged, smiling at me while she answered.

"You're in a good mood." I stroked the exposed skin of her leg where her skirt rode up.

"It helped immensely knowing I would see you again so soon." She covered my hand with hers.

"I'm in love with you." I brought her slender hand to my

lips and kissed the back. Her fingers were like icicles.

"So you keep saying." She watched my mouth move over her skin.

"When are you going to say it back?" I pestered. "And why are your hands so cold? They keep that air conditioning too low. You should bring a sweater."

"Mmmmm, I don't know. I kind of like keeping you guessing." Surprisingly, she returned to the original question instead of dodging it like she usually did.

"Really? So this is a game now?" I kept my tone light so she knew I was teasing too.

"You know what they say. Good things come to those who wait."

"Who is *they*, exactly?" I volleyed.

"I'm not sure. *They*, they."

"Well, *they* are full of shit. Waiting sucks. I want you to tell me right now. Say that you love me. Say that you will love me forever. Like I will love you forever." I tugged her hand, pulling her closer until her seat belt stopped her progress.

She looked at me solemnly.

My heart literally jumped to my throat. I contemplated pulling over. Oh, fuck. This was going to be it. *At last.*

"Did you know the human head weighs eight pounds?"

I burst out laughing. My breathtaking, bold, astonishing, amazing little *brat*. "I actually do know that. Neurosurgeon"—I pointed to myself—"remember?"

"Oh, yeah. Wrong crowd to dazzle with that fact, I guess." She slumped back in her seat dramatically, as if I'd popped her balloon.

I just started laughing again. She was the most adorable woman I'd ever known. I knew in my heart she loved me. I also knew she had her reasons for holding back on saying it. I wasn't sure what they were, but I had a feeling we were getting really close to reaching whatever invisible milestone she had set before saying it. The air around her was lighter despite the goddamned mire we were going through. Correction. *Mires.* But here we were, in the best place we had ever been relationship-wise.

The crucibles had honed us. Had turned our clay into stone.

Had lit the way for our lost hearts to find each other.

Even as we walked hand in hand through the front doors of the police station to face the damages and ramifications of her fucked-up stalker, I felt like I was on top of the world. Nothing could tear us apart. Not now. Not ever.

Cocky as fuck? Probably. But I didn't care.

I probably should have.

The shitstorm was just getting started.

CHAPTER ELEVEN

Taylor

It was remarkable how quickly a great mood could be soured when faced with the reality of a stalker.

We were met by a middle-aged detective named Ron Johnson. Of course, I had a private laugh at the close brush to Don Johnson. But the cute little rhyme was where the similarities ended. This detective had a spare tire around his midsection and the fashion sense of my grandmother's German Shepherd. None of that mattered though, as long as he was tits at his job.

Four chairs were arranged around a square metal table in the center of a room not much bigger than the eat-in kitchen of my apartment. Mac and I declined the refreshments the detective offered, wanting to just get on with the matters at hand. Another gentleman walked into the room unannounced and sat at the table, occupying the fourth chair.

"This is my partner, Detective Munson. Taylor Mathews"—he pointed to me—"and Dr. Maclain Stone." He nodded toward Mac.

"Thank you for coming down this morning," Detective Munson stated. "I'm sorry you had to cut your vacation short, but we appreciate you taking the matter seriously."

"Absolutely," Mac answered. "Taylor's safety is my biggest

concern at the moment. It's my understanding that no one has been apprehended? What's being done to rectify that situation?"

Mac's normal inclination to take charge of a situation had the detectives bristling. The older of the two wasn't about to have his turf trampled. I seriously wanted to roll my eyes—in triplicate. And yeah, that meant including Mac in the assessment. I was so tired of men and their tree-pissing.

"Dr. Stone, if you wouldn't mind"—the guy shifted in his chair, rolling his weight around and visibly puffing his chest—"since this *is* an official investigation, we need to follow certain protocol. First, we need Ms. Mathews's permission to record this conversation, and then we will begin with routine questioning. When we are through with our questioning, you will be able to ask any follow-up questions that you may still have. Ms. Mathews, if you prefer to have an attorney present, you have the right to do so."

I took a deep breath. His blustery speech was just pissing me off more. "An attorney?" I spat. "Why would I need an attorney? That asshole broke into *my* apartment. Why the hell would I need a lawyer?" I could hear the rambling panic rising in my voice, but the mere mention of an attorney freaked me out. "Am I being charged with something?" I dashed a frantic stare between Mac and the detective. Mac's gaze matched my confusion, which was oddly comforting. At this point, I'd take it.

"Please forgive me," Detective Johnson offered. "I didn't mean to upset you or confuse you. Many people prefer to have an attorney with them simply when they walk through our door these days just to cover their bases. We've gotten in the habit of saying that spiel to everyone. You aren't being charged with anything at this point."

At this point. Though his demeanor shifted to good cop, that little tidbit didn't escape my observation. Maybe I was just edgy and a bit paranoid, but I'd bet my paycheck Mac noticed the wording too. But when I made eye contact with him, he'd already shoved aside his bewilderment for a steady, reassuring gaze, imbuing me with all the courage I needed to continue.

Habitually, I reached for his hand beneath the table. His huge, strong grip was already waiting. At once he wrapped me in his warm, secure hold. I needed it—more than I'd ever thought I would.

"So, if I understand you correctly, Ms. Mathews, you consensually went on a date with Mr. Busby just days before you left on vacation with Dr. Stone?"

"It wasn't a date," I volleyed.

"I'm not following." He speared me with a puzzled expression, his beady eyes narrowing. "You just said you went to lunch with Mr. Busby, alone, just the two of you, on Thursday afternoon."

"Yes, I did. Lunch. Two friends. Just as if you and I went to lunch right now. Nothing more, nothing less. When you use the word date, it implies a romantic situation, and it was not that. I had just given blood, and he was getting off for his lunch hour. He asked me to grab a bite with him. That was it. I made it repeatedly clear that the situation was as friends only."

"Did you ever get the impression that Mr. Busby was interested in being more than just friends?" Detective Munson asked while focusing on his notepad.

"Yes. On a few occasions, Mr. Busby made comments—but I told him I wasn't interested in being in a relationship with him. Additionally, he knew I was involved with Mac. Pardon me. Dr. Stone." I squeezed Mac's hand again under the table.

"So even though you knew he wanted to be more than friends, you still led him on and went out with him?" Johnson pressed.

"Excuse me?" Mac interrupted this time. It was probably a good thing, so I could check my instinct about slapping the man so hard his head spun.

"I was asking Ms. Mathews the question," the detective clarified.

"I know who you were speaking to, Detective." Mac punctuated it with heavy breaths from his nose while keeping his lips in a board-straight line. "And you are pushing the line of inappropriate implications with these questions to her. It's imperative that is heard on this recording. If you insinuate, or even come close to it, that Ms. Mathews led that asshole on, or was asking for it, or whatever it is you're getting at with this line of questioning, we're going to leave and follow your suggestion to return with an attorney. I hope I've made myself clear." The glare he leveled at the detective was enough to strip him of his attitude.

The man physically shrank back from Mac's stare but only by an inch or two. Nothing like the way a man like John would have, for example. Clearly he was used to dealing with all types of personalities, including much more aggressive styles than Mac.

"Dr. Stone, I again regret any misunderstanding. We're here today to gather facts. I'm just trying to establish a timeline. An exact course of events that led to the evening of the break-in. We can't be sure at this point that Mr. Busby is even a suspect." He paused for a moment and then angled himself toward me. "Now, Ms. Mathews, after you had lunch with Mr. Busby, what happened? Did you go straight home from the restaurant?"

"No," I responded, focusing on the hand I still had resting on the table. *Be calm. No fidgeting. You haven't done anything wrong.* "I went back to the hospital," I calmly continued. "I'd driven both of us to lunch, so I brought Mr. Busby back to the hospital. When I dropped him off, I...umm...ran into Dr. Stone, in the parking lot. And then—"

Before I could continue, the detective interrupted again. "That's quite a coincidence, isn't it? I mean, given the size of the hospital and the number of different parking lots on that campus, that you would just happen to see him in the parking lot?"

"I...agree," I mumbled. "Quite the coincidence." What else was I going to say? That Mac was in a jealous rage and came charging across the parking lot to tear John's head from his torso? Didn't think *that* part really added to the investigation.

"Can you explain that, Dr. Stone?" Detective Munson asked. "What were you doing in the parking lot at that exact moment? Seems odd, wouldn't you agree?"

"Not odd at all. I left some files in my car that I had taken home to review. My surgery rotation is on Thursday, and I often take patient files home on Wednesday night to prepare for the OR the next day. You understand, get in the right frame of mind and all. I mean, after all, I operate on people's *brains*. It's serious business."

He stared at the detective, almost daring him to have an opinion on what it took to prepare for brain surgery. Dear *God*. He was laying it on so thick, I wanted to smack him in the back of the head. I knew he was doing it to annoy and intimidate the detective, but now was not the time for the God complex. I tried communicating as much with a fast glower his way, but he just stared with droll serenity in return. *Arrogant, adorable ass.*

"Doesn't the hospital have a separate lot for physicians? Why would you be in the lot where Taylor had parked to donate blood that morning? I'm guessing the Bloodmobile doesn't do their collection drive in the doctors' parking lot?" one of the cops asked. I was too busy staring at my boyfriend to pay attention to which one.

"You're correct," Mac said without skipping a beat. "I'm still fairly new to the campus, and I don't know if you've been there before or not, but honestly, it doesn't make the most sense regarding layout. I still get turned around from time to time. I had come out a side door from an interior stairwell, expecting to be one place and ending up in another. I saw the Bloodmobile first, and then by luck, Taylor and John happened to be standing there talking. She and I had some confusion in plans we made the previous weekend and were having a hard time connecting since, so I took the opportunity to speak to her in person. I had some downtime before my next case, so it all just worked out."

He shrugged, making it all seem so innocent and plausible. And really it was, if the jealous rage part was taken out. And then the hot monkey sex in his office part.

But none of that mattered in the facts causing John to lose his freaking mind and vandalize my home.

"Did you have an altercation with Mr. Busby the day in question?" Detective Johnson asked.

"Did I?" Mac dramatically asked. "No. Why would I? As I recall, he went inside the RV before I even spoke to Ms. Mathews. I don't think he even knew I was there."

"Did you go home at that point, Ms. Mathews?"

"No. I went with Dr. Stone to his office inside the hospital. Like he said, we had some things to...umm...discuss. I left about two hours later. The blood drive had ended, so Mr. Busby and the rest of the crew were gone from the hospital property by then."

"And that was the last you heard from Mr. Busby?" Munson scribbled notes as fast as his number-two pencil would allow.

"No," I answered before swallowing the lump in my throat. Remembering listening to John's creepy messages made goose bumps rise on my arms. "While I was with Mac in those two hours, John left sixteen messages on my phone." I waited to see the detective's outraged response, but his face didn't change at all. Not even surprise or disbelief. No change at all.

I was furious.

"Come on!" I cried. "That is *not* normal! Sixteen phone calls in two hours? All left on voicemail?"

"It's not for me to judge what's normal or not normal. Just collecting the facts. Did you save the messages?"

"Yes. Of course I did," I snapped. "After he showed up at my apartment that night, I was freaked out. I knew he was a complete lunatic and figured if things escalated, I would need to get the police involved."

"How did he have your phone number, Ms. Mathews? Did you give it to him?" Detective Johnson asked, using the same condescending tone with which he'd started the interview.

"No. He said he got it from my paperwork from the blood bank. I think he says that on one of the phone messages." I looked to Mac to confirm my memory.

"Yeah, I think he says it on there. Idiot." Mac shook his

head in disgust.

"So, you said he showed up at your apartment that night?" Munson asked next.

"Yes. I went home and took a nap. During that time, Mac called—or texted...I really don't remember—to ask if he could come over for dinner, and of course I said yes." I squeezed his hand that I was still gripping in my own. "We decided to order Chinese when he got to my place, but Mac went and picked it up instead. When someone knocked on my door, I figured it was Mac, but I still just opened it as far as the chain would allow. It was John. I thought I was going to have to call the police, but Mac, thank God, arrived at the exact same time and made sure he left." My sentences ran together in one long rush. When I finished, I just looked between the two officers, now knowing better than to expect them to be shocked.

"He also took her address off the paperwork from her health records. Complete HIPAA violation. If nothing else, charges should be filed for that," Mac added, tapping on the table at the end of his statement as if punctuating it.

The younger detective interjected regarding my health records. "I believe that needs to be initiated with the place that maintains the records, but I can look into that for you to confirm that. You're absolutely right—something needs to be done regarding that abuse of privacy, even if he isn't charged with anything else by our department."

"All right, connect the dots for me. How did you go from Mr. Busby showing up at your door uninvited to a spur-of-the-moment vacation in the Dominican Republic?" Johnson steered us back to the subject at hand.

Even though he directed the question to me, I looked to Mac to answer. Since it was his actions and the resulting disciplinary action that led to the idea of taking off on an unscheduled trip, I figured he'd be better at explaining the whole thing.

"We found out somewhere in all of this that John-Boy works at Scripps Green. The Bloodmobile is a volunteer gig he does on the side, and he also said at some point, he only signed up for shifts when he knew Taylor would be donating. We looked on her online account on the flight home, and up until recently, she was a regular donor. Therefore, he could estimate when she'd be in to give blood with pretty decent accuracy."

"Who would've guessed that would turn out to be a bad thing?" I mumbled.

"It's still very noble, baby. It's not your fault you caught the eye of a psychopath." Mac kissed the backs of my fingers while I watched with hunger growing inside me. I wanted to be done with this damn questioning and return to the private poolside of our hotel in the DR.

One of the detectives finally cleared his throat, causing both Mac and me to jump a bit. Maybe we'd been staring into one another's eyes longer than they were comfortable with.

"You were saying?" Detective Johnson prompted Mac to continue his explanation.

"What was I saying?" he asked with a grin.

I fed him the reminder. "That he works at Scripps."

"Right. The day after he showed up at Taylor's apartment, I ran into him on the elevator at the hospital. I told him to stay away from Taylor. It was pretty cut-and-dry." Again, Mac shrugged as if it were all in a day's work.

"Did you threaten him?" Detective Johnson asked.

"Can you define threaten?"

"Don't fuck around, Doctor."

"I'm serious. What is your definition of the word threaten?" Mac replied sternly.

"Did you say you would cause him bodily harm if he didn't do what you told him to do?"

"I told him to stay away from her. I suggested he not mess with me. I don't recall anything other than that. However, he went to our HR department and told them I was creating a hostile work environment. I was put on a ten-working-day suspension without pay. That prompted Taylor and me to leave town for a bit. We both really needed a break. She had some serious vacation time accrued, and she happens to work for my cousin, who is also her best friend's husband, Killian Stone. Since they knew what had been going on with the stalker asshole, he let her go without prior notification."

"Mr. Stone seemed like a really great guy when he was in here the day after the break-in. Very polite and cooperative," Detective Johnson said respectfully.

"Yeah, everyone loves Killian. That's for sure." Mac's sarcastic tone made me squeeze his hand tighter. I didn't let up the pressure until he shot his gaze in my direction, allowing me to give him a slight shake of my head. The last thing we needed was to raise suspicion about Mac's temperament. If it seemed like he had trouble getting along with people, especially his own family members, what would that say about him threatening John?

"Detective? Is it appropriate for me to ask how you found out about the break-in at my apartment?"

"Oh, of course. A call came into the switchboard early Wednesday morning. At that point, it had been close to a week since you had last seen Mr. Busby, is that correct?" He looked back and forth between Mac and me.

"Yes. We left for the Dominican Republic last Sunday. We were there eight days when we had to leave. Today is Friday, right?" I laughed a little. "Sorry. My internal clock is still a little goofed up from the travel."

"It is, thank God. I'm so ready for the weekend," the detective replied. "Anyway, apparently you have a very observant neighbor who noticed your door wasn't closed all the way. She said she knocked a few times and called your name. When you didn't answer, she pushed the door open and immediately saw the place had been vandalized. She called 9-1-1 right away. We were really glad she didn't go inside and disturb the crime scene."

I leaned forward. "When can I go there? Are you finished with your investigation?" I was anxious to get my belongings.

"We should be wrapping up there today. I'll make a phone call before you leave today and verify that. I should warn you though..."

The detective trailed off, not finishing his sentence. He made eye contact with Mac, some unspoken message passing between them. Mac gave a quick nod, and the detective moved on with a new topic.

What the hell?

"Excuse me?" I voiced before he considered starting a new line of questioning.

"Yes, Ms. Mathews?" He sounded bored and bothered at the same time.

Too bad.

"You didn't finish your sentence. You said you needed to warn me and then didn't say anything in the way of a warning."

Mac spoke up instead. "I'll go with you when you go to your apartment, Sassy. That's all. I think the detective was just wanting to make sure you stay safe with John still running around and didn't want to say it." He motioned toward the recording device on the center of the table with his chin.

I looked at the black, three-armed object and then to the detective for some sort of confirmation that Mac was on the right track, but he had turned to Detective Munson and was having a separate conversation altogether.

"I think you're full of shit," I whispered to Mac. "But we can discuss this further in the car. I'm so ready to be done here."

"You and me both. Seriously, what more do we need to say at this point for them to haul his guilty ass in here?"

"I can't believe they haven't already. Is it going to take him raping me or killing me for this to be taken seriously?" My emotions and lack of sleep were getting the better of me.

My voice must have been louder than the whisper I intended because Detective Munson replied quickly, "Of course not, Ms. Mathews. We take every case seriously. We understand your concern and frustration. As soon as we have enough evidence to make an arrest, it will be done. No matter who it is." For some strange reason, he was staring at Mac while he spoke.

"I know, I know." I put my hand up in surrender. "I apologize. I shouldn't have said that. You have to realize, I'm running on less sleep than normal and way too much adrenaline. My body still thinks it's in a different time zone, and my nerves are shot. Again, my apologies." If I could crawl under the table and hide, I would.

"Gentlemen, are we done here? I think Miss Mathews and I would really like to head home," Mac asked, putting his best manners forward.

"I really need to go by my apartment first," I reminded him.

"It's going to put us in the middle of rush-hour traffic. Why don't we just do it tomorrow when we have all day? We don't have anything else planned, and it's the weekend. Oh, actually, one last question for you, Detective, if I may?"

"Go for it," Detective Johnson answered, looking a bit worn out too.

"Have you, meaning the police in general, informed the hospital of Mr. Busby's involvement in all of this? I'm a little frustrated that I was given an unscheduled vacation, as we're affectionately calling it, and that fuckstick is walking around proud as a peacock. All the while, he's a first-rate stalker and has violated her personal information, property, privacy, and who knows what else."

The detective grunted. "Luckily, as far as stalkers go, this guy isn't even close to first-rate. And that isn't to say what's going on isn't frightening for you, Ms. Mathews. We guarantee that charges will be pressed if we can collect evidence at your apartment that will stick to him. But it is a blessing that he's very minor league in the world of stalkers. We've seen some really creepy shit in our day. Some really sophisticated, highly evolved methods of spying and invading people's personal lives. This guy is peanuts. We'll catch him if he's the guy. He's sloppy and lazy, I can tell you that much," Detective Munson said while closing his notebook and pushing back from the table.

"Okay, that's all great. Was that a yes? Yes, you've informed his employer? Or no, you haven't?" Mac's patience was as thin as I'd seen it.

"No. We haven't. The investigation isn't at that stage, Dr. Stone. I have to advise you to not do any part of our job for us, either." Detective Johnson smirked while answering.

Again, the two stared at each other, our time at the station concluding much the way it began.

I let out a heavy sigh, breaking Mac from his tree-marking moment. When he looked in my direction, I just shook my head. No doubt he'd question me about it in the car. I'd be all too happy to let him know what I thought about the bullshit male posturing I had to witness on repeat.

"Let me just wrap all of this up with a word of warning, Ms. Mathews," Detective Munson said. "Our team has been in and out of your apartment collecting evidence, but they remove only what they need, and they generally leave a scene just the way they found it. They are not a cleanup or repair crew." He shrugged on his suit coat while issuing his final words of advice. "Whoever did this to your place left quite a mess, and it's not pretty. You may want to mentally prepare yourself before you head back there."

"I'm inclined to say thank you because I was raised to have good manners, but when your words register in my brain, it doesn't really feel like something I'm grateful for." I was too exhausted to sugarcoat my reply.

We stood, shook hands with the detectives, and exchanged cards so we could get in contact with them if we thought of anything that might be relevant to the case. They agreed to keep us informed as the case moved forward but cautioned, "These things take time, so try to be patient."

"Will you please call whoever you need to and find out if I can go into my apartment?" I reminded Detective Johnson with a sugary—albeit phony—smile.

He excused himself and walked away, ducking into an office off the hallway to make the call.

"I'm going to use the restroom before we get on the road.

Who knows what traffic is going to be like." Mac gave my forehead a quick kiss before heading toward the men's room.

"Good idea. I'll go after you get back." I watched him walk away, thinking I could watch that man's backside for hours. The thought of digging my nails into it while he drove into me made heat flare through my bloodstream.

"Ms. Mathews?" I jumped when I heard my name from behind, totally expecting to see Detective Johnson come out of the office he went into up ahead. Instead, it was Detective Munson standing a few feet away.

"Oh, sorry, I was waiting for your partner to make that phone call." I smiled.

"Right, I didn't mean to startle you."

"It's fine. I was daydreaming. It's been a long couple of days."

"I can imagine. I just want to say I'm sorry you have to deal with all of this. I know it can't be easy. We see a lot of stuff like this go really bad, so I just want to advise you to be extra vigilant over the next few weeks. I know my partner didn't talk about that at all while we were in there." He thumbed over his shoulder toward the room we'd just left.

"I appreciate it. Mac is super protective." I laughed. "You may have noticed."

"Well, he should be. If this guy is half as crazy as it seems, you can't be too careful. That stuff on your apartment walls... well, he definitely has a colorful imagination."

"Ms. Mathews?" Just as I was about to ask Detective Munson to be more specific, Detective Johnson called my name from down the hallway.

"Thank you again, Detective." I shook his hand and smiled. Genuine concern was etched on his face.

Mac joined me as I walked to where Detective Johnson stood outside the office door. "Well, looks like you're in luck. They finished gathering evidence this afternoon. You'll want to contact your homeowner's insurance before doing anything so they can see the extent of the damage before you start cleaning it up. You'll probably be inclined to just start picking things up, but don't. A lot of times they won't file a claim if it's disturbed before they see it firsthand. Trust me, we've heard it from victims over and over. It's just a few more days, and if you have a place to stay, what harm is there?"

"Thank you for the advice. I wouldn't have thought of that," Mac replied. "You're hearing him, right?" He ducked his head down to be eye level with me.

"Yes. I hear him." I peeked around his big fat head and thanked the detective myself. "Now please, just take me home."

"Did you want to use the restroom?" Mac reminded me.

"Yeah, I'd better. I'll be just a minute." I said it quietly, not trusting my voice to stay steady.

I will not start crying. I will not start crying. I will not start crying.

Until the moment I pushed through the ladies' room door and burst into tears. At least the men didn't see me lose it. I'd held my shit together all afternoon, and for some reason, the wall crumbled, and I went to pieces. Thank God it wasn't like my breakdown on the jet home from our trip—but a mini-version. So much stress, so much tension and drama I didn't want to be dealing with.

Fucking John Busby.

I hadn't even known his last name before this afternoon. Now the bastard was keeping me from my home, my clothing, and even my car! I wanted to rip his nutsack off and bounce on it with a pogo stick.

I was so enraged, I couldn't even cry anymore. I started trembling instead. All over. Before I knew it, waves of hot and then cold began coursing up and down my body. Oh, holy shit. I was a damn basket case. But I needed to calm down before going back out to Mac. He'd seen more than enough of my hysteria in recent days. I took a few deep, cleansing breaths, trying to release the negativity into the universe before whipping my head up and staring at myself in the mirror.

"You'll deal with this," I gritted out to my reflection. "You always have, and you will again."

And I believed it. Mostly. Life had tried to kick my ass more times than I could count. I still got back up and continued to come out on top. Now I had an incredible man in my corner, fighting right beside me. There was no way I'd be knocked down and stay down.

We could conquer anything.

My new mantra.

I just didn't expect to have it tested so soon.

CHAPTER TWELVE

Mac

Wild horses couldn't have held her back from that damn apartment the moment the sun came up on Saturday morning.

"Rise and shine, sleepyhead." She was standing at my side of the bed with a steaming cup of coffee in hand. Fully dressed, hair done, ready for business.

"What the hell time did you get up?" I squinted to see the clock on my nightstand, eyes not wanting to be open, whatever time it happened to be.

"It's already eight. You've never slept this late as long as I've known you." She handed me the coffee and went around to sit on her side of the bed. "I sleep so well in this house," she said wistfully. "I think being so close to the ocean is good for my soul."

"It wouldn't have anything to do with me? Or the multiple orgasms you *endure* just before bed?" I took a sip from the cup, keeping my eyes on her over the rim.

"Mmmm, maybe. You make good points. Maybe I should conduct a study. You know, for scientific reasons." She tilted her head to the side, index finger pressed to her chin as if she were really contemplating the idea.

"In the name of science, of course." I set the cup down on my nightstand and turned toward her, throwing my long arm across her middle and dragging her up against me.

"Whoaaaa there, Clown. We have things to do." She halfheartedly batted at my arm.

"But science needs us. The whole scientific community is counting on your research."

She giggled as I tickled her sides, burying my face in her neck. She smelled so good, all fresh from the shower. I loved that she was rolling around in the covers, knowing her scent would linger when she left the bed.

"Maclain Stone! I am very serious!" She tried pushing out of my embrace but got absolutely nowhere. I outweighed her by at least a hundred pounds, and she was no match in the strength department either.

But suddenly I stilled, and she did too. I wondered if we were thinking the same thing. I hoped like hell we weren't, because my thoughts had just taken a really dark turn.

"Do you know how helpless I am? I mean, really, when it comes down to it?" she asked quietly.

How did that happen? Like she crawled right into my head and plucked the thought like a daisy.

"I'm not sure this is the exact time to marvel at it, but generally speaking, it's awesome that we are so in tune. Specific to this particular topic, however, you're right. It is a little frightening how easily you could be physically overpowered by someone, and that's especially scary considering our current situation." I stroked her shoulder with my thumb while she rested her head on my chest. It seemed like a topic better discussed without eye contact, for some reason. I knew she wasn't a fan of admitting vulnerability in any form, so for her to open up to me was extraordinary progress in its own right.

"I think we can talk about two things here," I continued.

"I'm not sure which one will make you leap out of this bed in denial faster, so I'm going to just blurt them out and see which one sticks."

She laughed her sexy, throaty laugh, which, of course, shot straight to my cock. I reached down between my legs with my free hand to adjust myself in my pajama pants.

"Easy there, big guy." She patted my chest in sympathy.

"It's that laugh. It does things to me," I admitted without shame.

"My laugh?"

"Who am I kidding? It's everything about you. I'm in *hopeless* territory, woman. I have no defense to offer."

"Try to focus, Mac. What were you going to say before Big Mac got your attention?"

"Big Mac? Like the burger?" I joked, not thrilled with the nickname for my manhood.

"I don't know? That sounds kind of cute, doesn't it?" She looked up at me through the curtain of her bangs.

"I've always thought a pet name for your dick was ridiculous all around. I don't think I can sign on for calling mine a heart attack waiting in sandwich form."

She sat up and laughed again. This time, it was the laugh where she threw her head back and closed her eyes, and her hair shook free and hung loosely off her shoulders.

Yeah—hopeless, party of one.

"You tell me to focus and then do *that*? I don't think you're playing fair, Ms. Mathews." I said her name in my best impersonation of Detective Johnson's stuffy-from-being-overweight voice.

"Oh, my God." She covered her mouth with her hand. "You sounded just like him. That was so creepy. Do it again."

She closed her eyes and waited.

"Ms. Mathews, are you saying you knew Mr. Busby was a total loser-douchebag from the first moment you met him?" I said the whole sentence while channeling Detective Johnson.

Her eyes sprung open, and she stared at me. "Can you do that with other voices? Seriously, Mac. Super. Creepy."

"I used to call my mother and pretend to be people she knew. I fooled her every time. Killian and his brothers, Trey and Lance, and I would do it for hours. But I was the best at it. Lance is terrific too. You would like him." I thought for a few beats. "I should call him, see how he's doing."

"You should. A good family is too valuable to let go. They seem so few and far between. Oh, my God, though. Can we stay on one subject? We're worse than Margaux and Claire right now. What were you going to suggest regarding ways for me to defend myself? I think this is serious enough to talk about."

"I couldn't agree more. But you need to really listen to me and not huff off," I chastised before she even did it.

"Huff off? I don't *huff off*." She put her hand on her hip in defiance.

I tilted my head, my unspoken message clear. *Are you fucking kidding me?*

"Maaaaaccc!" she burst out. "Come *on*. Suggestions. Speak them. Now."

"All right, all right. Just stop with the bossy stuff." I adjusted myself again while she flopped back in the stack of pillows. Her blond hair fluffed all over her face. "That shit does funny things to me too."

I couldn't help but roll on top of her, pressing my semi-erect cock into her belly. When I eventually uncovered her face from under the mess of hair, she was grinning like a fool.

"You are in hopeless territory, Clown. No doubt about it."

"Yes, but do you love me anyway?" I kissed her pert little nose, barely resisting the urge to bite her.

"Wouldn't you like to know?" Her blue eyes twinkled with mischief as she looked up at me.

"God, you're killing me." I looked to the heavens for strength before continuing. "But really, while I have you here and you can't get away, illustrating my point beautifully, you need to really consider letting me hire someone to protect you when I can't be with you."

As predicted, she balked.

She couldn't get me off her, but she wanted to argue fiercely. So, I did the only thing I could. I covered her mouth with a passionate kiss, dissolving her ire quickly and swirling it into sensual heat. When I ended the kiss, she opened her eyes and her mouth at the exact same time and launched into a tirade.

"There is no way in Sam Hill I'm going to have a fucking bodyguard. Can you imagine how ridiculous that would look? Walking into work with some gorilla-sized man following me around? For Christ's sake, do you even think before you suggest things sometimes? Seriously, Clown, this one might take the cake."

My grin started small, but as her rant continued, it spread until I felt like my face would split in two.

"And what, exactly, is so funny, Dr. Stone?" She tried to imitate Detective Johnson with terrible results. "God, that was awful. You're so much better at it."

"Be honest with yourself, Sassy. I'm so much better at a lot of things."

"I would knee you in the balls if you didn't have me pinned

down right now. In fact, that was such a dickhead thing to say, I may still do it when you finally let me up and have forgotten all about it, just to remind you what a dick you really are." She gave me a quick kiss to ensure I caught the mirth beneath the blustery threat.

"My second suggestion is, maybe you should take a self-defense class or possibly carry a weapon of some sort. I don't know your stance on any of that—the weapon thing—or even the laws in this state...what you can or can't have on your person. But you *must* do something to protect yourself, damn it."

The words couldn't tumble from me fiercely enough. All I could think about was how much I was going to worry about her. I was already dreading Monday morning, when she had to go to her work and I to mine. The only saving grace of all this? I'd be able to keep a better eye on John at the hospital, at least to a small degree. Hell, it was something. I was grasping at any straw I could. Even though she was adamantly opposed to the bodyguard idea, I was considering talking to Killian about it anyway. I was sure it was grounds for an enormous fight between Taylor and me when she found out, but I had to find some sort of peace of mind.

Somehow I convinced her to go out to breakfast before we went to the apartment. I knew she couldn't resist the offer of chocolate chip pancakes. They were her favorite. Maybe it was a dirty move, but I never said I played above the board *all* the time.

With full stomachs, we headed toward Mission Valley. The chorizo burrito I'd chosen from the menu churned in my gut with each mile we covered on the way.

"Why are you driving so slowly? Are you nervous about

getting there?" She looked at me over the top of her sunglasses.

"What are you talking about? The speed limit is seventy. Just not in the mood to deal with more cops. Kind of had my fill lately." It seemed like a decent reason, even if I just made it up on the spot. Of course, she saw right through it.

"Uhhhh, okay. If I didn't know better, I'd say you're full of shit."

"Well, good thing you know better, then."

She was totally right. Killian had told me a little bit of what to expect when we got there, and it was about to be a really long day.

"Damn it," she said suddenly while looking out the window.

"What's wrong? Did you forget something? Do we need to go back?" A man could hope, right?

"No. I just realized I never asked Detective Johnson about Sally. It would've been better to know what to expect going in, you know?"

"I hear you. I'm not sure anything can prepare us for this, though."

"Why do you say that?"

"Well, the only thing I can draw from is the one time I've had something stolen. I was doing my residency in Philadelphia. The hospital was in a bad part of the city, and a lot of the residents parked on the surrounding streets because the parking passes for the parking structure were expensive. At that point in your career, you don't have two nickels to rub together, so any opportunity to save money seemed like a good idea."

"Was it a flashy car like the ones you have now?" she asked, always interested in the small details of a story. She should've been a detective herself.

"It was a BMW, but a used, older model, apparently easy to break into." I laughed but thought back affectionately to the little 3 series. "I came out one night after my rotation, and it was gone. The cops recovered it within a few days, but I didn't really want it back." I shrugged. "I felt so violated. It smelled like weed and cheap beer. That's all I can remember. The seats were all marked up, and I just couldn't stop imagining all the things they must have been doing in my car in the few short days they had it."

"What did you end up doing with it?" she asked, genuinely interested in my story.

It took me a few moments to remember. "I think I sold it to one of the orderlies for way less than it was worth. I just wanted to get rid of it at that point."

I took the exit off the freeway and pulled into her apartment complex before I could come up with any other excuses to delay the inevitable.

"Well, here we are. Were you able to get in touch with your homeowner's insurance folks?" I asked, circling the property looking for a parking spot.

"Mac, be serious. I'm a renter. I have nothing. That chessboard was the most valuable thing I own. Well, that and Sally. I didn't say anything yesterday while the detective was saying all of that because it's embarrassing." She stuffed her phone in her purse as we parked.

"Why would you be embarrassed?" I asked.

"Well, let's see. I'm twenty-five, work like a dog, and I literally have nothing to show for it. You don't find that cause for embarrassment?"

I waited in front of the car until she got out and closed

her door. I set the alarm with the key fob and stashed it in my pocket.

"No. I know people twice your age in the same situation. People with salaries probably three times yours. People who don't have addict mothers sucking them dry. You are an amazing, responsible, level-headed young woman. I can't think of a single thing you have to be embarrassed about. Well, maybe your singing voice." I gave her a sideways grin, and she smacked me in the chest with the back of her hand.

"Ouch." I rubbed over the spot. "Maybe you don't need self-defense classes after all."

The telltale yellow crime-scene tape was easy to spot from across the apartment complex. As we approached, Taylor twisted her hand tighter against mine.

"Are you sure you want to do this?" As hopeless as the cause likely was, I wanted to give her one last option to back out. "We don't have to go in there, baby. I can send a cleaning crew instead. They can pack up your things and have them sent to my house."

"No. I need to do this. It...it just looks so ominous...with that tape. Like you see in a movie," she said as she dug through her purse for her keys.

"I don't think you're going to need those."

"Why?"

"Looks like the door is already ajar."

"Are you kidding? They left my door open this whole time? I'll be lucky if whatever crap I do have hasn't been stolen."

As we got closer, I could see the wood around the door frame was splintered. Clearly Busby used a crowbar or some other means to force the door open.

I pulled the yellow tape down, crumpled it up into a wad,

and then tossed it on the patio. I hadn't even thought to bring trash bags with us for the cleanup. "We're going to have to run up to the store and get trash bags. We should've stopped on the way. I should've thought about that."

"Well, let's take a look around first and make a list. That way we make just one trip," she replied, pushing the front door open.

"Good idea."

I followed her inside.

But neither one of us were prepared for what we encountered.

Her once cute and tidy apartment looked like it had been through a 7.0-magnitude earthquake. Things that had previously hung on the wall were on the ground. Furniture was overturned. Even the contents of the kitchen cabinets were strewn about.

"I can't imagine the reason for all of this. He must have been in a full psychotic episode when he broke into this apartment," she muttered, turning in a full circle.

"Are there security cameras on this property?" I asked, doing the same turn-and-gawk.

"I think out in the parking lot. Maybe in the common areas. This is unbelievable." She turned to look at me, shaking her head in disbelief. "What would make him do this?"

"I can't imagine."

"Why did you ask about the cameras? They won't show what happened inside here."

"I just thought it would be interesting to see his demeanor—you know, his general state—as he approached your apartment. Maybe we could see if he was agitated or spoke to anyone. Or if he was acting strangely." Then I quickly added,

"Well, stranger than normal. And, now that I'm thinking about it, if he were shown on video here, it would blow a hole in the alibi he fed the cops."

Taylor started to ask more about the alibi comment, but all train of thought was lost when we rounded the corner and went into the bedroom. This must've been what Killian warned me about. Taylor's bed looked like a human sacrifice had taken place. Her bedding was covered in what looked like blood. So much blood, it soaked through to the mattress. The smell was overwhelming.

"Oh, my God!" She covered her nose and mouth and turned away, burying her face in my chest. I wrapped my arms around her, shielding her from the horror of the sight and stench.

"We can leave. Let's just go." I started stepping backward out of the bedroom, but she stopped our progress.

"No. He's not going to win like this."

"This is not a contest."

"That can't possibly be real blood," she said, looking back at her bed.

"The asshole works at a blood bank. If he's as sick as I think he is, it's probably *your* blood."

"Oh God, Mac, don't say something like that. Why does it smell like that?"

"There are a number of reasons. But oddly enough, the predominant odor doesn't smell like blood." I looked around the room from where we were standing in the doorway. I didn't want to voice my thought out loud, but it smelled like decomposing flesh more than blood. Both had very distinct odors, and I was shocked some of this hadn't been cleaned up by the police department when they collected evidence.

"What on earth is that?" Taylor pulled from my embrace and started across the room. On the wall was line after line of chicken-scratch handwriting in what looked like black marker. Killian had warned me about that as well.

"Let's just start packing up the stuff you want to take and get out of here." If I could dissuade her from reading the messages, she'd be better off.

"Oh, this is disgusting. What a pig. He's more delusional than I thought. Oh...yeah...*no.*" Her eyes grew wider the more she read.

She turned to me where I was still standing in the doorway. "He's really disturbed. This..." She pointed at the writing. "If they don't arrest him after seeing this, I will lose all faith in those who are paid to protect the citizens. I mean, he's written threats here, on my fucking bedroom wall. How he's going to fuck me and kill me and then fuck my dead body. That's not enough to arrest him? Really? What's it going to take? My actual dead body?" Her voice stepped up in pitch with each question, panic transforming the features of her face.

"Taylor. Taylor, look at me." I strode across the room when she kept staring at the wall. Physically turning her by the shoulders to face me, I bent down to be directly in her line of sight. Her eyes were brimming with tears. "Listen to me." She still didn't meet my regard. "Baby. Look at me. Taylor!"

Fully yelling her name snapped her to attention.

"What?"

"Get what you want to get from this place, and then we're leaving. I won't take no for an answer this time. I don't want to stay here. I don't want *you* to stay here. Tell me what you want to take, and I'll help you pack it up."

She stared at me for a few moments before saying,

"Clothing?"

"Okay, let's look in your closet. You walk over there with me. No more looking at that wall. Do you understand me?" I kept my face right in line with hers, not letting her eyes drift anywhere else.

A quick nod of her head was all I needed to see before I towed her with me toward her closet. I carefully slid the rear door open on its track and was so thankful to see the things inside had been untouched.

"Okay, we can do this," I declared. "Do you have a suitcase around here? It will be easier to pack your things that way." I felt like I was talking to a small child, but she was so spooked, and neither of us knew what we would find around the next corner.

She answered like a robot. "Under the bed."

"I'll get the suitcase. You start taking what you want from your closet out to the other room, and we'll make space out there to fold."

My natural inclination to take charge worked perfectly in the situation. She was in the ozone, and I couldn't blame her. I got on my knees beside the bed and lifted the bed skirt to look underneath, and I almost threw up from the smell that blasted me in the face. Something was under her bed, and it was definitely dead. I pulled my phone out of my back pocket and pressed the icon to make the flashlight illuminate. I saw the suitcase first and pulled that out of the way, dragging it to the middle of the bedroom floor. I ducked back down, shining the flashlight into the space left from where the suitcase was.

"Oh, Jesus Christ," I grumbled.

"What's wrong? What is it?"

Taylor had come back into the room for another load of

clothing. She was walking past just as I was cussing about my discovery. I rose to my knees and looked at her, trying to decide if I should tell her or make something up.

"What's under there? The smell is like thirty times worse since you pulled the suitcase out." She was definitely doing better than when she first read the threats on the wall.

"What does Mrs. Miller's cat look like?" There was no way I was going to be able to hide this from her. The smell was taking over the room.

"Jonah? He's a big orange tabby. The biggest lover boy you've ever seen. Why do you ask?"

The look on my face must have clued her in. That and the unmistakable smell of a dead carbon-based life-form.

"Noooo. No, Mac. *Nooo*. That cat was all she had. Why would he do this? What am I going to tell her?" She held her face in her hands and dropped to her knees, sobbing. I quickly got up from where I was kneeling beside the bed and went to console her. Of course she pushed me away at first, in perfect Taylor fashion, but I knew better than to let her. I pulled her into my lap, cradling her in my arms, and let her cry it out.

"Ssshhhh. It's going to be okay, baby." I knew things were far from being okay, but I didn't have much more to say. Really, what kind of human being killed an innocent pet to prove his disturbed point? Which brought up an even more frustrating question: What point was he trying to make with all this destruction? That he was a tough guy? He was big and scary? Interesting how he had to do all of this while we were halfway across the world. Fucking coward. Like every other bully, nothing but a fucking coward.

Her sweet sniffles shook me from my internal rant. "I'm okay." She patted my chest softly. "I'm okay." I leaned her back in my arms so I could look down at her face.

"This is a lot to deal with. We can leave, and I can have people come do this."

"It's all right. Let's just get the stuff packed up, and then we can go. I'll figure out a way to tell Mrs. Miller about Jonah." She sniffed again and pushed up to stand. I followed suit and was reminded of the problem under the bed.

"What do you think I should do about the, umm..." I motioned with a tilt of my head toward the bed.

"I don't know. If we leave him under there, that smell is just going to get worse. But I don't have any trash bags."

"Okay, I'm going to go to the store on the corner for trash bags. Can you think of anything else we need? Wait. I can't leave you here. Come with me."

"No. That's ridiculous. I'll stay here and pack stuff up. It's just around the corner. You'll be gone for fifteen minutes, tops. I'll be fine. Here... Let's go see if Mrs. Miller is home, and then you'll know I'm not alone."

I stood rooted to the spot, indecision paralyzing me. This was precisely what I was afraid of. The thought of leaving her alone anywhere terrified me. Going to work Monday was going to be impossible.

"Mac. Be reasonable. Don't let him win. We cannot be terrorized like this. Come with me next door. We'll see if Mrs. Miller's home."

We crossed the shared front stoop and knocked on her elderly neighbor's door. The old woman peeked through the curtains on the transom window before opening the door.

"My goodness, you're a sight for sore eyes," she said, her gentle smile adding more wrinkles to her face. "I've been so worried about you, dear." She wrapped Taylor in a motherly hug. "The police have been here so many times, asking questions but never telling me what happened in there." She pointed past us toward Taylor's front door.

"I know, Mrs. Miller, and I'm so sorry you've been worried. Someone broke into my apartment and trashed the place. I'm afraid I'm going to have to move out." Taylor patted her hand while she held it in hers.

"Oh, dear. That's such a shame. Where will you go? It has gotten so expensive everywhere in San Diego."

"I know. But I'm going to move in with Mac. He has a great house in Oceanside. Right on the beach. Maybe you can come over one night for dinner?" Taylor asked hopefully.

"Oh, I don't know about all of that." The old woman waved her hand. "I don't see well enough to drive that far."

"That's okay. We can come to get you, couldn't we, Mac?" She looked over her shoulder to me.

"Yes, of course, anytime. Okay, I'm going to run to the store. I'll be right back." I kissed Taylor's cheek and pointedly showed her my cell phone. She would understand what I was getting at—that I was just a phone call away if she needed me.

"It's going to be fine," she reassured me. I heard her explaining my worries to Mrs. Miller as I walked away toward the parking lot.

I'd never hustled through a grocery store quicker in my life. I hadn't received a text from Taylor saying we needed anything else, so I made a beeline for the trash bags, used the self-checkout, and was back in my car in less than ten minutes. If all the traffic lights worked in my favor, I would be back to the apartment complex in record time.

The sooner the better.

Especially with a guy like John Busby still roaming free.

CHAPTER THIRTEEN

Taylor

What the hell was taking him so long? After twenty minutes, I found myself checking my phone obsessively, almost minute by minute. I was doing exactly what I scolded him for. Allowing myself to be terrorized by John the jackass. I set my phone on the kitchen counter and went to the horribly stinky bedroom for another armful of clothing, One or two more should wrap up the clothes packing, and then I would start on shoes and personal items. Like I'd repeatedly told Mac, I didn't have a lot of material possessions to worry about, so we should be finished and out of the apartment in another hour. Two at the most.

The front door was propped open to allow fresh air to flow through the small space. Anything to help clean, healthy smells replace the foul stench in the bedroom would be a blessing. Plus, Mrs. Miller insisted I keep the door open so she could hear me if I yelled for help. She had hers propped open with the precast concrete frog I'd given her last Christmas. It usually sat proudly on her front stoop, but it now made a handy doorstop until Mac returned.

Finally, I heard him jingling his keys in the living room just as I rounded the corner, arms piled high with as many pairs of shoes as I could carry in one trip. The voice that greeted me was the last one I ever expected to hear in my own home. Dropping my payload where I stood, I was shocked to find Constance Stone among the chaos in my shabby apartment.

"What are you doing here?" I asked as impolitely as possible.

"Orrrrr 'Hello, Mrs. Stone.' Or maybe 'Hi, Constance,' if we were more closely acquainted. Either of those would be appropriate greetings, Taylor." She shook her haughty head in disapproval.

"Like I said, what are you doing here? How did you get my address?" How could this even be happening? And where the *hell* was Mac?

She took a few steps farther into the room, stepping carefully over the items still lying on the floor. Where her face wasn't pinched from age-erasing procedures, it was from disgust of the conditions she stood among.

"I really like what you've done with the place," she said dryly. "I've heard of shabby chic, but this seems to be more...I don't know...dare I say, trailer trash?"

"Can I help you with something in particular? Your son isn't here at the moment. He went to the store to pick up some trash bags, as a matter of fact. My apartment was broken into, as you can see." I turned in a semicircle with my arms stretched out wide, as if showing the place proudly. "He should be back any minute, though. You're more than welcome to wait in your car. I'll text him and tell him to hurry. I'm sure he'll be glad to know you've stopped by. Completely uninvited, I might add."

I strode over to where my phone sat on the countertop, but she stepped in front of me to block my path. Wow, this woman had bigger balls than I'd seen in some time. If I weren't so completely in love with her son, I'd level her ass right then and there.

Yes. I just admitted I loved him. Maybe not right to him, but it was a start.

"I'm sorry. How did you say you got my address again?"

Because my front door was wide open, I heard the very distinct sound of Mac's car as he entered my apartment complex. I had no idea how long it would take him to find a parking spot, as they were usually in high demand on the weekend, with many of the residents at home rather than at work. With any luck, he would soon be walking in on his mother's antics.

"Oh, dear," she said in her best patronizing tone.

"Cut the bullshit. I'm not your dear. I'm not *your* anything. Why are you here?" Knowing Mac was close by gave me a whole new level of bravery.

"Excellent point. Money talks, Taylor. That's probably a concept you can relate to, am I right?"

"I'm not following." I wanted to drag this shit out so he would hear, firsthand, whatever bomb she was about to drop.

"Well, that's what you're doing here, isn't it?" She continued with her accusations.

"Still not following. Spell it out for me, Constance. I'm not very bright. I'm not overprivileged and overeducated like the people you're used to hanging out with. You have to really dumb it down for me." I crossed my arms over my chest and leaned against the wall, settling in for an epic speech.

"Don't play coy, girl. There have been a dozen others like you in my son's life. Probably more. All you see are dollar signs. I mean, look at this place. This dump. Look at *you*, for heaven's sake. What does a woman—no, a *girl*—like you have to offer a man like Maclain?"

Mac had quietly walked in behind his mother, now

so engrossed in her speech that she didn't hear him in the doorway. I saw him over her shoulder, and he quickly put his finger to his lips, signaling for me not to let on that he was there. I was all too happy to go along with his plan. Nothing would make me happier than to watch this cunt dig her own grave.

"Maybe you're a hot little number in bed." She gave a careless shrug while sneering the rest of her speech. "But after all that dies down, what's left? Can you even hold a decent conversation? My guess is probably not." She made a practiced charitable grimace—one I was sure she saved for moments like handing some spare singles to the homeless man in front of the grocery store.

"There's more to life than shoes and Starbucks, sweetie. My son needs to be stimulated intellectually. He will grow tired of the likes of you." She wrinkled her face like she just tasted something sour. "He always does. I will make sure of it. I mean, that's what mothers are for, among other things, of course. But you should do him and yourself a favor and go on your merry way now. You're just holding him back from real opportunities of meeting quality women who deserve his attention."

Apparently, my ridiculously-sexy-when-he's-mad boyfriend had heard enough. He held his hand about two feet above my tile countertop and dropped his keys. The clatter made his mother jump from her skin. Damn it! Why didn't I think to catch that on video? It would've been brilliant Snapchat fodder.

"Maclain! I didn't hear you come in!" Her facial expression along with her body language changed a hundred eighty degrees from the cunty shrew who had just been lecturing me to the loving, doting mother who rushed to her son to greet him with outstretched arms.

Arms he batted away and dodged as if they were Medusa's snakes trying to strangle him.

"What's wrong? Why won't you give your mother a hug? Aren't you pleased to see me?" She made this absurd puppy-dog face, and I actually burst out laughing but quickly covered my mouth to stifle the sound, knowing it wasn't helping the situation.

"Now, I was just walking up the sidewalk, so I could've heard what you were saying incorrectly," Mac said very seriously to his mom, "but did I just hear you say you *paid* someone to give you Taylor's home address? You better tell me the fucking truth when you answer."

"Do *not* speak to me with that sort of language, mister." She tried to divert the subject and focus on his swearing.

"Tell me. Now."

Did she know her own son? At all? The man was like a dog with a bone when he wanted something.

"Well, yes. I did. But only because you didn't return my calls. You gave me no other choice." She shrugged, so much like Mac did when he stated a simple fact. The similarity was eerie.

"And I figured she was the reason." She turned and glared at me. I returned an innocent *who me?* mime.

"She's been keeping you from your own mother. I did what I had to do. You know I can be resourceful when I have to be. It's a trait you've inherited from me, you know." She straightened her posture, gloating with pride.

Mac's glare, however, cut her right back down to size.

"Do you realize that Taylor has a stalker right now? A legitimate freak that has been terrorizing her? That's who did this in here. She doesn't live like this normally. She's one of the neatest, cleanest people I've ever met. Annoyingly so at times." He winked at me over his mother's head. "Who gave you the information? Again, I caution you to tell nothing but the complete truth."

"I really don't appreciate these threats, Maclain." She picked at a nonexistent thread on her sleeve.

"And I really don't care what you appreciate and don't appreciate. Tell me who you paid to give you Taylor's address. Immediately!" He bellowed the last word so loudly, both Constance and I recoiled from his outburst.

With her hand over her heart, she panted, "For heaven's sake. *So* unnecessary. It was her mother."

"What?" Mac and I burst it out at the same time.

Constance whirled around to face me with a Cheshire cat grin stretching across her lips. "Yes. Your mother told me." Then she turned back to Mac, as if she were a tattling schoolgirl. "Didn't take much either. You know, I'm pretty sure the woman has a drug habit of some sort. I was prepared to pay her more, but at the mention of twenty-five dollars, she sang like a canary. I wired her the money at a Western Union or something similar." She waved her hand dismissively, recalling the bothersome task. "And it was that simple. Can you imagine? Twenty-five dollars for your own daughter's safety? She didn't know who I was or what I planned to do with the information. Didn't even ask, if I recall correctly." She shrugged and turned back to me while the words sank in, watching me with scrutiny as the effects of her bitter information wore away at my heart. A cruel smirk played on her lips as we stared at one another.

"Leave." Mac's voice was lethally calm. The sound was so quiet and level, it was scary in a different way.

Constance quickly turned back to Mac, and he repeated his words. "Leave. Now."

"But—"

"Get the fuck out of this apartment before I drag you out of here myself. And if you ever come near my girlfriend again without her permission and mine, I will call the police and have you arrested myself. Are we clear?" Rage was bubbling just beneath the surface of his calm tone. Why she continued to push him made me question her sanity.

"Maclain. Be serious," she tried to reason.

"Get the fuck out!" This time when he yelled, I wanted to cheer him on. Complete with bicolored pom-poms and a cartwheel. My hero not only saved my heart but whatever tiny shred of what was left of my dignity too.

His mother walked through my front door, and he slammed it so hard behind her that the window beside it rattled in its old frame.

When he turned to me, I could already feel the goddamn waterworks coming on. How many times would he see me go to pieces before he cut bait and ran? But I couldn't stop them if I tried. I had been dealt another critical blow, and I honestly didn't know how much more I could take. My knees buckled the exact moment he swept me into his arms.

It was pretty much the last thing I remembered until I woke up later in his bedroom—our bedroom—in Oceanside. He was spooned behind me in the big bed, just the sheet over both of our still fully clothed bodies. He was running his fingers through my hair, from my scalp to the ends, over and over again. It was so hypnotic, I didn't want to move for fear he would stop. He knew how to make me feel so cherished. He was the *only* one who ever made me feel that way, actually. The only one who took the time or cared enough to even try.

If he didn't own my heart before today, he certainly did now.

"Are you hungry?" he asked, keeping his voice quiet and even. I thought I'd done a good job at playing possum, but nothing slipped past this man.

"No. Thank you, though." I couldn't bring myself to face him.

"Will you try to eat something anyway?"

"My stomach hurts," I whispered.

"You cried so much. Maybe a smoothie? I'm worried about you."

"Please don't worry." I turned in his arms to face him. The green eyes that normally danced with life were flat. I stroked his cheek with my thumb. "Why do you look so sad?" I wanted to heal him the moment I saw the pain in his gaze.

"I feel like I really let you down today. I've been lying here thinking of ways to make it up to you." He barely kept eye contact while he spoke. So not my Clown.

"How can you say that? How can you blame anything that happened today on yourself?"

"That devil's spawn is my mother. Mine. I have the privilege of saying that's the woman who gave birth to me. That wretched hag who treats innocent young women like you the way she did? That's the woman who raised me. That's how I can blame myself."

"You are not responsible for her behavior, Mac. Surely by this point in your life, you understand that." I sat up higher and immediately regretted it. Stabbing pain in my temple reminded me of all the crying I'd done. The dizzy spell that quickly followed reminded me of the food I hadn't eaten. I closed my eyes and willed the room to stop spinning.

"I'm going to get you something to eat. I won't take no for an answer."

"Bossy," I mumbled, keeping my eyes closed.

"Call me what you will, you need food. First some ibuprofen."

"Actually, do you have Tylenol? I always think it works better for a headache."

"I do. You stay here." He trotted off toward the bathroom and returned quickly with two little white tablets and a glass of water.

"You don't have to stand there and watch me. I'm going to take them."

"I was just going to take the glass when you were done, smart mouth. But I do want you to drink all that water, please."

"I have to admit, this caregiver bit you have going on is kind of sexy." I gulped the water down and handed him the empty glass. "Thank you." When he went to take the glass from me, I held on to it until he met my gaze. "Seriously. Thank you. I'm not sure how I got from that apartment to this bed. I'm sure it will all come back to me once I really think about it, but thank you for taking care of me and making sure I made it safely. I've been depending on you a lot lately. And you've been letting me." I handed him the glass after I said what I needed to.

"Because I love you. I want to help you." He let that sink in for a second and then added, "I'll be right back with some food."

I thought for sure he'd use that opportunity to go into some speech about taking care of me, how I needed to let him handle the hard things for me, some other chest-beating talk like that, so I was pleasantly surprised when he showed the restraint he did.

Something had changed today. Something wasn't right in his eyes, and it worried me. I was very concerned that today was the straw that broke the camel's back for him. He might have decided I was just more trouble than I was worth. Or maybe the things he overheard his mother saying had sunk in while I was sleeping. Perhaps he'd decided I wasn't what he needed in a partner. I came with a shit ton of baggage, and right on cue, Janet proved that point once again.

My own mother had sold my personal information for a bump of meth. The stabbing pain returned to my stomach and temples. I scooted down lower in the covers as a wave of icy chills rippled through my body. I completely refused to cry again. Frankly, I was pretty confident I was too dehydrated to form any more tears, even if I cared to.

I couldn't let myself dwell on what my mother did. If I made a list of all the times she hurt me throughout my life and mentally played it on repeat, I'd probably never get out of bed in the morning. But I needed to take the advice I'd just given Mac. I was not responsible for that woman's behavior. I couldn't allow her to hurt me anymore. She was sick, and she was an addict. Maybe one day, if she decided to get help and go into treatment, she would realize all the times she had hurt me and would find some way to atone for her mistakes. In the meantime, I couldn't live with that pain defining me. That was just a recipe for a miserable life.

Mac walked back into the room with a bed tray piled high with food.

"Oh, my God. That's for both of us, right?" I peeked out from under the edge of the covers.

"What's wrong? Why are you back under the covers like that? I'm going to get a thermometer." He set the tray on the dresser and dashed back out the door before I could stop him.

When he returned, he had—no joke—a black leather doctor's bag in his hand.

"Okay, first of all, I thought doctors only had those bags on TV. Second, you look very sexy with that bag, Dr. Stone. Do you make house calls?" I sat up tall, hopefully looking anxious for my physical exam.

"I'm about to make my very first one."

"Oh, goodie." I rubbed my hands together in front of me. "Should I get naked for this? You know, just to be a cooperative patient?"

"As much as I love the idea of playing doctor with you, I want to see you eat some more of that food. Then"—he paused dramatically—"let the games begin!"

He went back to the dresser and picked up the tray. "In all seriousness, are you cold? Do you want me to turn down the air conditioner?"

"No, it's perfect in here. It's me. I'm all over the place with my emotions. And I'm sorry about that. I'm sorry about earlier too. I'm sorry you keep having to see me lose my shit."

"No more apologizing. For any of it." He nodded at the tray. "I brought a little bit of everything. I have no idea what you're in the mood for."

"I see that. What's on the sandwich?" I looked over the small buffet on the tray, zeroing in on the sandwich first.

"Turkey and avocado."

"What kind of bread?" I quizzed.

"Squaw."

"Let's split it. Did you put salt and pepper on it?"

"Just the way my queen likes it."

That dumb little fact made me so happy, I felt tears welling up in my eyes again. Just when I swore the well was dry.

"Honestly, maybe I should take a pregnancy test," I joked as I reached for half the sandwich.

My statement made Mac choke on the drink he'd just taken, which made me burst out laughing.

"Are you okay?" I patted his back.

"Are you late?" he finally asked when he could speak again.

"No. I was saying that because I've never cried as much in my life as I have in the past month." I mentally counted days as quickly as I could. "I mean, I don't think I am. What's the date today?"

His eyes grew so wide I started laughing again. "Are you serious?" he asked with a grin this time.

"We definitely have a lot of sex. That *is* how babies are made, last I checked."

"Today's the twelfth."

"Well, good. I'm not late. Should be happening any day now, which really would explain the excessive waterworks in addition to everything that's been going on." I took a big bite of the sandwich to avoid having to speak on the subject further. He did the same thing, and we both sat chewing in silence. His initial reaction surprised me, though. He seemed almost happy about the possibility.

"Do you want to have kids?" I asked bluntly.

"Someday. For sure. Although when I think about it, it's so scary. I don't want to be a screw-up like my mother was. Seems like no matter how hard you try, your kid ends up resenting you for something."

"My theory is to take the example I was given and do everything opposite. That way it can only be better, right?" I smiled before taking another bite. "This is really good," I mumbled with my mouth full.

"What do you want to drink? I brought a beer and a lemonade, and I have water up here in the fridge." He was already standing, waiting to get my selection.

"I think I'll just have water. I feel dehydrated. Why can't I remember how we got home?" It was starting to bother me that my memory wasn't coming back.

"Sometimes our brains just protect us that way. You were really upset at first in the apartment, crying pretty hard. You wanted to leave. You grabbed your keys to go out to your car, and I went after you because there was no way you should be driving while that upset. And then you saw Sally..."

I put my hand up to stop him.

The memory came flooding back. *Sally.*

"Oh, God. Mac." I felt like I was going to throw up the half sandwich I'd just eaten.

He sat down beside me and took my hands. "Listen. We can try to have it fixed if that's what you want to do. I'm sure I can find a good body shop."

I saw it all in my head now. I had rushed out to the parking lot, keys in hand, bolting in my typical fight-or-flight fashion, and I came around the corner and saw Sally for the first time. My worst fear had come to life. John had scrawled the word *whore* across the hood in red spray paint. Two of the four tires were slashed, and the windshield was smashed.

I think Mac had Mrs. Miller sit with me in his car while he did his best to lock up the apartment, and then we drove home in silence. For me, it was more like some strange catatonic state, but until he'd just spoken of it, I had erased the experience from my memory completely.

"No, that doesn't make a lot of sense. Mechanically, I think she was on her last leg anyway. It's time to put on my big-girl pants and face the music. Why didn't the cops say something about it? I mean, that was extensive damage. I have auto insurance, so I will definitely have an adjuster come out and file a claim. Not that I'm going to get very much. It should be enough, at least, for a down payment on something new. I wasn't looking forward to a car payment, though. Oh well. If that's the worst that comes out of all of this..."

I had to find a bright side somewhere. It would be impossible to be without a car, especially once Mac went back to work.

"We'll get it all figured out. In the meantime, you can use one of mine. That way, you can take your time finding something that's right for you. Please don't argue with me on this."

"Thank you so much. I really appreciate it. Do you have something that isn't fancy, though? A Hyundai or something? Maybe a little thing that a bunch of other clowns climb out of when you open the door?"

"I see you're feeling better." He grinned. "How about some of this?" He held out a bowl of fruit salad, and I wrinkled my nose. "Or these?" The second offer was more to my liking. I snatched the red package out of his hand.

"Where were these hiding? I haven't seen these in the cabinet before." My favorite peanut butter cookies, the same kind I was eating outside the Bloodmobile the first day he came and spoke to me, were like crack to me.

"I keep them hidden in the way back so you don't see

them. They're for special occasions."

The light was returning to his green eyes.

"Dude! Every day is a special occasion that calls for Nutter Butters!"

This time he took a turn at the wrinkled-nose look.

"Have you ever tried one? Although I have to warn you—you can't have just one. And honestly, the wafer ones are better than these." I worked on opening the package while I extolled the more exceptional points of the peanut-buttery awesomeness.

"I think I'll take your word for it."

"No, I think you're about to pop your Nutter Butter cherry." I handed over one of the peanut-shaped cookies and watched him turn it over and over in his fingers, examining it from every angle.

"For Christ's sake, Mac." I giggled it out. He was so cute, gazing at the damn thing as if it was about to turn into a spider or—*gasp*—a condom. "It's a cookie. You *have* seen a cookie before, right? She wasn't *that* ghastly of a mother, or was she?" My eyes grew wide as I thought of the horror of a childhood without cookies.

"Of course I've had cookies before. I'm just not a connoisseur like you apparently are."

"Well, stick with me, kid. I'll teach you what you need to know. Now, these aren't the best for dunking, but you can if you need to. I like to take the tops off two"—I demonstrated, separating two cookies as I explained—"and then put them back together so you get twice the peanut butter in one. Like so." I bit off half the new cookie I'd created and handed him the other half. He looked at me skeptically before taking it from my fingers and popping it into his mouth.

About halfway through chewing, he couldn't hold back the smile. "Okay, that's really good," he mumbled around the cookie in his mouth.

I clapped my hands together with delight. Sharing something I loved with him gave me more joy than I expected. "See? Right?"

Now that my blood sugar was up, all sorts of thoughts were running through my brain, crisscrossing one another and shooting out in no particular order. "Oh, I just thought of something. Aren't all your cars at the house in Thermal? You only have the M2 here, and there's no way I'm driving that."

"That's a good point...about Thermal, I mean. You could totally drive the M2 if you wanted to, though. I don't know why you're so afraid of it."

"I didn't say I was afraid of it. I just know how much you love it. And you know people drive like assholes on the freeway. If something happened to it, I would feel terrible."

"Okay, how about this," he said, wiping his hands on a napkin. "You take one more day off on Monday, we drive out to Thermal tomorrow, and Monday we bring one of the cars back for you to drive until you get something new?"

"Baby, I can't keep taking days off work without notice." I rubbed my hand on his leg while I spoke.

A goofy grin took over his entire face, making me very self-conscious and causing me to pull back my hand, trying to figure out what I'd done or said to get this out-of-place reaction.

"What?" was all I could really say.

"You called me 'baby.' Not Clown. Not Mac. Not some other derogatory name or insult. Just a sweet, normal term of endearment. I can't help the reaction, and I'm sure I'll pay for it here any moment, but yeah. *Baby*. I like it." Now the dancing light was fully back in the green depths I loved to stare into.

By that point, I was wearing the same goofy grin. He was so adorable. And handsome. And beautiful. This man, who sat opposite me on the big comfy bed, making sure I ate and drank enough to sustain good health. The same one who'd held me in his arms—countless times now—while I cried from a broken heart or fear that shook me to my very bones. This man was mine.

Big plans formed in my head for tomorrow night. I would make sure he knew how much he meant to me and how much I needed him. He would know we'd always find our way through whatever storm life sent our way. Together, we would never feel lost again.

CHAPTER FOURTEEN

Mac

The villa was a bit of a from since the last time I was here. I'd left in a fit, knowing I had really fucked things up with Taylor. I tried calling my housekeeper in Indian Wells, but she couldn't get out to the place on such short notice. Consequently, I spent half the drive to Coachella Valley explaining and apologizing to Taylor for what we'd probably walk into.

"Would you relax?" She toyed with my free hand while I drove. "Just yesterday, we discovered a dead cat under my blood-soaked bed. How bad can this place be?"

"Good point. When you put it that way, there's nothing to worry about. Nothing at all." I brought her hand to my lips and kissed her slim fingers. One day there would be a ring on the fourth one, announcing to the world how much I loved her. It would be one of the best days of my life. I already knew it with all the certainty in the world.

We pulled up to the gatehouse at the villas, and I showed the guard my identification and club membership card. After he opened the gate, we drove to my place, enjoying the quiet beauty of the property while at rest. When the track was empty, it gave the park a whole other appearance. The sun was low over the hills, picking up purple and copper hues in the rocks.

The desert landscape here was different from anywhere else, and it had its own natural beauty and appeal.

"It's so beautiful here." Taylor gazed out over the acreage when we got out of the car. I had gone around to the trunk to get our bags, and then I continued to the passenger side to enjoy the view beside her.

I dropped the bags and wrapped my arms around her waist. "Even more so with you standing here." I kissed her slowly, enjoying a lazy tangle of our lips and then tongues. We had fallen asleep without making love the night before, and my cock was needing attention in the worst way.

"Let's go inside," I suggested, hoping I could take her directly to the bedroom and spend some time worshiping her body.

"Okay. But I have some special plans for tonight. And I don't want you and impatient Big Mac ruining them. So no funny business," she dictated while playfully pushing me away.

"Funny business?" I asked, looking over my sunglasses. I wasn't even acknowledging the "Big Mac" nonsense.

"Don't act innocent, mister." She grabbed her bag from the ground and led the way up to the front door but then stepped aside to let me unlock it.

While I opened the door, I started badgering her with questions about her comment. "So? Big plans? Like what? Give me a hint. What if I try to guess? Will you tell me if I'm hot or cold?"

"Do you hear yourself right now?" She laughed. "You're like a little boy on Christmas Eve begging to open his gifts early." She turned in a full circle when we got inside the front door. "This isn't so bad. I mean, there are a few things out of place, probably some dishes in the sink. But you made it sound like we were going to walk into the aftermath of a frat party or something."

"I just like things to be perfect for you. All the time." I looked down at my feet, hoping I didn't sound too mushy. The strangest things set my girl off.

"Well, my sweet clown. You have to be realistic. Especially now that we're—oh, my God, I can't believe I'm about to say this—living together."

The grin that took over my face probably made me look deranged, but I couldn't help myself. The reality of our relationship status was finally settling in for both of us, and we both stood there beaming like lovestruck fools.

I pulled her into my arms, much like I had out front. "About these plans, then."

"Patience is a virtue. Or so they say." This time, she initiated the kiss...but also ended it much too quickly. "Do you want to have dinner here or in town tonight?" she asked, leaning back to look up at me.

"Let's see what Grubhub will deliver here. There definitely isn't edible food here, unless you want ramen. And I don't mean the trendy hipster stuff. I'm talking ten for a dollar."

She giggled but wrinkled her nose, so I pulled out my phone to check the food-delivery app. We were limited to about a dozen choices for delivery from a restaurant since we were pretty far from Palm Springs and Indian Wells. We settled on a little Italian place, and Taylor went to shower while we waited for the food to be delivered.

I used the time to go down into the garage and check on my babies. The space was as pristine as the living area of the villa, and I could see through the ceiling to the living space above. I had the perfect car for Taylor stored here, and I couldn't wait to show it to her. I'd been thinking about it much of the drive from San Diego, and I was sure she was going to love it.

It was very unassuming in appearance. While most people didn't expect much from the Ford Focus RS—direct from the American manufacturer's economy line—car enthusiasts knew better. This little rocket packed three hundred fifty horsepower under the hood right off Ford's assembly line. With a minor tune, it could easily keep up with its big-sister Mustang without breaking a sweat. Taylor would have the get-up-and-go she needed to be safe on the freeway, though she'd be comfortable driving the car too.

When the doorbell rang, I quickly hustled upstairs in case she wasn't out of the shower, tipped the delivery guy, and brought the food into the kitchen. I was getting plates from the cabinet when Taylor came out of the bedroom, still in her robe but looking fresh and gorgeous.

I stopped what I was doing to simply stare at her.

"What's wrong?" She peeked into the brown bag. "Did they forget something? That's the only bummer about these delivery services. They always leave something off your order." When I didn't respond, she finally looked back up from the bag to find me still gazing at her. "Mac? What's wrong? Did something happen?" The panicked look was adorable but made me realize I needed to set her worries to rest.

"No. Nothing's wrong. Nothing at all." I tried an easy smile, hoping it helped.

"Then why are you just standing there staring at me like that?" She wasn't buying it for a second. Too much had happened in the past few weeks for her to believe me.

"I was just thinking how lucky I am." I walked around the counter to where she stood. I wanted to touch her while I spoke my next words. I took her hands in mine. Her skin was always so soft, like fine silk. "It's been a long week. It feels so good to be here with you. Just us. Not having to worry what's around the next bend. Just to be here, you and me, and to be able to just breathe, you know?"

"I couldn't agree with you more. And yes. It's been one of the longest weeks of my life. I really want to eat this food, because it smells amazing. And then I want to give you your surprise. But we have to do it in that order."

"Ooohhhkaayy." It was my turn to be skeptical.

"A very wise doctor once told me you should carb-up before big nights like the one we're going to have tonight." She winked at me, grabbed the brown bag off the counter, and headed to the table. I stared at her sexy little ass, barely covered by the silky kimono-style robe she wore, as she walked away. I knew the exact conversation she was recalling, and I could remember the night it led to. The very first night I touched her. Tasted her.

The night my life changed forever.

I wanted to throw all the food in the trash can and drag her to the bedroom right then and there. But I had to show some restraint. Clearly she had a plan in her mind of how she wanted the night to play out, and I had a feeling it would be in my best interest to go along with the program.

Although I could feel my dick swell past comfort in my cargo shorts, I grabbed the other bag and the plates I had taken from the cupboard and joined her at the table.

"Very wise, huh?" It was so rare that she issued me a heartfelt compliment, I had to fish around a bit more to see if there were more where that one came from. She just grinned and continued serving our dinner though.

Conversation escaped me as we ate. All I could think of was laying her out on the table and having her for my meal. Feasting on her pussy until she called my name with her climax. Italian pasta and meatballs just didn't hold the same appeal.

Scraping forks and clinking glassware were the only sounds filling the villa now. I was trying not to scarf my food down, but I was certain I finished my meal in record time.

"I'm going to go shower, if you don't mind?" I asked, not wanting to wreck any part of the big plan.

"Actually, can you give me a hand cleaning up first?" She smiled sweetly, and I felt like a first-class jackass. Where were my manners? Also, if she kept up with that sexy little smile, I'd walk across hot coals barefoot if she asked me to.

"I'm so sorry. Totally rude of me." I shot up out of my seat, grabbing my plate and hers, now overcompensating for my boorishness.

"Hey, don't overreact." She put her delicate hand over mine when I went to take her plate. "We'll do it together." She took care of the leftovers while I scraped and rinsed the plates and loaded them into the dishwasher. We had the table cleared in no time.

"See? Now we can get to the good stuff." She widened her eyes while taking my hand. "How do you feel about a bath?" We started down the hall toward the master bathroom. There was an enormous Jacuzzi tub in there—one I'd thought was a waste of space when looking to purchase the home.

"I can't remember the last time I sat in a bathtub. Maybe when I was five?" My imagination was already coming up with better ideas than working math problems on the tile walls with dry-erase markers.

"I guarantee this will be a much different experience," she promised as I trailed behind her into the large en suite bathroom. I watched while she produced some sort of hamburger-sized object from her overnight bag. She ran the water to fill the tub and unwrapped the patty from the tissue paper that covered it.

"What the hell is that?" Curiosity had finally gotten the better of me, and watching without asking a million questions just wasn't my style.

"It's a bath bomb."

"A bomb? Yeah, definitely didn't detonate bombs when I was five. Fifteen? Maybe. But that's a story for another time."

"No, this will make our skin soft and smell nice." She dropped the "bomb" into the water, and it fizzed like a giant Alka-Seltzer, turning the whole tub an odd, bubbly blue.

"Is that really safe to submerge ourselves in?" Now the scientist in me took the driver's seat.

"I do it all the time. Come on. Off with the clothes." She tugged my shirt upward, and I helped by lifting my arms. She wasn't tall enough to finish the job, so I pulled it over my head and tossed it onto the floor while she set to work on the button on my shorts. I stood still and watched her slim fingers work the fastener loose and pull down the zipper. She made the most mundane tasks sexier than I could withstand. I closed my eyes and dropped my head back while she slipped her hand into the waistband of my boxers, running her fingers around to the back before stopping.

We just stood there. Taylor's hands in my underwear, while she was still covered in her slinky little robe, bathwater running and fizzing in the background. All the while, I concentrated on not ejaculating from the mere anticipation of her silky skin touching mine.

Her warm breath on my neck caught my attention, and I opened my eyes gradually. She licked my neck while she pulled my boxers down, carefully freeing my cock when it got hung up in the fabric up front.

"You need to watch where you point this thing, mister. Someone could lose an eye." She grazed her fingernails lightly over my shaft before abandoning me to turn off the faucet. I caught a stellar peek of her ass when she bent over to test the bathwater, making sure it was ready for us to get in.

"After you, handsome." She swept her hand out in front of her, inviting me to get in first.

"All right. And you're sure my skin won't look like a Smurf when I get out?" I asked one more time before stepping into the bubbling blue water.

"Well, just for a few hours, but it fades," she answered smartly. "Oh! I almost forgot! I made a playlist for tonight." She darted out to the bedroom and came back with her phone and a Bluetooth speaker. She set the two on the bathroom counter and pressed Play. After dimming the lights, she came and stood beside the tub where I was now completely submerged.

"Mind if I join you?" she asked while working the knot loose on her robe.

"I'd be terribly disappointed if you didn't."

She unbelted her robe and let it slip from her shoulders, revealing her creamy skin. I offered my hand to steady her while she climbed in behind me.

"I think you'd be more comfortable in front, no?" I asked.

"No, I'm taking care of you tonight."

I turned my head to look at her, puzzled.

"All week, you've been taking care of me. One thing after

another. So tonight, I want to just say thank you. Just indulge me a little. Let me care for you."

I leaned back against her, and she wrapped her long legs around my waist.

"See? That's not so bad, is it?"

I ran my hands up and down her smooth legs. "Not at all."

She used the big sponge that usually sat on the side of the tub as decoration and squeezed water over my shoulders and chest, time and time again. It was relaxing and hypnotic. Combined with the dim lights, soothing music, and the scent of the bath bomb, it was a very calming experience.

"I like this song. It really says a lot of what I think I would say to you if I wrote a song." She seemed to be thinking out loud, or just talking absentmindedly, the way her voice sounded so far off in thought. So instead of questioning her more, I just listened to the words. It was a young guy singing—and hitting a fierce falsetto, I might add. He sang about his lover being patient with him. The chorus repeated as he begged his lover to be patient while he made the changes she needed him to make to be the kind of man she wanted him to be. Shit, even I felt bad for the dude the way he plaintively delivered the lyrics after the second go-around.

"Who's singing this?" I finally asked.

"Charlie Puth. Have you heard of him?"

"I think so. I think I've heard him on the radio. Not this song, though."

"Yeah, it's a deeper track," she answered wistfully. "I thought of you the second I heard it. I really couldn't have said the words better myself."

"But Taylor, you are what I need. You're everything to me exactly the way you are," I insisted. Why couldn't she see that?

"But when you wrote that letter—"

"I could cut my own hand off for writing that damn thing. It feels like twelve years ago at this point, doesn't it? We've been through so much since then. You've been. I've been. And together, *we've* been. I wouldn't change a second of it, as strange as that sounds, because it's all part of *our* story now." I toyed with her fingers under the water while I spoke.

"You shouldn't regret telling me those things, though. I needed to hear them. It was hard at the time, but if you hadn't had the courage and the strength to say what you did, when you did, I don't think we would be here right now. Together, I mean. I had a bad history of running away when things got tough. I tried doing it the other day again. But you showed me you would be there to help me through it instead of me having to face it all by myself. I owe you so much more than a thank-you for that, Mac."

I wanted to see her face while we were having this crucial conversation. I wanted to hold her in my arms and kiss her and tell her how brave she was being and how much I loved her. The current setup in the tub was preventing all of that from happening, however.

"Let's get out of the tub. The water's getting cold." I didn't wait for her response. I lifted the drain, and the water started to whirl down to the end of the tub.

I stood up first and grabbed two towels off the rack on the side of the tub. I helped her up and wrapped her in one of the cloths before wrapping one around my waist. She reached for a second one, patted the water droplets off my chest and shoulders, and then ran it up and down my arms.

"Turn. Let me get your back too."

I did as she asked, and she took gentle passes over my back

and shoulders again, making sure I was perfectly dry before asking me to bend forward so she could dry my hair. I did the same for her and left hers looking like a fluffy cloud around her angelic face.

"I think this is a new look for you," I said, smiling down into her eyes. She leaned past me to look in the mirror.

"Yeah, I could totally rock this." She gave herself a nod of approval before digging into her bag for some lotion. "Come on. I'll give you a little massage."

Who was I to turn down an offer like that? But I really needed to acknowledge everything she'd just said to me in the tub. It was a turning point for us, and I didn't want it to go unspoken that I'd heard everything she'd said.

Leaning against the counter, I took the lotion from her hand and set it down beside me. I pulled her between my legs and wrapped my arms around her.

"First, I want to say a few things in response to what you said in the tub. I don't want you to think you just opened up to me like that and it didn't register with me or that I don't value your honesty. It means more than anything, Taylor, that you trusted me with your heart and your safety. We've been working really hard to get to this point." I paused for a few beats, not wanting to sound like a politician giving a campaign speech. The words were truly from my heart.

"I will do my absolute best to never take any part of what you trust in my care for granted. I know that a lot of this has been hard for you. You know, so much about our relationship has been uncharted territory for me too."

"Really?" She seemed astonished by my admission.

"Why does that surprise you?"

"Well, you've been engaged before. I mean, that's pretty

serious as far as relationships go. I've barely lasted more than six months with the same guy before freaking out and finding a reason to break up with him."

Strangely, that just made me feel better, not worse, and I grinned accordingly.

"Is that funny?" She tilted her head to the side with wonder.

"Not funny... It just makes me feel—I don't know... Special?" I smiled fully. "But seriously, when I was engaged... and it seems so silly to even call it that now"—I made a face of distaste, hating that I ever cheapened the very notion of engagement and marriage—"it was for show more than anything. It was..." I paused, trying to think of the right words to use, being very careful to not trivialize the very thing I wanted with her more than anything. "How do I explain this? In that circle of people, at that point in my life, it was the next logical step? You date for a certain period of time, check all the relationship-milestone boxes, get engaged. Does that make sense?" God, I hoped I didn't just fuck myself with all that.

"Well, I can't say that it makes sense, necessarily. But I do understand what you're saying. Isn't that terrible, though? That's how relationships progress? Like ticking things off your grocery list? It shouldn't be that way." She shook her head, and I totally agreed.

"No, it shouldn't. But you see? That's why I'm standing here with you and not in some cookie-cutter suburban home in the outskirts of Chicago. She wasn't the right girl. She wasn't 'the one.'"

Taylor took my hands from her waist and held them in her own. I still marveled at the size difference between us. She was so slight compared to me, yet so fierce and so strong in will and temperament. She was brave and bright, even though this week showed me a rare peek at the vulnerable side of her I hadn't seen before.

Once again, as if wading into the stream of my thoughts and fishing out the catch of the day, she squeezed my hands and spoke. "You know, this week was very trying for me. For us both, really. There were some really shitty moments, but every one of those was balanced out by a beautiful gift from you."

I looked at her, not hiding my puzzlement. Okay, there had been the wardrobe replacement, but that couldn't be what she was talking about. When push came to shove, she'd finally seen the necessity of all that. Moreover, she wasn't typically fixated on material things. Was all of this just because I'd sprung for some work ensembles and yoga pants?

Luckily, she saved me from having to solve the riddle on my own. Pretty quickly, she went on. "Every time I was scared, Maclain Stone, you were there to calm my fears. You held my hand and showed me we would get through the darkness to the light on the other side in one piece, and I thank you for that."

She lifted my right hand and turned it over, placing a very tender kiss on my palm. When she was done kissing my palm, she put my hand on her sternum, right over her steadily beating heart. It thumped so strongly, I could count the thrums through my palm. I looked up to meet her bright ocean-blue eyes staring back at me. God, this beautiful queen captured every good thing in the world. Every good thing in *my* world.

"And every time I was sad this week, Maclain Stone, you were there to hold me and to care for me while I cried. You made sure I ate and slept and had a safe place to exorcise my emotional demons where no one else would see. You healed my heart by making me believe there are good, kind, loving people in the world who do things for one another just because they care about them. For that, I thank you."

She left my right hand on her chest and lifted my left one to her lips, just as she had moments ago with the other, turning it over and kissing my palm with veneration, maintaining eye contact with me while doing so. Then, as before, she placed it over her heart, right on top of my other hand.

She then covered my hands with her own and looked up to me. "Every single time you were there for me this week, Maclain Stone, my heart knew I was no longer lost. That I had finally found my true love. You've given me the strength to believe that I'm good enough. That I deserve to be loved, and I deserve to give love in return." She paused, staring at me while a slow smile spread across her lips. "I love you. I love you with all my heart. Can you feel it? It beats for you. Only you. My arrogant, sexy clown. I love you, Maclain Stone." She stretched forward and kissed my lips, and I wrapped my arms around her waist and pulled her against me.

I was absolutely, undoubtedly, the happiest man alive.

CHAPTER FIFTEEN

Taylor

Every classic love story had that one moment. A look across a crowded room, the sprint through a crowded airport, or a tearful reunion just when all hope seemed lost.

I was pretty sure our perfect moment occurred when I saw the look on Mac's handsome face as my words registered within his very complicated mind. I would hold it in my heart forever. I'd thought about the way I would tell him I loved him for so long, and when I finally said the words, it went nothing like I'd planned. But letting my heart speak for itself, and really tell him how much his support meant to me, turned out to be the best way to express my feelings when all was said and done. Sometimes, overthinking things was one of my biggest character flaws.

"Now that I've told you how much I love you and how much I appreciate you, let me show you." I backed out of his embrace, grabbed the lotion from beside him on the countertop, and walked toward the bedroom. I heard him following close behind me, so I loosened the towel that was wrapped around me and let it fall to the ground as I walked. I heard Mac inhale sharply when I bent forward to take a few of the pillows from the head of the bed and tossed them onto the floor.

"Lie down so I can put some lotion on your back. No one

likes dry skin, you know."

He followed my instructions judiciously, dropping his towel and scampering onto the bed like an eager little puppy. It was so adorable, I had to hold back a giggle as I sauntered to the other side of the bed to remove the pillows there as well. I dimmed the lights at the wall switch and climbed onto the bed, meeting Mac in the middle.

He automatically reached to touch my thigh, and I swatted his hand away. "You don't touch your regular masseuse that way, do you?" I teased.

"I'm hoping like hell this won't actually be like a regular massage," he answered, his voice already low and rumbly like it always got when he was sexed up.

"Hmm. Good point," I conceded easily. "Now lie flat so I can start on your back. You'll have to tuck Big Mac up under you or something." Honestly, lying on an erection like that couldn't be comfortable, but I wasn't about to be derailed.

"Why don't you start on my front, and I can put it up in you?" He wiggled his eyebrows suggestively and grinned.

"While that idea has merit, I don't think we'd get very far with the lotion." I squirted a good amount in my palm and rubbed my hands together, making an obscene slick sound.

"I'm not complaining," he said, stroking his already fully erect cock.

"Yes, but this climate is terrible for our skin. If you'd stop arguing, I'd be halfway done already. Turn. Over."

"Killjoy," he mumbled into the pillow after doing as I told him.

I started on his shoulders, depositing the majority of the lotion there. Working up into his hairline with my thumbs, I concentrated on the thick cords of muscle that made his strong neck so prominent. He moaned into the pillow, so I continued with the long strokes, moving from his hairline down and across the top of one of his shoulders in one fluid motion. I worked until the lotion was absorbed, eventually transitioning from just using my thumbs to using my entire hand. His moaning and my bare pussy against his firm ass were making me incredibly aroused.

"Christ, that feels so good. I can feel the heat from your cunt on my ass," he said, turning his face to the side. "Kneel up for a sec. I need to turn over."

I rose up tall on my knees, lifting my weight off his body, and he flipped over beneath me. Now lying on his back, his cock jutted up from his body and nudged the entrance of my sex.

"Let me in there," he said roughly. "I can feel how wet you are. Ride me, Taylor. Baby, please."

"You don't have to beg to fuck me, Mac. Put it in." I squirted more lotion into my palm and squished it between my two palms. I leaned forward, balancing myself on his chest with my lubricated hands while he lined himself up at my opening. When he guided me down onto his shaft with his hands on my hips, I slowly shifted my weight back, taking his dick into me entirely.

"Christ, woman. Fuck that feels so good. Why does it feel like the first time every time with you?"

"I have a magical vagina. Didn't I tell you?" I massaged his pecs each time I leaned forward on his length and again when I slid back home. A massage for my inside walls and for his strong, masculine chest all at the same time. Again, I used a combination of my thumbs to press deeper into his muscle tissue, relieving the stress and fatigue of everyday tension and use and then the heels of my hands to even out the sensation.

He was working some sensation tricks of his own down below. Combining hip movement and finger stimulation of both my clit and back end to overload my nervous system with pleasure.

"Oh, my God. Mac. Jesus, that feels so good."

"You like that, don't you, my love? You like your ass played with. So tight back here." He was pressing in and around my anus with his fingers as he gripped my ass cheeks to move me up and down on his cock.

We had touched one another there before, but he'd never really penetrated me with anything. I had never had it done. Ever. By anyone. And honestly, never had any interest in it. He was slowly changing my mind to the idea, and I had a sneaking suspicion that was his devious plan. At the moment, I didn't mind at all. I was entirely on board. It was a whole new world of sensation and confusing pleasure. At the pace he was taking it, there was no pain involved, but I still couldn't imagine his dick going in there without it hurting.

"Stay with me, Sassy. Feels good, right?"

"Yes. So good."

"Then don't get all worked up and worried." He pulled me down to meet him for a deep kiss, exploring my mouth with his tongue like a hungry savage.

"Who said I was worried?" I asked when I could finally catch my breath. Christ, the man could kiss.

"It was written all over your face. Neon-blinking-sign style." He swiveled his hips up into me, reminding me that his cock was still buried deep within my body. He hit a particularly sensitive spot when doing so, making me unexpectedly cry out.

"Well, what do we have here?" He grinned, anchoring my torso to his with his arm slung low around my hips. Once he had me secured to him, he repeated the rotation of his hips, hitting the sensitive spot again. This time, because I anticipated it, I stifled the yelp but felt the incredible surge of pleasure regardless. My eyes rolled back, stars replacing the normal light in the room.

"That is ridiculous. I don't think you should continue doing that." I gasped between sentences, trying to control my erratic breathing.

"Oh, I definitely think I should. The sweat breaking out on your forehead is a clear sign I should," he answered smugly.

"No, Mac, seriously. Way too much. The neighbors will hear me." I panted through the words again.

"That's perfect, then. They'll know I'm a god on and off the track."

He repeated the motion, and because I was just about to chastise him for the arrogant comment and wasn't prepared to hold back the animal sound, it escaped full force.

"Fuck me! Shit. I'm not sure what's happening, but please, you need to stop doing that. Mac, seriously, I think I'm going to pee in this bed or have the biggest orgasm of my life. Maybe both. Please, don't—"

Before I could complete the sentence, he became possessed, fucking me repeatedly, nailing that same spot, over and over. I screamed at the top of my lungs, incapable of stifling the sound brought on by the sensation ripping through my lady parts. I'd never felt anything like it in my life.

When my orgasm broke free, fluid squirted from my pussy, covering Mac's torso and soaking the bedding.

Mac stared up at me with his green eyes wide and amazed, mirroring what I could only guess my gawk looked like.

"What the hell just happened?" I demanded in a fierce

whisper. "Did you break my vagina?"

He chuckled, sitting up a bit to get a better view of the mess covering both of us. "That was incredible. You are the sexiest fucking creature I've ever laid eyes on."

"Are you kidding me right now?" I croaked, looking down at the same area.

"No, I'm serious. I've only seen women squirt in porn. That was so hot. Feel how hard I am." He moved inside me, and I squeaked because my pussy was so sensitive it was almost unbearable.

"Oh, shit. I feel like the slightest move is going to set me off again," I said.

"Really?" His eyes lit up.

"Don't be insane. I'm not doing that again. Switch with me. Something. Please." I went to move off the top of him and could not believe how wet the bed was. "I'm so sorry. I think the bed is ruined."

"Totally worth it."

"Insane clown posse in the house" was all I could add before he kissed me, taking my mind off everything but him.

Him and his unyielding demand for my focus, my awareness, my presence of mind on what we were doing at that moment. On everything we symbolized with our union there in that bed. Our love for one another and our commitment to each other. Our gratification, our enjoyment, and our rapture. All those amazing things we so willingly shared and gave openly to one another. The absolute joy and adoration we allowed to blossom in our hearts and in our souls because of one another.

Those were the things, the feelings, and the gifts that Mac would always make sure we took the time to treasure.

Together.

After spending the past week of trials with this amazing man by my side, I was as sure of those things as I was sure of the air I needed to breathe to sustain life.

I loved Maclain Stone. He loved me just the same. There was also as much certainty that if he didn't have an orgasm in the very near future, his poor balls would be bluer than my eyes by the time we fell asleep. I went with the rip-the-Band-Aid-off approach and popped off the top of him and onto the floor at the side of the bed in an almost Olympic-gymnast-worthy maneuver. He didn't have time to protest or stop me with one of his mind-altering kisses.

"Where are you going?" he asked, grinning.

"Away from that mess and in a different position. Come over here and fuck me, Clown." I leaned on the edge of the bed with my forearms and swayed my bare ass from side to side.

"Mmmm, I do like it when you're bossy." He rolled off the bed, not nearly as impressively as I had, I noticed, and then took up position behind me. "And this ass. How do I say no to this ass?" He stroked his strong palm down my spine to the roundness of my ass cheeks and then ran stroke after stroke down the slope of my back, warming my flesh with his hands and my heart with his words. "I love you, Taylor. Every single inch of you."

Mac trailed kisses along the same path his hands forged, making goose bumps erupt on my skin when the cooler room air wafted over the moisture left behind by his lips. Leaning his whole body over mine, his cock rested naturally in the crack of my ass as if it had found its way home. He slid down my body, kissing, rubbing, grinding as he went, creating a need inside me again where only minutes before I thought would've been impossible.

When the absence of his warmth registered, I looked back to see where he had moved to and was slightly panicked to see him sinking to his knees behind me. Now his face was level with my ass and pussy, and he was eyeing it like an all-you-can-eat buffet.

"Mac."

"Yeah, baby?"

"What are you—"

His mouth on my oversensitized labia cut off my ability to speak, and a deep moan replaced the words that would've completed my question. I pressed my forehead into the bunched-up bedding and absorbed the sensory onslaught that hit from below.

With his hands gripping onto my thighs—he reached around about two-thirds of the circumference because of our size difference—he anchored me in place and feasted on my pussy. His nose and mouth were pressed entirely into my soft tissue, slurping and nuzzling my juices like ripe fruit.

"Jesus, Sassy, so good. You're so wet from coming, and you taste so good. I will never get enough of this pussy." Sporadic parts of the sentence came between him licking and sucking at different angles.

I looked back at him again just as he leaned back from his feast and wiped his face on the back of his arm like a little boy after enjoying melting ice cream. The grin that followed was comparable too.

"Mac! Please. Pleeeeeaaassseee," I whined with a touch of begging thrown in.

"What, baby? What do you need? Tell me, and it's yours." He was moving to stand, so he already had an idea of what I was going to request.

"Fuck me. God, just fuck me. I need you to fill me," I demanded.

He stroked his erection a couple of times with one hand and placed the other on my ass, using his thumb to swipe through the wetness from my pussy and drag it toward my anus.

"In here?" He pressed at my back hole and looked to me hopefully.

My answering look was filled with concern. I just didn't think I was ready for that. "Can we work up to it somehow? My parts have already had such a workout today."

"A man can dream, right?" He slid two fingers into my pussy, and my eyes shuttered closed. Things felt so good when done the way nature meant them to be done. He finger-fucked me repeatedly, toying my clit with his thumb simultaneously. I pushed back against his hand in rhythm with his thrusting, and I quickly built to a second climax.

"Mac! Please!" I pushed my ass higher in offering when he stopped fingering me, letting the climax wane just as I was ready to go over the edge.

"Shhhhh. Baby, just relax and enjoy it." He finally replaced his fingers with the head of his cock and slowly pushed in. My pussy quickly sucked him in, welcoming him home.

"Yes! God, yes! Thank you. So good!" I babbled into the bedclothes while resting my head on the mattress, creating a gentle slope in my lower back.

"Goddamnit, woman. You're so sexy. So feminine and sexy." He ran his hand down the line of my spine and back again as he thrust in and out of my body. "I'm the luckiest fucking man on the planet. Without a doubt."

I just wanted him to stop talking and finish us both off.

I didn't know what else to do. I'd begged, I'd been gracious. Then an idea struck. I reached between my legs and through to his body and found his ball sack. I cupped his balls in my hand and squeezed them like I did when I sucked his cock. He liked when I did it then, so it would probably feel good while we were fucking too.

"Ooooh, Taylor," he moaned, his voice so low he sounded possessed. "Shit! Christ! Killing me. Right now. Killing me. Fuck. Yeah, baby. Like that. Shit."

A cocky grin spread across my lips. I had him by the balls now.

Ha! Pun intended!

"Fuck me harder, Mac! Make me come again!" I was right on the edge, and having this power over him, holding his balls in my hand, was making me crazy.

He pounded into me while I squeezed him a bit harder, doing my best to maintain my pressure and not dislocate my shoulder at the same time.

"Taylor, I'm going to come. Are you close? I can't stop. Baby, I can't stop."

"Do it! Do it, Mac! Yes!" I was right there with him, feeling his urgency set off a fantastic orgasm along with his.

I let go of his balls and braced myself to take the last few strokes as he worked through his release, pumping every drop from his cock deep into my body.

Finally, we sagged forward onto the bed, and Mac rolled to the side of me, pulling me up against his sweaty body. We were both panting as we calmed down from the powerful ending to our lovemaking.

"Jesus Christ, Sassy, that was hot. Like, crazy hot." He buried his face in the back of my hair, nuzzling through until he found my nape.

"I do what I can," I said when I caught my breath.

He kissed me a few times before nibbling the thin skin of my neck.

"Oh, my God, don't start again. Although, Christ, that feels so good," I said, my voice scratchy from shouting during the last round.

He sank his teeth in deeper, and my fucking traitor body broke out in goose bumps. I reached over my shoulders with both hands to grab his face. Not necessarily to stop him but just to be touching him as much as possible.

He moved down the back of my neck and shoulder, trailing bite after bite as he went. Little marks would be left behind for how hard he was going at it, but I couldn't bring myself to stop him. He had created an addict in me with the sensation a while back, and now I craved being bitten as much as he desired biting me.

"Mmmmm. Mac?" My tone was a mixture of inquisition and pleasure.

He held me closer, thumbing across my peaked nipples. "What?" he finally answered, wholly distracted by arousing me all over again.

"I love you. I'm totally in love with you. Completely, one hundred percent, head over heels in love with your clown ass."

"That's what I've heard. Isn't it great?" He pinched my nipple between his thumb and index finger, making me squeak before answering.

"It really is. Thank you for bringing me out here. Getting out of San Diego is great. I mean, I know we just got back from the DR, but, well, you know what I mean. What we came home to and all."

He pulled me even closer to his body. "I know exactly what you mean. But I just remembered, there's something I want to show you downstairs." He sat up abruptly, almost tossing me to the floor as he hopped off the bed. "Throw on some sweats or a robe and come with me."

"Can't we do that in the morning?" I whined. I was so after-sex-sleepy, I didn't want to get out of the warm bed.

"Nope! I'm too excited. I know you're going to love it. I won't be able to sleep until you see the car I want to give you." He quickly held his hand up when I started to object. "The car I want to loan you. Sorry. Sorry. Don't get your dander up there, little kitty."

I couldn't help but laugh at his use of the southern expression, which sounded so out of place from his pedigreed mouth. I grabbed a pair of yoga pants and a tank top from my bag and followed him downstairs into the garage. He flipped on the lights as we went, and the pristine garage lit up like a car dealership's showroom.

Three or four of his favorite BMWs had pride of place as we entered the ample space. The first one I recognized from the initial day we came to Thermal. I knew it was an M something or other, but not the same as the M2 he drove in San Diego. This had bright-orange trim and no back seat. A brilliant orange tubular bar structure filled much of the interior.

"What is all of this for?" I peered in the open window and pointed at the bar.

"It's a roll cage for on the track. If the car flips over, it maintains the integrity of the structure so the driver doesn't get crushed."

"Oh. Good to know" was the best response I could muster while panic swelled inside at the thought of him pinned beneath an overturned car.

"Well, safety first." He winked at me sarcastically.

At the speeds those cars whipped around the track, safety was the last thing on their minds, and I knew it.

We walked around the back of a few more cars and came to a halt behind an adorable little white hatchback.

"Mac," I said with an overly dramatic tone in my voice, gripping his forearm. "Don't look now, but someone has sneaked an American-made vehicle into your garage. I mean, I'm not sure how they did it, but there is an F-O-R-D in here."

"Very funny, Sassy. What do you think of this little beauty?" He was grinning from ear to ear, looking like a proud papa pointing to his newborn through the hospital nursery window.

"I think it's adorable. Looks like something I would drive. But seriously, why is it in your garage?"

"It's mine. But now, it's yours. I mean, if you'd like it to be. I mean, I'd like it to be. Well, what I'm trying to say—"

"Yes!" I had to let him off the hook. I couldn't take the stumbling and stammering a second longer. Even though it was pretty adorable watching the mighty Dr. Maclain Stone looking so unsure of himself.

"Really?" He was nearly bouncing on the balls of his feet.

"Yes! I love it." I was as excited as he was but quickly sobered. "But I insist on paying you for it."

"Well, let's worry about that later. I'm stoked you like it. I was afraid you were going to give me a hard time. You're going to really love driving—" Something made him pull up short in the middle of his sentence.

"What's wrong? Honestly, babe, I think it's great," I said, rubbing the arm I had playfully clutched moments before.

"I wasn't even thinking. Can you drive a manual? Stick shift?" he asked with worry etched on his handsome face.

"Of course I can! That's a poor person's standard, Mac. Not everyone has all the money in the world, you know? My first car was manual because that's what I could afford to buy with the money I saved up from babysitting and waitressing. Automatic transmissions cost more."

"I wish I could erase all the hard parts from your life and make them easier." He pulled me into his embrace and kissed my forehead. I wrapped my arms around his waist and inhaled his perfect Mac smell. I didn't know what it was exactly—some combination of the soap he used in the shower and his laundry detergent. I didn't know him to use cologne. It was just...him.

"But if you changed those things about me, I wouldn't be me." I leaned back to look up at him.

"True. I just want to give you everything. The world. I want to make you my queen." He smiled down at me, his green eyes twinkling under the florescent lights of the brightly lit garage.

"Well, let's just stick with this cute little hatchback, and we'll both be super happy. How's that?" I grinned, so happy with the idea of a new car, especially one that was his.

"I'll take it!" he shouted as if winning a game show bonus round.

I stretched up on my tippy-toes and kissed him. "Thank you. For everything."

"You're very welcome. Tomorrow we'll take her home."

"Does she have a name already?" I asked.

"Nope. The honor will be yours," he said, bowing low at the waist to formally bestow the duty upon me.

"How exciting!" I clapped my hands tightly in front of my chest. "Well, I'll have to drive her for a while. Get to know her personality. We'll also need to discuss a payment plan. Come up with something that fits into my budget." We left the garage and headed back upstairs to the living space.

"I've been thinking about it, and I'd like to pitch in with the rent too. Oh, and the utilities. Obviously groceries, but that's just a no-brainer." I was prattling on and on, and Mac was unusually quiet. When I looked back over my shoulder to see if he was still behind me, I caught him staring at my ass while we were headed to the bedroom.

"Hey! I'm talking! Have you heard a word I've said?" I chastised, already aware of the answer.

"Uh...no?" he answered with very little guilt.

"What has gotten into you?"

"It's those damn yoga pants. Your ass looks phenomenal in them. I don't think you should wear those outside the house anymore." He couldn't peel his eyes off my butt even while he spoke to me.

"Maclain Stone. Can you hear yourself right now?"

"Yeah. I hear it. It sounds like M-I-N-E. And I don't share. At all." He smacked my rear right when we got into the room, and when I whirled around to retaliate, he grabbed me around the waist and kissed me so thoroughly the room spun.

"Holy Jesus," I finally said when we came up for air.

"Now, if these look this good on *you*, let's see how good they look on the floor," he said with a wolfish grin, tucking his fingers into my pants at the waistband.

The next round of lovemaking was as stellar as the first but not nearly as sweet as the third. By the time we slept, the clock had struck midnight, and we had both passed out like babies.

Happy, sated, and deeply, madly in love with one another.

The world could try to break us down, but together, we were stronger than good *and* evil.

CHAPTER SIXTEEN

Mac

We took the longer route home to Oceanside late the next morning. I planned on reorganizing some things in the garage once we got home so both cars could fit inside. The salty air was brutal on everything, including car exteriors. Taylor did great with the manual transmission once she worked out the rust.

"Just like riding a bike," she bragged over the Bluetooth phone connection once we were well established on the 10 freeway and on our way out of the Coachella Valley.

"Well? What do you think of the car so far? Do you like the way it handles?" I was anxious to hear her review of the Focus RS.

"Yes!" she answered enthusiastically. "I think I'm a little bit in love, actually."

"Do I need to be jealous?" I teased.

"Nah, this stick has nothing on yours, Clown." Her adorable giggle filled the cabin of my M2 as I glided along in traffic behind her. Once she was more comfortable with the car, we would have a lot of fun in the canyons through Temecula and Fallbrook, but for now I kept a safe distance behind her, and we held steady at the speed limit as we made our way home.

She'd had a voicemail message this morning from Detective Johnson saying there was new information about her case. We'd told him before we left San Diego that we were headed to the desert for a couple of days, so he said to call the station when we got back into town. We debated driving straight into the city and checking in with him in person, but with two cars and the shitty parking situation downtown, we decided to stop at the beach and call first.

It was close to two in the afternoon when we pulled into the driveway. I opened the garage door with my clicker, and she quickly snaked the available spot inside with her Focus.

"Brat," I muttered as I swung into the driveway behind her. I made a mental note to find the other garage-door opener as we both slammed our car doors and met at the entrance to go inside the house.

"Are you ready to hear what Johnson has up his sleeve?" I asked as I sorted through my key ring to find the right one for the house.

"As ready as I'll ever be, I guess. But before we do that, I want to say something to you."

I unlocked the door and held it open for her to go inside. I pressed the lock icon on my key fob and closed the garage door before following her inside. When I finally looked at her, she was waiting patiently for me to finish my coming-home ritual.

"Sorry." I grinned and quickly stole a kiss. "What do you want to say?"

She'd kept her arms locked around my neck from when I kissed her, and her face sobered. "Thank you for loaning me that car. I love it. And, if I haven't said it yet today, I love you. Very, very much." She stretched up and kissed me this time, and I was delighted to indulge her.

"You're welcome, sassy girl. I love you too. Very much. It was one of the best experiences following you home in a safe, freeway-capable car. I could breathe so much easier knowing you would make it the entire way without overheating or breaking down on the side of the road before we got here."

"But you loved Sally as much as I did." She pouted, and I couldn't resist nipping at her lower lip. It was like dangling a pot of honey in front of a bear.

"I did, you're right. But the old girl had seen better days. Very soon after I met you, I fell in love with you, and with that came a very primal need to take care of you and keep you safe. That car was a roadside incident waiting to happen."

"Well, like I said, thank you. You know I was just busting your balls by pulling into the garage in front of you, right? I don't expect to take the M2's spot. After we call Johnson, we can swap them." She released her arms from around my neck and stroked them up and down my arms a few times.

"I think if I do some rearranging out there, there should be enough room for both cars. They're both so small, they should easily fit."

"I like that they're both white. Kind of like his and hers." Her grin was so adorable, I couldn't help squeezing her closer to me. "Is that dorky?" She looked up to me, starting to get embarrassed.

"Not at all. I love it." I pulled her into me by handfuls of her perfect ass.

"I have a confession—of sorts." She backed out of my embrace, picked up her overnight bag, and headed toward the staircase. I followed with mine, wanting to hear what she had to say.

"Oooooh, is this going to be juicy? Tell me! Tell me!"

She laughed. "You might be disappointed if you're looking for gossip. Or hot-sorority-girl-pillow-fight-type secrets."

Looking dramatically disappointed, I trudged up the stairs behind her, acting like my duffle bag weighed eighty pounds all of a sudden.

"You're such a dork." She laughed.

"But you love me, you said so yourself. Just a few minutes ago," I reminded her in a playful singsong tone.

"Yeah, I guess I did, didn't I?" She made a face like she'd just eaten something spoiled.

"Yep. And no take-backs either," I teased.

"Wow, you're a tough player, aren't you?" She dropped her bag on the bed and flopped down beside it.

"In all seriousness, tell me what you were going to say. I'm all ears." I knelt down at the side of the bed and nudged my way between her legs. Holding her hands in mine, I waited for her to speak, honestly wanting to know everything there was to know about my amazing girl.

She looked at me for a moment or two. Really just studied my features—to the point where I began feeling a bit self-conscious.

"You are so beautiful, Dr. Stone. Honestly, you are the most handsome man I've ever laid eyes on." Her blue eyes were the color of denim in the afternoon sun shining in off the Pacific.

"Thank you, baby." I was touched by her genuine compliment.

"My whole life, I've put a lot of effort into knowing what I didn't want. I knew I didn't want to end up like Janet, for example. Didn't want to depend on my children to survive, didn't want to be an addict or a loser." She grinned. Something about that was funny, apparently.

But then she continued, still holding my hands, even tighter than before, and still looking me straight in the eyes. "I knew I didn't want to live in a double-wide, and I didn't want to trip from one man to the next, making promises I'd never keep. I didn't want to let people down time and time again. I definitely knew I didn't want to be a burden. On anyone."

"That all makes perfect sense," I said quietly, sensing there was more to what she was trying to say.

"But I never spent time thinking about the things I did want in life. Doing that meant I had hope that I would get those things. And hoping always led to disappointment. *Always*. So I stopped having hope."

Tears welled up in her eyes, and I wanted to take her in my arms and make all the pain in her crappy adolescent years go away. I wanted to erase it all and give her the perfect do-over right then and there.

"Until I met you," she said as one lone tear ran down her soft cheek. Usually she would angrily swipe tears away the minute they were shed, but that tear was a trailblazer, and it deserved to run free. I watched it streak down her face and curve around her jaw, finally dropping off onto my wrist where our hands were joined on her lap. It was like she had given that little bit of herself to me as a symbol. A small offering to show me how open her heart had become, how her once unavailable emotional existence had been resuscitated. Where there was once a barren and desolate wasteland, there was now a lush and fruitful meadow just waiting to be cultivated and harvested and thoroughly enjoyed.

"Thank you," I said. It almost seemed banal. But really, nothing more was needed. It encapsulated so much of what

I felt for so much about her—about her mere existence in my life.

She chuckled. "What are you thanking me for? I feel like I should just play a recording of me saying thank you to you on repeat, over and over. You've given me so much already, Mac. So much. Things I can't even articulate. Things I just feel in here." She released my hand to touch her chest, on top of her heart. "You've given me life."

I laid my head in her lap like I've seen children do with their mothers. Of course, I didn't remember ever doing that with my own mother. She probably would shoo me away and complain I was wrinkling her designer clothing. Or, God forbid, someone might see me doing it.

Taylor stroked my hair, and my eyes closed automatically. When she added her fingernails to the motion, I was in blissful heaven.

"Oh, that feels so good. I could do this for hours."

"What do you mean 'do this'? You aren't really *doing* anything," she teased.

"Okay, I could let you do that for hours. Better?"

"Grammatically, yes. But practically? No." She laughed. "I have to call Detective Johnson before he leaves for the day, remember?"

"Damn it. I knew I didn't like that guy. Just another reason," I mumbled into her thighs.

"Well, if we're living right, he's going to have good news for us. Let's just get it over with. Then we can work on the garage."

"I can do that. You don't have to worry about it," I said, sitting back on my heels and then rolling up to stand.

"I don't mind helping. Two of us can get it done quicker than one, right?" she asked with a cheery tone as we both headed back to the kitchen.

"So the saying goes. Do you want a drink? Beer?"

"Nah, I'm just going to grab my phone," she said, looking around from side to side. "Where the hell did I put my purse?"

"Did you bring it in from the car? You had the key and your phone in it, and we talked on the phone during the drive and you had the ignition on, so I know you didn't leave it in Thermal."

"God, wouldn't that suck?"

"Yes—and no. We'd have to go spend another night. And honestly, last night was one of the best nights of my life." I was not exaggerating. The woman nearly fucked me to death, and I would've died with a smile wider than the Grand Canyon.

"Okay, I'll go look in the car," she said, heading to the garage. She returned in less than a minute with her bag in hand, cell phone already held to her ear.

"Hello. Detective Johnson, please. Yes, this is Taylor Mathews returning his call. Yes, thank you." She held the phone away from her mouth slightly and said to me, "I'm on hold while they page him or whatever."

"Would you mind putting the call on speaker? I'd love to hear what he has to say." I was hoping I hadn't stepped over some personal space line by asking.

"Oh, good call!" she said enthusiastically, laying my worry to rest. She set her phone on the kitchen island and pressed the icon for speakerphone, and we both sat down on stools around the counter.

"This is Johnson." The detective's voice filled my beach house kitchen.

"Hi, Detective Johnson. This is Taylor Mathews, and Dr. Stone is here with me as well. If you don't mind, we have you on speakerphone so we can both hear the call."

"Well, that's up to you, Ms. Mathews. It's your case," he answered nonchalantly. This guy seriously got on my nerves. I rolled my eyes at Taylor, and she responded with an eye roll of her own.

"Oh, okay. So your voicemail said there was new information. What's going on?" Taylor got straight to the point, and I was really grateful. The last thing I felt like doing was making small talk with the asshole.

"Let me just grab your file here, to keep everything accurate, you know. I have a crazy caseload at the moment. Well, who am I kidding, with budget cuts, it's always like this."

Taylor and I just stayed silent while he fumbled around, filling the phone line with noise from shuffling papers and drawers opening and closing. Finally, he cleared his throat a couple of times and got back to our conversation.

"The lab reports came in late on Friday. Munson was working, but I was already gone for the day. My kid had a soccer tournament, and I promised her I'd be there. So anyway, looks like we have more than enough evidence to bring Busby in for the break-in and vandalism at your apartment. I thought you'd want to know we're going to his place of employment this afternoon to arrest him."

"Well, what do you know," I said. "Can we go there and watch?"

"Isn't that also your place of employment, Dr. Stone?" the detective asked, not understanding that I was joking. Sort of.

"Yes, it is," I answered dryly.

"Well, nothing's stopping you from being at your job. You can do whatever floats your boat."

Taylor shook her head from where she sat. Apparently she

thought the whole thing was a bad idea. We could talk about it when we hung up with Barney Fife.

"Detective, I forgot to ask you about my car when I was at the station last week. When we went to my apartment to clean up and get my belongings, I saw that my car had been vandalized as well. Did you also find he was the one who did that?"

"Ummm, I don't recall seeing anything about a vehicle in any of the reports, and I didn't personally write up anything about a car in my report. I can check with Detective Munson and see if he did any work-ups on a car at the scene and get back to you."

"Thank you. I'd appreciate it," Taylor clipped.

I couldn't believe what I was hearing. How could they have missed the damage done to Sally?

"Is the vehicle still on-site now?" the detective asked.

"I believe so?" Taylor looked at me, and I nodded yes. I hadn't made arrangements to have it towed as of yet, still under the impression it was police evidence. Maybe it would be better to just scrap Sally and put it all behind us. Another thing to talk about when we hung up.

"So what happens after you arrest him today?" Taylor asked.

"Well, he will be held until an arraignment can be scheduled," Johnson responded.

"What does that mean?" she fired off before he had a chance to explain.

I was a little surprised by all the run-ins her mother had with the police that she wasn't more familiar with the judicial system.

"That's when he is formally charged with the crimes he's

committed. We will file our case with the prosecutor's office, and they have up to seventy-two hours to formally bring their charges to the judge at an arraignment."

The man was prattling on like he was giving a lecture to a room full of high school students. Clearly he loved the sound of his own voice when in know-it-all mode.

"I doubt he will be released without a bail hearing. That may or may not be done in conjunction with the arraignment. The court system is so impacted, we see separate dates more and more lately. So, at a second court date, a bail amount will be determined. If he can post bail, he will be able to leave lockup until his trial date, usually with restrictions such as no leaving the state, he has to check in with a probation officer weekly, or more often, et cetera. If he cannot post bail, he will remain in jail until his trial."

"How long does it take until the actual trial?"

Shit. He finally came up for air, and Taylor fired another question at him, sending him into a second lecture.

"That depends on the caseload of the court system. If he can't afford an attorney and has a public defender assigned to him by the court, the case is typically tried sooner. Fancy-pants private attorneys typically file continuance after continuance to uncover additional evidence or drum up character or expert witnesses. There are all kinds of games the attorneys play with the system."

"Detective, I have to say, I'm honestly concerned for my safety."

She caught me completely off guard with the comment. I didn't say anything but waited to hear his response with very interested attention.

"Has Mr. Busby contacted you again?" he asked without

inflection.

"No, he hasn't. But you were at my apartment, were you not?" Her tone was clipped, and I knew her patience with the detective was thin from conversations we'd had over the weekend.

"I was, yes." He would mind the condescension if he were smart.

"Did you read the messages on the wall in my bedroom, Detective? They were very explicit, very graphic and violent. Not to mention disturbing and completely unhinged. How would you feel if you were in my shoes and a person wrote those things on *your* bedroom wall, and they were walking around freely among the general population? Free to just show up on your doorstep at any time?"

I reached across the island and touched her forearm. If nothing else, just to lend some support. She was getting riled up, and while I completely understood why, I also figured a man like Detective Johnson probably bristled when a woman became emotional.

What? she mouthed to me, bugging her eyes out to go along with it.

I held my hands up in surrender. She needed to believe I was one hundred percent on her side on this one. On every issue, actually. Every single time.

"Ms. Mathews, we've got this guy by the balls. Excuse my French. He was very sloppy at your apartment. He's a rookie at this stalker thing, and for all of us involved, that's an excellent thing."

"Are you saying you have enough evidence to send him to prison?" I asked bluntly. I didn't need another lecture on Criminal Law 101. I just wanted a straight answer.

"Well, nothing is written in stone. Ha! No pun intended. I mean, look at OJ Simpson, right? Of course, I can't discuss particulars until after the evidence is revealed in the trial. But you have to trust me on this. I've been doing this for close to twenty years. This is as close to airtight as a case gets," Detective Johnson blustered.

"One last thing before we hang up. I don't really feel like we've gotten a solid answer. How can we be sure, if he posts bail, that he stays away from Taylor?" I pressed again.

"If he makes bail—well, let me rewind. I'm going to recommend to the DA that bail is denied in the first place. Of course, they do what they want, but I will impress upon them that he is violent and that you've expressed significant fear and such."

"Thank you." Taylor's soft voice barely reached my ears, so if he heard her over the speakerphone connection, I'd be surprised.

"No worries," he mumbled in response and then continued. "Like I was saying, *if* he makes bail, I suggest you file a restraining order at the station in the next few days. It can only help in getting your message across that you want nothing to do with him."

"Really? That's your suggestion?" I was outraged. "This jackass broke into her apartment and soaked her fucking bed in her own blood, and you think a piece of paper saying stay away is going to stop him? Wow. Just...yeah...wow." I was furious. I had reined in my temper up to that point, but where Taylor's safety was concerned, I couldn't sit by and listen to such nonsense.

"Thank you for the information, Detective Johnson. Would you be so kind to text me when he's in custody? It would just help me sleep better. Or I can call the station and confirm for myself?" Taylor's saccharine-sweet question even rubbed me the wrong way at that point. Why was she so kind to the asshole?

"Yeah, if you don't mind calling back. Once we bring him in, there will be a lot going on with the booking process and all. I'd appreciate one less thing on my plate."

What a lazy asshole.

"No problem. Thank you for everything. Have a great afternoon." Taylor managed to stay poised until ending the call, but when she pressed the icon on the screen to end the call, her hand was trembling with rage. As soon as the call was completed, she put her head down on her folded arms and hid her face from me. I wanted to throw that fucking cell phone out the plate-glass window that made up most of the west-facing wall of my living room and watch it sink into the three footers currently crashing to shore in my "backyard."

"What a fucking piece of shit." I really didn't have anything else to add, and clearly Taylor was already upset. Me getting wound up wasn't going to help her at all.

I walked over to her end of the island and touched her arm, and she looked up at me. "Come here."

"I don't need a hug," she said quietly.

"I do."

She stood automatically and wrapped her arms around my waist, pressing her head to my chest. Holding her against me was one of the most calming sensations I'd ever known. No matter what the situation, she made the perfect soothing balm.

"I'm so thankful they're arresting him today," she said against my T-shirt, and I could feel the warmth of her breath through the fabric.

"So am I. I kind of wish I was there to see it. I wonder if the hospital will apologize to me now?"

She pulled from my embrace and sank down onto the island stool nearest to where we were standing. "It will definitely be interesting to see how it plays out. They moved pretty swiftly when they punished you, so I doubt you'll have to wait too long to find out."

"Good point. Still want to help with the garage? At least it'll keep our minds off John-Boy."

"Absolutely. Then we can get both cars inside. I don't think the salty air is good for the paint. I've seen what happens to people's cars around here." She wrinkled her nose at the thought of ruining either car.

"Yeah, me too. Isn't that crazy?" We continued chitchatting as we went out into the garage—and throughout the next two hours while we reorganized. We threw a bunch of stuff away that I never really needed or understood why I was saving in the first place, and before we knew it, the two little white speed demons were parked side by side inside the garage.

My cell phone rang just as I was getting out of the shower after cleaning up the garage. I saw my cousin's number on the display screen and thought it rather odd that he was calling me in the middle of a business day.

"Don't you have a world to dominate? People to boss around at this hour of the day?" I jabbed.

"Good point," he laughed in greeting. "Although, shouldn't you be digging in someone's brain at this very moment? Saving a life or two?" he poked back.

"Fair enough. Fair enough. What can I do for you, cousin? We got back from Thermal earlier. Taylor agreed to bring one of the cars back for her to drive, so we were just straightening out the garage a little bit so they can both fit inside." I voluntarily filled him in on what I'd been up to.

"Listen to you. So domesticated."

"I know, right? Loving every second of it, too."

"I wouldn't trade it for anything, my man. But listen, the reason I called... I have some ears to the ground down at SDPD, and I hear they brought your boy in a little while ago. Thought you and Taylor would want to know."

"Yeah, we talked to the idiot detective earlier this afternoon when we first got home. He said they'd be making the arrest today. Glad he didn't get stupid and try to bolt," I said to Killian.

"Well, I won't keep you. I'm sure you two have some celebrating to do." His comment was heavy with innuendo.

"Not exactly in the partying sort of mood, you know? She's still pretty worked up about the whole thing. If that asshole makes bail, I'm not convinced he won't come after her again. I can barely sleep at night now. I don't know how I'm going to go back to work wondering if she's safe all day."

"Why don't you put someone on her? I have people who do that sort of thing," he offered, as though he were offering to loan me a cup of sugar. You know, just another day, another bodyguard.

"Trust me, I've thought about it. But the moment I mentioned it to her..."

"Mistake number one. You don't tell her, dumbass. She's a very independent woman. She would never agree to have a bodyguard. Even *I* know that. Let me take care of it. She won't suspect a thing."

"Bad idea, Kil. I'm telling you. She's way more street-smart than Claire. She'll see through whatever harebrained idea you're thinking of." No one could say I didn't try to warn him.

"I don't have harebrained ideas." He tried to sound offended.

"Duuuuddde. You totally do. Remember the time you put the potato in the tailpipe of your dad's Bentley?" I reminded him with a chuckle.

"That was a classic. Not harebrained in the least," Killian defended.

"Except when the whole family nearly coughed to death from the carbon monoxide that backed up into the car when he started the engine!" I laughed wholeheartedly then, and he joined in.

"Well...that part...maybe that wasn't thought out so well... but you have to admit, we all laughed our asses off afterward!" he said when he could speak between laughing.

"Yeah, we did. Hey, my other line is ringing. Looks like the hospital. I better take it. Talk to you soon."

"Bye."

I clicked over to the incoming call, chuckling at the memory I'd shared with my cousin. We'd really had a good time when we were kids.

"Hello? Dr. Stone," I said, trying to transition into a serious tone of voice.

"Oh, hello, Dr. Stone. This is Mrs. Sanchez from human resources at Scripps Green Hospital. How are you doing? Hopefully well." The woman's professional demeanor sobered me quickly.

"Yes, I'm fine, thank you. How can I help you? I'm aware I'm due back to work first thing in the morning. My ten-working-day suspension ends today." Honestly, at the moment,

I couldn't recall if I was supposed to call them or just show up to work. Reviewing the paperwork I was given when I was put on leave was next up on my agenda.

"About that..." She paused, seeming to measure her words carefully. "I'm afraid the hospital has a big mess on our hands, and we need to start with an apology to you. We'd like to do it in a formal setting, so the administration has asked me to extend an invitation for a face-to-face meeting with you first thing in the morning. Does that work with your schedule? Maybe eight o'clock?"

Since I had cleared my schedule completely when placed on leave, I had nothing pressing first thing in the morning. "Sure, that's fine. May I ask what this is regarding? I'd like to be prepared for the meeting. The last time I received a notice from your office, it was an unscheduled vacation without any spending money." I chuckled uncomfortably, trying to make light of my disciplinary action.

"Well, you may have heard by now—since the gossip machine inside this facility is a swift and well-oiled one, indeed—John Busby was arrested this afternoon. I haven't heard what the formal charges are, as of yet, but we are having a meeting with the police department shortly, so I'm quite certain we'll have more information for you in the morning."

Well, that was a professional non-answer if I'd ever heard one.

"Thank you for calling me, Mrs. Sanchez. I'll see you and the other administrators in the morning, then."

"Great. I will email you a calendar invitation with the location when we secure a meeting room. Have a good night, Dr. Stone."

I hung up and went to find Taylor to tell her the news.

Everything was falling into place. Killian was going to handle her safety while she was at work, I was going to receive a formal apology at my place of employment, and John would be behind bars.

If the earth would open up and swallow both our mothers, we'd be living large.

"Uh-oh... What's that smile all about? You look like you're up to something." She eyed me suspiciously over the top of her sunglasses. I found her lounging on the deck off the master bedroom. We both favored the location over any other in the house.

"I was picturing a giant sinkhole swallowing my mother and then yours."

"I like the way your mind works, man. For many reasons, but that is an excellent one."

"Guess who I just got off the phone with?" I asked, plopping down onto the lounge chair beside hers.

"Please don't say your mother." She rested back, eyes closed behind her shades, face pointed toward the late-afternoon sun.

"It would make sense that you'd guess that, but no. It was the hospital. They want to have a meeting first thing in the morning to formally apologize to me. I didn't press for details, but the HR rep said the police came in to arrest John today."

"Niiiicccee. Congratulations! Maybe after they apologize, they will offer you department head, after all?" She turned in her chair to face me again. This was everything we had hoped for.

"Well, let's not get ahead of ourselves," I cautioned.

"Ha! Get it? A 'head'?" She laughed at her own joke, therefore making me grin too.

"Clever girl." I tweaked the end of her nose and leaned closer to kiss her. "I love you so much, Taylor."

"I love you too."

"I think everything's going to work out just fine for us. Our very own happily ever after," I said, holding her hands in mine. I kissed her knuckles like I loved to do.

"And if it doesn't? We'll just keep fighting until we get what we want. Because that's how we do things around here." She leaned over and kissed *me* this time—officially making me the happiest man alive.

ALSO AVAILABLE FROM

VICTORIA BLUE

A washed-up model at the age of twenty-seven, Oliver Connely has gone from being a household name to barely making the rent. It's time to think fast—and cash in big—with a can't-miss idea inspired by the passion he sees in a handful of romance novel fans. Book Boyfriend Incorporated is born.

Can't. Miss.

Right?

Except for the unexpected glitches Oliver's business plan doesn't cover—like falling for one of his "lonely lady" clients, Bailey Hardin, who's as smart and driven as she is beautiful and sexy. Their chemistry is instant and scorching, but everything's turned on its head when LA's city manager—Bailey's scoundrel of a husband—turns up dead.

The mess intensifies when Oliver's roommate sets her sights on the freshly vacated political position, thrusting Oliver into a test of loyalties between his longtime best friend and his new ladylove. Tough decisions must be made, and for the first time in Oliver's life, matters of his heart are on the line.

Keep reading for an excerpt!

EXCERPT FROM
MISADVENTURES WITH A BOOK BOYFRIEND

CHAPTER ONE

I was Oliver Connely, for Christ's sake! A household name—especially if the house had women living in it. For the past decade, my face had been plastered on billboards and buildings around the world and every magazine cover from *GQ* to *Esquire*. I'd walked for top designers in Milan, Paris, and New York. I was at the top of my modeling game.

But today?

Today I could barely pay my rent.

I'd heard of the proverbial "wall" from others in the industry but smugly laughed it off, never believing it would happen to me. After all, I was the most sought-after model of my generation. But my twenty-seventh birthday loomed like a dark cloud on the horizon, and the blustery wind that blew in before the storm took all the modeling jobs out to sea with it.

And now I was the guy scraping together change to pay his fucking cell phone bill.

Well, my agent, Harrison Firestein, might not be calling, but my favorite lounge chair at the pool in my condo complex certainly was. I'd been setting up shop there a few times a week to perfect my tan, relax, and forget about the stress in my life.

Since I actually *was* expecting a call from Harrison, I made sure my phone was charged and then grabbed my backpack and strolled across the complex to the pool.

I usually had most of the place to myself during the week. Everyone in Southern California was so health conscious and worried about wrinkles that sun worshipping had fallen prey to self-tanners and fake 'n bake salons. But I'd grown up in rural Iowa, where the summer was barely a quarter of the year and not a decent four-fifths. I hadn't yet given up appreciation for how the sun warmed my skin and gave me a sense of peace like nothing else in my regular routine.

I usually worked out five days a week, but I took an extra day off this week because—*honestly?*—I just wasn't that into it. It was so much easier for me to get motivated when I knew I had a shoot coming up or a show to walk. Since my phone had been unusually silent, I lacked the drive to hit the weights. Where were the job offers from Harrison?

The pool was particularly busy, and I questioned if I'd mistaken today for a weekday when it was actually a weekend.

No. Definitely not.

Skye Delaney, my best friend and amazing roommate, had been out the door at five thirty this morning like she was every workday without fail. Her punctuality used to annoy me, but I'd learned to admire her for her dedication to her career. I might not like the asshole she worked for, but she loved what she did and made a great wage doing it.

We'd been best friends since sophomore year at UCLA, and she'd been my rock when my family abandoned me for dropping out—and also through the crazy ride of my modeling career. It probably looked like we should've just hooked up and called it done. Been there. Tried that. We had less sexual chemistry than the leads in a bad rom-com. We could laugh about it now, but at the time, it was a disaster.

As I surveyed the crowd at the pool, a vacant lounge chair near the deep end called to me from across the deck. Three little shithead kids were screaming "Polo" in the shallow end while one of their pals turned in haphazard circles randomly shouting "Marco" to coax out their clap backs. Who was the sadistic bastard that came up with that game in the first place? I sent up a mental *thank you* to the ingenious creator of the AirPods in my backpack that were about to drown out the racket.

A cluster of empty chairs just a few feet from mine could pose a potential problem if those kids took a break and decided to camp out there, but a quick scan of the rest of the pool-goers yielded a view of their mothers across the deck. Two were absentmindedly watching the game in the water; the other two were huddled together, obviously talking about something they didn't want the others to hear.

I loved people watching. I'd done a good amount of traveling in the last few years, and often times I was alone. Making up people's backstories had become one of my favorite pastimes. I didn't even try to get it right. I just tried to make it interesting.

My own parents were two of the most boring adults I'd ever met. They met in high school and had been stuck with each other ever since. When I'd come along as an unwelcome party favor from their senior prom night, any hope of leaving that small town and making something of their lives went down the toilet with the first flush of morning sickness.

If the rest of middle-class America were in the same boat, I'd have begged that sucker to pull a Titanic. In the stories I created, people were happy, had adventures, and made the most out of every day.

A nasally voice broke through I Prevail's rendition of "Blank Space" being belted into my ear canal. "Anyone sitting here?" Judging by the "annoyed mom" look on the woman's face when I opened my eyes, she had already asked more than once. I pulled the little white pod from my ear and gave my practiced grin.

"Oh, excuse me. I didn't realize you had— Hey, what is that?" She pointed at my AirPod.

"They're the new AirPods. Perfect sound without the bothersome cord. They connect to your phone or any other device by Bluetooth."

"Well, I'll be... Janine, check this out!" She looked over her shoulder to her three approaching friends. Apparently, the leader of the posse was named Janine.

The bedazzled word *Diva* on her impossibly white ball cap threw tiny rainbows on her friend's face and chest as she spoke to her. "Honey, don't point at him like he's a piece of meat. I'm sure he has a name. And I saw him the minute we walked in. You'd have to be unconscious not to." Janine gave me a conspiratorial wink, like we were sharing a joke at her friend's expense. Except, when I thought about it further, it was really at mine.

She pushed her way past her friend and offered her hand. "Forgive my friend here. She doesn't get out much. We signed her out for a few hours before the nurses came by with her medication."

I took the offered hand and turned it over to place a light kiss on the slope of her inner wrist, but not before noticing the enormous pear-shaped diamond on her ring finger. And I'm talking enormous, as in "my husband works like a dog and we never have sex, but he buys me whatever I want" enormous. The way her mouth hung open after I grinned at her reinforced my assessment.

"Pleased to meet you, Janine. Oliver—"

"Connely. Shit! You're Oliver Connely!" She stammered and stared, and I had to admit, the effect never got old. For all the emotional scars they'd dealt me, I was eternally grateful to my parents for the physical attributes they'd bestowed upon me. Gene pool for the win.

"I am." I grinned again, motioning to the ladies to make themselves comfortable in the neighboring lounge chairs. It was becoming clear we were going to be spending the afternoon together.

"You live here? In this complex?" Janine commandeered the seat next to mine.

"I do. I'm sorry, but I think you ladies have me at a disadvantage. You already knew my name, and now you know where I live. How about some introductions?"

ALSO BY ANGEL PAYNE

Secrets of Stone Series:
(with Victoria Blue)

No Prince Charming
No More Masquerade
No Perfect Princess
No Magic Moment
No Lucky Number
No Simple Sacrifice
No Broken Bond
No White Knight
No Longer Lost

The Bolt Saga:

Bolt
Ignite
Pulse
Fuse
Surge
Light

Honor Bound:

Saved
Cuffed
Seduced
Wild
Wet
Hot
Masked
Mastered
Conquered

Ruled

Misadventures:

(by Victoria Blue)
Misadventures with a Book Boyfriend
Misadventures at City Hall

(by Angel Payne)
Misadventures with a Time Traveler

Cimarron Series:
Into His Dark
Into His Command
Into Her Fantasies

Temptation Court:
Naughty Little Gift
Pretty Perfect Toy
Bold Beautiful Love

Suited for Sin:
Sing
Sigh
Submit

Lords of Sin:
Trade Winds
Promised Touch
Redemption
A Fire in Heaven
Surrender to the Dawn

For a full list of Angel's & Victoria's other titles, visit them at AngelPayne.com & VictoriaBlue.com

ABOUT ANGEL PAYNE

USA Today bestselling romance author Angel Payne loves to focus on high-heat romance starring memorable alpha men and the women who love them. She has numerous book series to her credit, including the action-packed Bolt Saga and Honor Bound series, Secrets of Stone series (with Victoria Blue), the intertwined Cimarron and Temptation Court series, the Suited for Sin series, and the Lords of Sin historicals, as well as several standalone titles.

Angel is a native Southern Californian, leading to her love of being in the outdoors, where she often reads and writes. She still lives in Southern California with her soul-mate husband and beautiful daughter, to whom she is a proud cosplay/culture con mom. Her passions also include whisky tasting, shoe shopping, and travel.

Visit her at AngelPayne.com

ABOUT VICTORIA BLUE

International bestselling author Victoria Blue lives in her own portion of the galaxy known as Southern California. There, she finds the love and life-sustaining power of one amazing sun, two unique and awe-inspiring planets, and four indifferent yet comforting moons. Life is fantastic and challenging and every day brings new adventures to be discovered. She looks forward to seeing what's next!

Visit her at VictoriaBlue.com